EXIT WOUNDS

ACID VANILLA BOOK 5

MATTHEW HATTERSLEY

BOOM BOOM PRESS

GET YOUR FREE BOOK

Discover how Acid Vanilla transformed from a typical London teenager into the world's deadliest female assassin.

Get the Acid Vanilla Prequel Novel:
Making a Killer available FREE at:

www.matthewhattersley.com/mak

CHAPTER 1

Farhad Mahmood turned around in the mirror to inspect himself, seeing the damp circles that emanated from under his armpits had now met in the middle of his shirt. He turned back, twisting on the faucet and letting the water run for a few seconds whilst he stared down into the porcelain bowl.

It had been one of those months where nothing seemed to be going his way. Everyone was having a tough time of it right now, he knew that, and he had to be thankful he still had a job, still had his health. But after losing his poor father and then his dear brother only two weeks later, surely he deserved a break? Some time off, at least?

But no. It appeared not.

Indeed, if Farhad didn't know any better he'd think Allah Himself was mocking him.

He'd already had his work cut out for him here at Tehran's Mehrabad International Airport – what with the entire building on high alert and every interview room and holding cell full of western travellers – but now the air conditioning had broken down. On the hottest day of the year so far.

He leaned into the basin and splashed cold water on his face, silently cursing his lot as he met his gaze in the mirror. It wasn't fair.

Since his recent (albeit rushed) promotion to Customs Security, getting the air conditioning fixed shouldn't have fallen to him, but with half the staff on rotation, no one else was available to contact the technicians. Now, on top of everything else, he had to go tell his superiors it would be another three days before they could be onsite. The pandemic, they'd told him. It had slowed everything down.

Voy, voy, voy.

Farhad understood the enormity of the global situation as much as anyone – it was important to stay vigilant, to follow procedures – but over the last few months he'd also seen a distinct decline in efficiency from certain parties and suspected the virus was a useful excuse for some lazy oafs to slacken off. But what could he do? Despite his promotion, he was still on the bottom of the ladder here. He still had a great many people outranking him.

He reached for a paper towel and released a heavy sigh. Three more days of heat and torment and sweating unbearably. Pandemic or not, it was enough to make anyone unwell. He wiped at his face before crumpling up the paper towel and chucking it at the large waste bin standing a few feet away. The balled-up paper hit the rim and bounced off onto the floor as he swivelled on his heels and marched out of the bathroom. Back to the toil and the stress. Back to work.

"Mahmood," a familiar voice came from behind, as he made his way through the labyrinthine corridors of the staff quarters. "Have you interviewed the English passenger in holding room six?"

Farhad slowed his pace before turning around and bowing to Saman, his superior officer here in the Customs Office. "No, sir," he stammered, focusing on a ripped carpet tile by his feet. "I have been arranging the cooling system repairs."

"Yes, well I need someone in there now."

He swallowed. "I haven't done an interview yet, sir."

"Don't worry, you'll have no problems. Find out everything you can about them. Why they're here, what their purpose is in our country. This is important, Mahmood. The eyes of the world are watching."

"Yes, sir. I will go there this minute."

Saman stepped towards him. "You work for me now, Farhad. Remember this. I understand the cooling system needs attention, but I need all staff focused on immigration and border control. Now more than ever. You know as well as I, since the distrust started to spread on social media we have been fighting an information war with our own people."

Farhad nodded. "Yes, sir. I understand."

"Do you?" Saman growled. "I trust you saw the Supreme Leader on Fars News last night, explaining how our enemies are once again spreading lies about us – saying we are letting down our people. That we are dealing badly with the pandemic. But this is not true. Is it?"

Farhad's mind drifted to the last time he saw his father. "N-No, sir."

"Exactly. So we need to be as vigilant as ever." He moved closer, not letting any social distancing rules get in the way of him shoving a fat finger in Farhad's face. "We are the first line of defence against the West's presence in our country, Mahmood. We must ensure everyone crossing our border is checked and double checked. This is a time of great crisis for Iran. Do you understand? If this continues we may have to shut our borders entirely to the West. And despite how we might feel about these people, this is not good for our economy. So do your job." He shoved a cardboard folder at Farhad.

"Yes, sir."

"Room six."

Farhad placed the folder under his arm and straightened his spine as Saman shuffled past. He waited until the gruff officer had disappeared around the corner before turning back the way he'd come and heading straight for the holding rooms.

Room six was at the far end of the last corridor. Once outside the door, he took a second to compose himself before opening it and stepping inside.

"Oh. I…"

He'd been expecting a man. So when he saw a woman sitting at the square interview desk in the centre of the room he was taken aback.

"Finally," the woman said with a sigh. "Can you let me know what's going on, please?"

"Yes… I… Of course," he muttered, closing the door and moving over to stand in front of her.

She was rather beautiful, which didn't help matters, and dressed in that loose western way that – whilst not angering Farhad the way it might older generations – made him uneasy. She was wearing denim jeans, gripped incredibly tight to her shapely legs, and on her top she wore a faded black t-shirt and a black leather jacket. Ridiculous attire for this heat, yet there wasn't a drop of perspiration on her. As she tilted her head to one side, her white-blonde hair grazed her jaw line.

"What is your name?" Farhad asked her, opening up the folder to examine the contents – a passport and visa, as well as a journalism permission document from the Iranian embassy in London. He removed the passport and thumbed to the ID page as she spoke.

"My name is Zora Dankworth," she told him, as he read the same on the passport. "And as I've already told two of your colleagues, I'm a freelance journalist with every right to be in your country. You can see I've got all the relevant paperwork with me. So what's going on?"

Farhad eyed the woman as she sat back in her seat and crossed her arms in a defensive gesture. He'd also noticed a distinct undercurrent of anger in her speech. He paused, figuring out how best to approach the interview and shifting his mindset into speaking English. Many of his older colleagues hated having to speak any western tongue, but it was something he enjoyed. To

Farhad it was a way of bettering himself, of stretching his knowledge and scope.

"I appreciate this is not a pleasant experience for you," he said, moving around the table to face her. "But you can appreciate this is an unusual time for everyone. We cannot let just anyone into our country unchecked, especially not a journalist, and especially not at this crucial time."

The woman sneered. "Right, sure. The virus. I get it. But please, I'm not here to do any sort of exposé or anything. I'm not interested in making your country or your government look bad."

"So, Ms Dankworth, what are you interested in? Why are you here in my country?"

"It's a long story."

Farhad bristled with a mixture of nerves and fury. This insolent woman, with her sneering expression and raised eyebrows. He wasn't having it.

"Well, I'm not going anywhere," he told her, sitting down on the chair opposite and relaxing into his role. "And neither are you until you answer my questions. So, talk."

The woman looked up, and for the first time Farhad noticed her eyes. They were big and round and had a wild intensity to them that left a ball of air caught in his throat. But this wasn't what was most remarkable. He could see now they were different colours. One blue. One brown.

"All right, fine," she replied. "What do you want to know?"

CHAPTER 2

The woman who wasn't Zora Dankworth sat back in the uncomfortable plastic chair and watched the customs officer fuss around with the contents of her file, eyes flitting back and forth as he speed-read her papers.

"You flew from London, Ms Dankworth?" he asked.

"That's correct." She raised her head and waited for his next question, tried to stay calm. It felt like a thousand hot needles were shooting through her nervous system. One wrong move now and it was all over, she'd be on the next flight home. Or worse. Much worse.

Because the woman's real name (the name she'd gone under for the last eighteen years) was Acid Vanilla, and she was arguably one of the deadliest and most skilled assassins in the world. At least, she had been. Now… well, she wasn't sure what she was. She certainly didn't kill people for a living anymore, although some days (most days, of late) she wondered if going back to her old life might be her only option. And as to why she was here – why she was anywhere – well, that was for revenge. But she wasn't telling this guy that.

He watched her over the top of his folder. "So, you are a journalist—"

"*Freelance* journalist."

"There is a difference?"

"Absolutely. I work for no one. No allegiances." She leaned forward in her seat. "Like I say, I'm not here to paint a bad picture of your country. I'm not interested in how you're dealing with the pandemic. I'm not interested in the bloody pandemic, period. I write people-pieces, op-eds. Think of me more as a storyteller than a news reporter."

He nodded but didn't seem convinced. "We now come back to my question, why are you here in my country?"

"Well it's not for the hospitality that's for sure."

Her mind flashed back to the sign she'd seen as she entered the airport, written in English in neon lettering:

In future, Islam will destroy Satanic sovereignty of the West.

It wasn't that she didn't get the sentiment (hell, she'd been around enough Satanic sovereigns to last a lifetime), and it wasn't even that she'd expected Iran to throw its arms around her. But right now it just felt like one more bad omen she didn't need.

"I mean, I wasn't expecting the red carpet treatment," she went on, doubling down on the snotty journalist schtick. "But I also wasn't expecting to be dragged through the airport and shoved in a locked room for the last three hours, without so much as a glass of water. Or anyone to tell me what the bloody hell is going on."

"Silence," the customs officer yelled, smacking his fist down on the table. "You are here because you will not give a straight answer. You are here because we do not take kindly to journalists here in the Islamic Republic, whether you are a reporter or a storyteller or whatever you say you are. And you are here because we have a crisis gripping our beloved nation and we do not accept just anyone into our country."

Acid sighed, inwardly cursing her rotten luck. The pandemic had been going on since the start of last year, and for most of that time she'd managed to swerve the hysteria. But even someone like her, who didn't watch the news or take any interest in current affairs, knew it was a big deal. They said it originated in bats and that didn't surprise her one little bit. She knew all about bats and what they were capable of.

The guy was still staring at her, nostrils flaring.

"Okay, listen," she said, lowering her voice. "I'm here because I'm writing an article on a man called Cyrus Heydari."

It was as if the name fell out of her mouth and landed with a clang on the metal tabletop. The customs officer stiffened.

Shit.

"I take it from your expression you know who I'm speaking of?"

A deep frown creased the young man's face. "What do you want with Cyrus Heydari?"

"I've just told you, I'm doing a piece on him. Nothing defamatory. But rather his rise to power and his growing influence on the region." She paused, letting the words land. "Look, you need to let me go. As you can see, I've got all the correct papers. Plus I've got a meeting set up this afternoon with Baraz Bayat, a local journalist who…" She trailed off as the customs officer snarled at the name.

"Bayat is a pig. He will only tell you slander and lies."

Shit.

She'd known it was a gamble, mentioning Bayat, a known critic of the current regime, but she also knew his name held some sway. Plus, this part of her story was true, their meeting today having been brokered by Sofia Swann, a journalist friend-slash-associate of Acid's (and someone who owed her a big favour).

"That man is not to be trusted," he added. "And maybe you aren't either."

Acid chewed on the inside of her cheek, considering how to play this for the best. Whatever she said next could make or break her case, and she had to get into the country. She had to meet with Bayat. Had to.

But, of course, there was no article, and she had no interest whatsoever in the sinister powers lurking in the shadows of the

Islamic Republic's regime. The reason she needed to meet with Bayat was because he had vital information on Cyrus Heydari's whereabouts – and more importantly, the whereabouts of Heydari's rumoured collaborator, Beowulf Caesar.

It was for this reason alone that Acid had risked travelling to the notoriously paranoid and hostile country in the midst of a global pandemic. To find Beowulf Caesar. Her old mentor. The man who'd betrayed her and killed her mother. Who'd taken everything from her. She was here to kill him. After that… well, there was no plan.

"I swear to you, I'm no threat to your country," she told him, casting her gaze down his body.

He was young, skinny with it, and she'd be able to overpower him in a second. A swift kick to the solar plexus would wind him enough she could grab him around the neck, and with enough pressure on his jugular vein he'd be sleeping like a baby before he knew what had happened. But what then? With the enforced lockdown these last few months she'd been training hard, eating well and getting enough rest, so she was on top form. Sharp and hard and ready for action. But even in her heyday she'd have struggled to take on the might of the Iranian border control if they discovered her trying to get into the country illegally. There had to be an easier way.

She opened her mouth to say more, but the customs officer held his hand up. "I have to speak to someone," he said. "I will return shortly." He stood and backed out of the room, taking her papers with him and locking the door.

"Shitting hell."

She let out a long breath as she scoped out the sparse room, hoping she might miraculously happen upon an air vent she hadn't noticed previously. But no. Apart from the table and two chairs, the room held nothing else of note. A fluorescent strip bulb, an old clock on the wall to her right, a yellowing sign above the light switch written in Farsi. That was it. The clock told her it was a few minutes after ten in the morning, local time. Meant she had nine hours before she was due to meet Bayat. Nine hours to escape.

She stuck a finger up under the blonde wig and scratched at her head. It was baking hot and airless in the room, and she wanted nothing more than to rip it off, her jacket too, but she resisted. It was all part of the façade and she couldn't let it slip. A minute went by. And another. With each second Acid grew more tense, the sweat soaking through her t-shirt the longer she waited.

When the click of the metal lock echoed through the silent room, she sat upright. The door opened and in walked the same young customs officer but now with an older guy, clearly his superior. He nodded at her and barked something to the youngster who shrugged and pointed into the open file in his hands.

"My name is Saman," the new guy told her, smiling knowingly underneath a thick black moustache. "I am head of customs here in Mehrabad International Airport, and you – you are a journalist? From England?"

Acid nodded. "That's correct. I—"

"Only, we have been looking into your papers, Ms Dankworth," he said. "And it seems you don't exist. Anywhere."

She bristled in her seat. "I don't understand."

"Don't you? You see, we have strict instructions to investigate all western travellers entering our country. Especially ones who might want to write evil lies about us. This is especially true at present, with this terrible plague sweeping the world. Brought to our shores, no doubt, by corrupt western blood."

Acid bit her tongue. "Okay, I get why you're tetchy," she told him, raising her head to look over the top of the folder. "But I've got papers, see, journalistic permission from the Iranian embassy in London. You have to let me in."

"Maybe I would," Saman said, with another repellent smile. "If any of your papers made sense." The smile dropped and he leaned forward. "You say you are Zora Dankworth, a registered freelance journalist. But there is no record of you on any list available to us."

Acid bit her lip as she stared up into his dark eyes.

Shit, shit, shitting shit.

This had been her biggest concern, and why she hadn't slept a wink of sleep on the flight over here. She only had herself to blame, of course. Ari Gold (her usual counterfeiter whilst in London) had disappeared, and rather than wait for him to show up, she'd hired an unverified forger Spook had found on the dark web. A guy calling himself The Fixer. The lousy cheap bastard, he'd screwed her. Normally, of course, it wouldn't have been too much of an issue, the passports were good quality, the papers too, but with Iran being even more paranoid than usual, they were digging deep. And whilst the actual counterfeiting was well done, the aliases and background were clearly gathered in haste.

"I am a journalist," she protested. "I am who I say I am, I swear. I don't know what you mean."

"Silence," Saman said, before barking something to his underling, who hurried out the door, only to return a few moments later flanked by two more officers who were decidedly bigger and meaner looking.

"What's going on?" she asked, her eyes flitting between each of the men.

"We must investigate your claims further," Saman told her. "Until we can be certain you are who you say you are, we must hold you."

"Hold me? Where?"

Saman turned to his men and spoke quickly to them in Farsi. As Acid watched, they nodded with grim intent before advancing on her, each of them grabbing an arm and lifting her to her feet.

"What the hell... Wait."

A thousand invisible bats screamed in her ears, and before she'd even properly acknowledged what was going on, her muscle memory kicked in. Driven by instinct and panic and an intense humming of manic energy, she lashed out, catching one of the guards with a sharp elbow to the chest and knocking the table over. A cloud of black rage overtook her as she went for them again, gnashing her teeth as Saman and the rest of her captors barked at her in brusque foreign voices. She felt her foot connect with something soft and fleshy, felt fingers digging into her arms and a hand around her throat. Then something hard smashed across her temple. As the room spiralled abruptly into nothingness, her legs gave way and she crumpled to the ground.

CHAPTER 3

Blinking herself awake, Acid was made instantly aware of a throbbing pain flooding her consciousness. As she sat upright and ran her fingers through her hair, a sharper, more localised pain revealed the source as a lump on her forehead. She groaned, tracing the line of dry blood running down her cheek while woozily scoping out the open-plan space in which she found herself.

It looked to be some kind of rudimentary cell. The sort of place you might see drunks being thrown into in eighties cop movies. Although there were no drunks here, not in Iran. But there were plenty who'd upset the authorities in some shape or form – she wasn't alone in her confinement.

Bollocks.

She leaned back against the wall as her recall of earlier events returned to hit her in the guts.

A cell.

Of course.

She glanced around and gave the room her full attention. In front of her the wall was made up of steel bars floor to ceiling with a few inches between each one, and a small door was cut into the metal on the right-hand side. A thin bench ran around the remaining three walls, on which she and her fellow prisoners were sat or slumped or lying. She counted seventeen other people in total. Men and women. All westerners as far she could tell. Everyone looked weary and broken. Some sat with their heads in their hands, others were staring blankly into space, but every face was rigid with a dark, unflinching despondency.

She groaned as more memories came to her. The customs officials had her papers and luggage. She reached up and touched her hair. Shit, she hadn't twigged before, but the wig was gone. It might be difficult explaining that away as the trappings of an innocent journalist doing her job.

"Miss? Are you all right?" She rolled her head to the side to see a man sitting a few feet away. "Are you hurt?"

If Acid had to guess, she'd say he was in his late forties, but he was also pale and gaunt and on a good day might have looked younger. His blond hair and accent gave him away as Scandinavian.

"I'm fine," she croaked. "Well, you know, relatively speaking. Where are we?"

"This is the local police station, but part of the airport," he told her. "My name is Lars Hansen. I am a doctor. Do you want me to have a look at your head? I have a mask I can wear."

Acid shook her head. "No. Thank you. I'll live." She sat upright. "So what's your story, Lars?"

"Excuse me?"

"What are you doing here, in jail?"

"Ah, well I hope it won't be for too much longer," he replied. "Originally I am from Norway but work for Doctors Without Borders. I travelled here last week to help with the pandemic. I have read reports stating Iran in particular have had a surge in deaths and are not coping well. I have much experience with respiratory illness and even virus control, but the authorities here are distrustful and over-vigilant. It seems they do not want the reality of their situation to get out into the world."

"Yes, I got that as well," she told him, before hammering her fists onto the bench either side of her. "Fucking hell."

Lars laughed nervously. "I can see you're angry. As was I. But this will not do you good."

Acid punched the bench once more, before leaning forward and resting her elbows on her knees. She glanced across at Lars. "You're right. I suppose. It's just, I need to get out of here. I've got a meeting with someone this evening across town. If I'm not there…"

"I'm not sure this will happen," Lars told her, before the door of the cell swung open and a man in a white coat entered followed by two large guards. They were each wearing blue surgical face masks and plastic gloves.

"What's going on?" Acid asked, as they headed towards her and the man in white produced a small box from his pocket.

"Don't be alarmed," Lars told her. "They are going to test you for the virus. It doesn't hurt."

The man gestured for Acid to tip her head back before going to work, quickly swabbing up her nose and down the back of her mouth.

Jesus. Christ. Fuck.

Once done, she sat back and glared at Lars through watery eyes. "I thought you said it didn't hurt."

"Maybe a little. But it's done now. You seem surprised?"

Acid shrugged, watching as the man placed the swab into a sealed bag. "I guess I'm still getting my head around all this. I've been a little… self-obsessed recently. Didn't realise the extent of the problem."

"Oh yes. A terrible thing. Which is why I am HERE TO HELP," Lars shouted after the man in white as he shuffled out of the cell and the guards locked the door. He turned back to Acid. "Sorry about that. Please, you haven't told me your name."

She wiped at her eyes. "Zora. Zora Dankworth. I'm a freelance journalist and I'm…" She trailed off as an idea hit her. Lowering her voice, she said, "Actually, that's a cover. Really I work for the British government. I can't say too much more as I'm in the country on a covert mission. But I do need to get out of here and meet my contact."

Lars listened intently but his expression didn't change. "I do not think this is possible," he told her. "Who is this person?"

She got to her feet and stretched. It felt better to move around. As she paced up and down in front of Lars, she told him the story, the same one she'd told the customs officer, albeit now with the slant she was… what? Special Forces? On a Black Ops mission? If his expression – half-way between shock and amazement – was anything to go by, the story seemed to do the trick. But when she mentioned the name of the man she suspected to be protecting Caesar, a thunderous darkness sagged his fine features.

"Cyrus Heydari," he repeated. But the way he said it, it was like the name was poison in his mouth.

"You know him?"

"I know *of* him. He's an evil and dangerous man. Once he was a mere thug, an insurgent. But now he has a lot of influence in the region. A lot of money behind him."

"Dangerous man? That's one way of putting it." She cricked her neck, thinking on her feet. "Word is he's planning something, an attack possibly, and I need to find him before it's too late."

"I see," Lars said, his voice dropping to a whisper. "So, you are here in Iran to assassinate him?"

"I need to find him first. But I can't if I'm stuck in this bleeding cage. Shit." A deep urge overcame her and she smashed her fist into the cell wall, before collapsing onto the bench and gasping back a deep lungful of air.

Come on, pull yourself together.

Don't let all your hard work unravel at the first setback.

The voice in her head sounded more like her friend Spook, but it was true, she had been doing well lately. Since returning to London from Spain she'd spent time working on herself, training hard and sorting through her feelings about her past and who she was, and about her relationship with Caesar – the man who'd given her everything and then taken it all away.

Rotten bastard.

The thought of him twisted her guts tight even now. She was getting there, but it was a work in progress.

A woman's cries snapped her back to the moment and she spun around to see that prick Saman bundling an older woman into the cell. Acid was over to him in two strides, jabbing her finger into his face.

"Hey," she hissed. "You have to let me out of here. Let me call someone, at least. I need to speak to my people."

"Oh yes? Which people are these?"

Acid flapped her mouth for a few silent words. "My… My agent. My friends. The Press Association." She was grasping at straws and they both knew it.

Saman grinned arrogantly behind his moustache. "I don't think so, Ms Dankworth. I have spoken to my superiors and you are to be deported back to the UK in the morning. To be handed over to your own authorities." His eyes narrowed. "From what I hear, they are keen to speak with you also."

Acid's heart dropped into her stomach, playing a tune on her ribcage as it fell. A death march in D Minor. "You piece of shit."

Saman snickered at her unease, his shrill laughter at odds with his appearance. "Farewell, Ms Dankworth. If we don't see each other again, it was good to meet you." He lowered his voice whilst shaking his fist mockingly in front of her face. "And it was even better to… how you say… take you down a peg or two. Stupid English bitch."

He barked something at the guards before turning on his boot heels and marching out of the cell, leaving Acid standing there with the very real possibility that tomorrow evening she'd be in the detention of UK customs. With records of who she really was having been wiped from the archives many years ago (and no easy way of explaining why she had no history on file), this was something she couldn't let happen.

Besides, she'd been searching for Caesar for too long and this was her strongest lead yet, she had to follow it through. She turned and walked back to the bench, cursing herself and her own rotten luck, but she was determined now more than ever. This had gone on long enough. She had to find her old mentor otherwise she'd remain in this oppressive and obsessive limbo state for the rest of her days, her energy and focus stuck in the past and her heart crushed under the heavy weight of unserved justice and simmering revenge. So deportation and pandemic be damned, she had to get out of this place.

She had to find Beowulf Caesar, and she had to kill him.

CHAPTER 4

The holding cell had only one window. A small rectangle of glass about the size of a laptop screen and placed so high up the wall it was impossible to see anything out of it but sky. Still, it didn't stop her from staring up at it every half hour or so, literally watching time drift away as the rectangle turned from sapphire blue to dusky pink.

"What a bloody carry on," she muttered to herself. "Typical luck."

As the hours had ticked away and the oppressive airless heat had grown in ferocity, it had become apparent her desire for vengeance might not be satisfied after all. Six hours in and it was all she could do to not smash her face against the brick wall.

It didn't help that the bats were back in force, bristling under the surface of her consciousness and telling her to act, to flee, to kill, to get out any way she could. This heightened, prickly part of her personality was so often a blessing, but it could also be a curse. Over the years she'd learned to hone the distorted spikes in her chemical make-up into something useable. Valuable, even. Like a superpower, she often said. But confine this agitated viper energy for any amount of time and it had only one way to go. Internally.

She was restless but with no means of an outlet. Her skin felt like it was vibrating whilst a million tiny fangs nibbled at her resolve, making her question herself.

Not what she needed right now.

Not one bit.

As Acid gazed up at the window an image flashed into her mind. A woman, with long dark hair and a smile halfway between caring and conniving. Dr Jacqueline Summers, her therapist in Crest Hill, the home for dangerous girls where she'd been taken after she killed Oscar Duke. It was Jacqueline who'd inspired the concept of the bats, as a way for Acid to deal with her Cyclothymia (a rare form of bipolar disorder), envisaging her hypomania and depression as outside forces – not a defining part of her, or who she was, just something she dealt with. She was also the woman who'd introduced Acid to Caesar, although introduced was probably the wrong word. Groomed her for him was a better description. But in the end Jacqueline had paid for her actions. Everyone did. In the end.

"Hello? Zora?"

Huh?

Acid snapped her focus back to the moment to see Lars sitting a few feet away, waving at her.

"Are you okay?"

She rolled her shoulders back. "I was away with the fairies. But yes, I'm fine. Just angry. And frustrated." She sniffed. "And feeling generally shitty."

She slapped her hands down on the bench and looked around. Everyone here in the cell looked wrecked. Sweat ran down grimy, sallow cheeks and their eyes held an empty quality she recognised all too well.

"At least you will be home soon enough," Lars tried. "I know it's not what you want to hear, but it could be a lot worse. If they'd marked you as a spy… Well, I think we both know what happens then."

"I can't go home," she replied through gritted teeth. "I have a mission to complete. I have to get into Iran."

"This is not possible. You must let it go."

"I can't."

Lars lifted his head, considering her with narrowed eyes. "This is very important to you? More than a job?"

"I told you why I'm here. What I have to do." She let her head fall back, resting against her leather jacket, which she'd balled up and was using as a neck pillow. "Obviously I can't give you too much detail, but you are correct, this is personal. I have to get closure on this job. Which is why I can't let them send me home."

Lars was quiet for some time, so she closed her eyes and listened to the gentle sobbing coming from the woman sitting on the opposite side of the cell.

This is personal.

There was the understatement of the decade. Acid had always prided herself on being able to expertly compartmentalise the many aspects of her life and career. Any assassin worth their salt did the same. If not you went mad. Properly mad. Yet ever since she'd pledged her vendetta against Caesar and her ex-colleagues, she'd felt this desire for revenge creeping into every aspect of her existence, taking over. If she wasn't careful it would become all she was. And she was so much more. So this mission was also about freedom. From her old self and also from hate.

"If you find Cyrus Heydari, what will happen then?"

She looked over to see Lars with his head in his hands, talking to the floor.

"It's not him I'm here for," she replied. "My sources tell me he's sheltering another dangerous man. Someone from my past. Someone who betrayed me." She coughed, cleared her throat. "Betrayed *my country,* I mean."

Lars lifted his head. His face said he knew exactly what she meant. "And this is why you are so angry? You were ready to face this person?"

"That's right."

"But this mission you are on, it is incredibly dangerous. I have met a lot of brave people in my line of work. Unofficial soldiers such as yourself, Mossad agents, mercenaries also. They are so often cold, silent, mean. Yet you strike me as a different kind of person. I see a tension in you. Strong emotions. I worry making this personal could be your undoing, no?"

Acid snorted softly. "You're a perceptive guy, Lars."

"It helps me get by."

"I bet. And you're right again. It could be my undoing. It probably will be." She shifted in her seat as he sat up and their eyes locked. "I've already made peace with the fact this could be a suicide mission. But I have to carry it out. My drive for completion is consuming me. It's going to kill me either way."

Lars nodded and looked away. Like earlier he fell silent, but it was clear now he was thinking deeply about what had been said. A few minutes went by before he spoke again. When he did, his voice had a different tone.

"I was working here in Iran four years ago," he said. "For Doctors Without Borders, same as now. There had been a lot of insurgency in the region – Islamic State mainly, but other, smaller organisations too. Whilst I was here I met a woman, Isla. She was a new doctor, from Canada. So full of life and virtue. She only wanted to do good in the world."

He paused, smiling into the middle distance, clearly seeing this woman in front of him.

"What happened?" Acid asked.

"Everyone loved her," he said. "But me, I fell in love with her too. We were inseparable. We even talked about living together when our duties finished. Then one day there was an explosion over in District 22, in the east of Tehran. The reports told of many injuries. Despite the reports also speaking of insurgents still in the area, Isla volunteered to go and tend to the wounded. She never came back."

Acid swallowed. She'd seen it coming, but the way Lars' voice quivered as he spoke hit her like a sucker punch to the throat. "I'm sorry," she croaked.

Lars shook his head, the sorrow in his eyes shifting to bitterness. "It was an IED on the roadside. When I got there I couldn't even identify her body. Their whole jeep was destroyed. One group took ownership of the original explosion and the blast that killed her. They called themselves Ezda-ha. Their leader, Cyrus Heydari."

"I see. So you've got some skin in this game too?"

Lars scowled. "If you find him, will you kill him?"

"Lars, the way I'm feeling right now, I'll kill everyone he's ever met."

The Norwegian laughed. It was good to hear. "You are certainly an interesting woman, Zora Dankworth. But I like your style. And you know what, I don't doubt you will. There is a fire in you like I've not experienced in a long time."

"So they used to tell me."

"Used to?"

"Forget it. But yes, when I find Cyrus Heydari I will kill him."

Lars nodded. "And if you get out of this cell, do you think you'd be able to make it out of the airport somehow?"

Acid rolled her neck from one side to the other. "I'll give it a damn good try. They also tell me I've got a death wish, but it's not let me down yet."

"Okay, good," he said. "Then I've got an idea."

CHAPTER 5

Lars Hansen flung himself against the steel bars of the cell. "Help, please. We need a medic in here. Now." He reached his arm through the gap, grasping out in desperation. The gruff customs officer standing guard on the other side eyed him suspiciously but didn't respond. Lars tried again, enunciating each word. "We need medical assistance. Now. She may die."

Now the guard looked troubled. He stepped over to the bars as Lars pulled his hand inside and gestured over to the far side of the room where his new friend, Zora, was lying unconscious on the concrete floor.

"What is problem?" the guard asked.

"She's had some sort of seizure and is now unresponsive. Please, go get help." The guard remained where he was. "She's a journalist, for heaven's sake, so she has international immunity. If she dies this won't look good on you. Won't look good on your country, either. So go, get help."

With a grunt the guard scuttled off down the corridor, shouting ahead of him in Farsi. Lars watched until he disappeared around the corner then hurried back over to Zora's side. Kneeling next to her, he lifted her head onto his lap and gently squeezed on her arm as if to say, *Keep it going.*

"Don't worry," he told the other inhabitants of the cell, who were now swarming around them. "I am a doctor. She will be okay. I hope."

The social distancing rules which had been drummed into the world's populace over the last six months meant they all kept a safe distance. Which was lucky, as one of them might have noticed Zora's eye flicker open a touch.

"Nearly there," Lars whispered. "You ready?"

"Did they buy it?" she asked, her voice a mere breath over rigid lips.

"The officials here know I'm a doctor," he replied. "I'll sell it to them. After that it's up to you."

She remained still, but Lars noticed the slight twitch of a smile playing across her lips. Lying here now in his lap she seemed peaceful. So at odds with the fiery woman he'd met a few hours earlier who'd prowled around the cell like a caged beast.

"Over here," he yelled, as the door of the cell swung open and three medics dressed in Hazmat suits and carrying a stretcher stepped inside. He called out again, beckoning them over. "This one. She is very unwell."

As they ran over, he laid her head down on the concrete floor and gave her arm another reassuring squeeze. *Good luck.*

"I am Dr Lars Hansen," he announced to the first medic. "Do you speak English?"

The medic, a middle-aged man sweating profusely in his white suit, nodded sternly. "What happened?"

"She collapsed a few minutes ago," he said. "I've examined her and I believe she's had an ischaemic stroke. Her pulse, it is incredibly weak." He held up her wrist, knowing the medic would have to remove the Hazmat gloves if they wanted to check.

The man shrugged. "You are certain of stroke?"

"Yes. I'm a specialist. She needs thrombolysis or a thrombectomy urgently." The medic looked from Zora back to Lars. "Urgently," Lars repeated.

The medic nodded and turned to his colleagues, shouting over and gesturing for them to get her on the stretcher.

"Can I come too?" Lars asked, as he watched them lift Zora onto the stretcher and secure her with straps. "I can help."

"No. You will stay," the medic said, holding an arm out as Lars stepped forward. "We will take it from here."

"Where are you taking her?" he asked, for her benefit more than his.

"She will be taken to the medical centre in the airport. If we cannot help her there, we shall take her to Emam Hospital. If they cannot help her…" He trailed off and nodded to the other medics now standing with Zora on the stretcher between them. "We go now."

Lars followed them over to the cell door and leaned his head against the bars as they rushed Zora down the corridor and disappeared.

"Good luck, my friend," he whispered after her. "I really hope you can pull this off."

CHAPTER 6

Acid remained as still as possible, peering out through her eyelashes as she was stretchered along the winding corridors. Some were so brightly lit with harsh strip-lights overhead that it hurt her eyes. Others – like the one they were racing along now – were dingy and grey, with no lights at all. They kept going, carrying her deep into the belly of the airport. A moment later they burst through a set of double doors into what was evidently the medical centre and the lead medic stopped his men to scope out the room.

Letting her eyelids flicker momentarily as if part of the seizure, she was able to make out a space not much bigger than the cell but enough for six cubicles, three down one side of the room and another three opposite.

The lead medic growled something at those carrying her and she sensed them taking her to the cubicle in the far corner and placing her down on a steel gurney. She kept her eyes closed and held her breath as one of the men leaned over to examine her. It wasn't easy for him to do through the Hazmat suit, and she felt the soft plastic of his face shield pressing against the tip of her nose.

Keep it together.

She relaxed her entire body and let her mind go blank, the way she'd been trained to do. Because despite what Hollywood might have you believe, the life of an elite assassin wasn't all machine guns and neon alleyways (far from it), there was also a hell of a lot of waiting around, mainly in cramped spaces. One of the first things Caesar had taught her all those years ago was how to remain composed and still, yet fully prepared. It wasn't always so easy. There were specific types of breathing techniques which tricked the brain and body into an incredibly calm, highly cooperative state. Except these were mostly centred around bringing your awareness back to the present moment, taking what was called SLLS breaks (stop, look, listen, smell). Difficult with your eyes shut and under the pretence you had a blood clot in your brain.

One of the medics grabbed her by the mouth and rolled her head around the stretcher before thumbing open her eyelids and shining a pen light into her pupils. She didn't flinch as the man let go and spoke rapidly to his colleagues, before she heard them shuffling out of the cubicle. A few seconds later she heard the double doors suck open. Then silence.

She gave it another few seconds, and a few more. Then slowly, carefully, she opened her eyes and peered about her. The men were nowhere to be seen, but that didn't mean they wouldn't return. They'd given no indication if they thought she was dead, or an emergency case, or if they simply didn't give two shits about the western journalist.

Sitting upright she swung her legs off the gurney and zipped up her leather jacket, glad she'd had the foresight to put it back on despite the heat. The jacket was her pride and joy and as much a part of her persona as her thick dark hair and *take-no-prisoners* sneer. Originally it had been Dr Jacqueline's but she'd taken it from her wardrobe – a trophy of sorts – on her first assignment. Her first professional kill. It felt like a lifetime ago now. As if it had happened to someone else entirely. But then, perhaps it had.

Staying low she moved around the room. She could see now

there were patients in the other cubicles, but all seemed unresponsive as she passed by. On the wall next to the exit was a large control panel with flashing green and red lights denoting different parts of the airport. Beneath this was a bench with white crates sitting on top, each one containing different items of medical equipment – gauzes, antibacterial swabs, syringe kits, and then, in the last one she came to, scalpels.

Jackpot.

She lifted out the top two and tore the metal blades from their sterile casing. The handles felt thin and unsatisfying in her grip, but at least she was armed. She had a chance. Each of the double doors had a round porthole window at eye level, and as she shifted over to the side of the wall she glanced out through the one on the right. Beyond the doors, a long corridor stretched off into the distance. Signs hung from the ceiling half-way along, written in Farsi and Arabic but with English translations too: *Main Hall, Airport.*

With the bats' brittle screeches fizzing across her soul, she leaned her shoulder against the door and eased it open. The air in the corridor was stifling, much hotter than in the cool chrome surrounds of the medical centre. She headed back towards the main hall, gripping the scalpels by her side and holding them with the blades pointing down ready to slash and tear if the opportunity arose. The end of the corridor split into a T-junction and she pressed herself against the nearside wall to scope out both directions. There were more signs here. One down to the left pointing to *Airport*, whilst another over to the left read *Staff Storeroom*. Someone had placed a new sticker on this sign that looked like a Hazmat mask with the letters *PPE* written underneath. An idea formed. Maybe she wouldn't need the scalpels after all.

Decision made, she was heading for the storeroom when a voice boomed, "Stop."

She spun around to see two customs officers rushing at her. Both male but with slight builds and not much taller than her.

What was that about not needing the scalpels?

Before the first guy was even on her, she stepped forward and kicked him sharply in the knee, snapping the joint with a disturbing crunch. He fell to the floor screaming as his colleague skidded to a halt, the look on his face telling her his bottle had gone.

Shocked and surprised.

The perfect state for one's enemy.

In one fluid movement she lurched forward and stabbed the scalpels into his chest, not deep but incapacitating him enough that she could shift around the back of him and get an arm around his neck. Once in position she pressed down on his carotid artery until he was limp in her arms. All done in under ten seconds.

She knelt by the side of his whimpering apprentice and lifted him up enough she could administer the same treatment. With an arm around his neck, the bats screamed in her head, the dark shadow side telling her to finish him off, snap his neck. She gripped the man to her chest as he gasped for air. One movement would be all it took, a quick jolt.

No.

Fighting the impulse with all she had, she squeezed his neck tight, sending him to sleep rather than to an early grave. This way was for the best. It was important she communicate to her subconscious that she wasn't that person anymore – someone who could kill indiscriminately at the drop of a hat. Besides, karma and all that shit.

She got to her feet, letting the man's lifeless body slump to the floor, and hurried back to the end of the corridor, taking a right. She'd travelled some way along before she saw a door up ahead carrying the same Hazmat sign as before. Stopping outside, she first tested the door was unlocked before barging her way in, already in attack mode, face rigid with penetrating rage. But the room was empty.

Two large locker units spanned the walls on either side of her, and on the wall directly opposite was a large metal shelving unit divided into squares. In each space was a pile of what looked to be protective gear – white Hazmat suits, gloves, face masks, visors, all sealed in clear cellophane. She was over at the shelving unit in a few strides, ripping open the bag containing a full suit and shaking it out. Holding it up in front of her body, she surmised it was about her size. She stepped into the rough crêpe material and pulled the all-in-one up to her waist. It was certainly going to be hot in the suit, but hopefully she wouldn't need to wear it long. She got her arms in the sleeves before flipping the hood over her head and zipping it up. As she pushed her hair up under the elasticated hood she noticed a mirror on the wall to her right.

Jesus.

Not the sexiest of looks, it had to be said. But needs must. Reaching down to the lower shelves, she grabbed an overhead visor and a face mask and unwrapped them to inspect the quality. Up to this point Acid hadn't engaged much with the potentially killer virus sweeping the globe. She wasn't a conspiracy theorist or anything like that (she'd been privy to enough actual conspiracies to see through the bullshit), but rather she just didn't have the time to worry about things like viruses and pandemics. The way she saw it, if she got sick, she got sick. If she died, she died. And maybe that was her supposed death wish coming to the surface once again, but for now she had a one-track mind. Her only concern was finding Cyrus Heydari and him leading her to Beowulf Caesar.

Once she'd strapped on the headgear, she moved over to the door and cast her hearing through to the other side. No voices could be heard, no footsteps either. So with her new disguise rustling annoyingly with each step, she left the storeroom and strode along the corridor, hoping to find a doorway that led outside. An emergency exit. Something.

Around the next corner the corridor opened up into a high-ceilinged room that appeared to be the main entrance for airport staff. A check-in desk was set within a hole in the wall, where two bored-looking moustachioed men were sitting behind a bank of computer screens. Across from them stood a six-foot rubber plant and a sorry-looking vending machine with a large proportion of its spiralised arms empty of produce.

As well as the two men at reception, she counted four more employees. Two wore the same customs officer uniforms as before, plus two men in darker uniforms, who she guessed might be air traffic control from the fraught energy coming off them. None of the men even glanced her way as she shuffled, head down, across the room, heading for the three doors adjacent to the check-in hatch. Crazy times, when someone dressed this way wasn't even considered unusual. But that was modern life for you. Crazy. The more Acid experienced civilian life, the more she realised it was as insane and messed up as anything she encountered in her life as an elite assassin. The only difference was the pretence.

As she got closer to the doors her heart sank. They were sealed shut and an electronic barrier system stood a few feet in front. The only way through appeared to be by way of an electronic key card, which of course she didn't have.

"Bastard," she muttered to herself, as she scanned the room for another option. She was so close now she could hear the working city drifting in through the doors. The clank and thrum from a nearby building site cutting through the drone of heavy traffic, the static hiss of voices and shouts from street vendors and pedestrians. Without faltering, she did a full sweep of the room before heading back the way she'd come. She'd had an idea.

Moving past the storeroom, she took a left towards the medical centre. The two guards she'd incapacitated earlier were nowhere to be seen and, pushing past any troubling thoughts about what that meant, she ran up the corridor and burst through the double doors of the stark, chrome room she'd been stretchered to earlier. The Hazmat suit and protective headgear offered little protection against the smell of ammonia making her eyes water as she sidled up to the control panel along the nearside wall. She narrowed her eyes at the black acetate displaying a white outline of the airport footprint, and the series of flashing lights, switches and dials set out to differentiate the airport zones. She moved her eyes around the panel, attempting to work out what it all meant, before thinking, *Screw it*, and twisting the dials and flicking the switches until she got what she'd hoped for.

Even wrapped in the muffled confines of the Hazmat suit, the alarm was ear-shredding. When the lights on the control panel all turned red, she ran for the door and joined the commotion in the corridor as the many cleaners, security officers and customs officials who worked in this part of the airport headed quickly for the exit.

Keeping to the wall, she hurried back to the entrance hall where she saw the magnetic seal on the doors had been deactivated and more staff members – front-of-house and even cabin crew – were filing out into the darkness beyond. A quick glance at the clock above reception told her it was nearly eight. *Shit.* She was supposed to be meeting her contact at eight and she still had to get outside and across the city. The knowledge sent a prickly energy zig-zagging up her spine, but she breathed through it, telling herself to stay calm lest this heightened sense of invincibility and profound nihilism drive her to do something rash. It wouldn't be the first time.

Instead she stood in line and lumbered forward with the crowds, keeping her head low and controlling her breathing as she heard shouting from outside. Four customs officials had taken position in front of the doors, herding people from the building. Another few steps and she felt a breeze coming up through the ankle cuffs of her suit. She was almost there. Almost free. Then she looked up. Straight into the eyes of the customs officer who'd interviewed her that morning.

Shit.

She snapped her face away, leaning into the person in front to try and hurry them along. Thirty seconds and she'd be clear. As she got past the first barrier she risked glancing back to see the customs officer still looking her way. His expression was one of confusion, as though trying to put something together in his mind.

And she knew just what.

For most people a full Hazmat suit plus visor and a mask covering your nose and mouth would have been ample disguise. But when uniquely coloured eyes were one of your most distinctive traits, that was kind of negated.

She pushed on as she heard the man yelling after her, the tone of his voice quickly shifting from confusion to realisation to anger.

"Hey... *Hey*... HEY!"

"Sod this."

Leading with sharp elbows, she barged her way along the lines of people and burst out into the Iranian night. Breaking into a run, she threw the mask and visor aside, thankful of the cool air on her face but not stopping as the customs officer began to bark after her in Farsi. She couldn't tell exactly what he was saying but the energy behind the words was enough.

Something like, *She's escaping. Get the hell after her!*

CHAPTER 7

hooting a furtive glance over her shoulder, Acid counted three of them. All armed. All in quick pursuit as she raced out of the airport grounds towards the imposing Azadi Tower. From there she was to travel west along the main road until she reached Bimeh Station. Her rendezvous spot with Bayat was a café in a side street nearby. If she made it that far.

She took a sharp turn down the side of the Iranian Aviation College, hoping it might throw them off. But risking another quick look behind her, she saw the three guards were still on her tail. Another minute and she reached the Azadi Tower and the main road that circled around its base. As Acid neared the impressive structure, she heard the familiar crack and whizz of a bullet flying through the air, over her head and off to the right. Getting across the road, she could see the guards were now only two hundred metres away. They weren't giving in. She followed the busy traffic around the circumference of the Tower before heading for the sprawling four-lane carriageway that led off from the opposite side. If her sense of direction was correct, this was the Lashkari Expressway and the metro station stood somewhere alongside it a few hundred metres away.

Pushing through the stitch in her side, she pressed on, but

could sense herself slowing down, getting wearier with each step. Despite training hard these last few months, eating well and laying off the booze, she would never be as fit as she had been in her day. Not as invincible either, despite the bats telling her otherwise. Although, she was always thankful for this aspect of her more manic personality – when the bats were visiting she felt she could accomplish anything, and experience had taught her when you believe you can do something, you're already half-way there.

She passed by a large mosque and took the next side street. It opened out into a residential area flanked with mid-rise flats and a series of smaller roads leading off the main one. Perfect for what she had in mind. It was also a heavily populated area and, even at this hour, the streets were full of people, young and old, some dressed in traditional Arabic dress, but many in jeans and t-shirts. Acid slowed her pace, confident the men wouldn't open fire in such a busy area. Walking backwards a few steps, she saw them cross the road two blocks away. She could now make out the indignant determination creasing their faces and wasn't surprised to see one of them was the same customs officer who'd interviewed her at the airport and recognised her as she fled.

As she watched, they barged their way through the crowds of people and crossed over to be on the same side of the street as her, less than a hundred feet away. With her own determination hardening her muscles, she slipped down the side of one of the apartment blocks and found herself in a narrow, unlit passageway with metal dumpsters on either side. At the far end the passage opened out onto another wider street.

Letting her instincts guide her, she slipped behind the dumpster to her right and knelt in the darkness. In this position she could remain out of sight whilst keeping watch on the entrance to the passageway as the three customs officers appeared. Acid held her breath as one of the guards pointed animatedly at the others. He looked to be suggesting they split up and that brought a smile to her lips. Two of the guards headed off either side of the passageway, whilst the third stayed put, scoping out the area with his pistol gripped tightly at waist height.

From this distance she could see the pistol was a Browning Hi-Power 9mm, as she'd expected. For once she'd done her home-work and knew these semi-automatics were a favourite of the Islamic Revolutionary Guard. Saddam Hussein had often carried a Browning HP with him. Ghaddafi had a gold-plated one with his own face engraved on the grip. A million thoughts raced through her mind as the young officer swayed around the space, eyes squinting into the blackness, body taut and ready, like he knew she was there. Acid tensed. She was still wearing the stark white Hazmat suit, meaning as the guard's eyes got accustomed to the gloom, the easier she'd be to spot. She sucked in a silent breath as he stepped towards her.

Now! the bats screeched. *Do it.*

Like a cat pouncing on its prey, she leapt from behind the dumpster and brought a hammer fist down on the unwitting guard's inner elbow. Before he had a chance to act, she followed this up with a pincer grip to the wrist which sent the pistol tumbling to the ground. He yelled out as she twisted his arm up around his back before stamping down on the backs of his calves and getting her forearm around his throat. Pressure applied, it took less than eight seconds for the man to stop thrashing around. As his unconscious body sank to the ground, she climbed out of the Hazmat suit and hurried over to retrieve the dropped pistol. A quick examination told her she still had all thirteen rounds in the mag. She stuffed the gun in her waistband and headed out of the passageway.

Once she'd found her bearings, she doubled back along the main strip towards the metro station. She'd just got eyes on it when she heard screaming from behind her, followed by the distinct crack of gunfire.

"Bloody hell."

Spinning around she saw a second customs officer running at her, aiming his pistol out in front of him. Their eyes met and he fired again but skying the round a fair way over her head. The idiot – all he was doing by opening fire was giving himself away. Acid had known people to be able to run and shoot on target at the same time (The Dullahan could do it, Spitfire too), but it was often a pointless exercise.

She held her ground as the man got nearer, his face morphing from furious resolve to something close to fear as she drew her own pistol and shot him through the shoulder. The force of impact knocked him over and sent his weapon skidding across the road.

Acid stepped towards him and raised her aim as the man mouthed whatever *Oh shit* looked like in Farsi.

The bats screeched for blood but her finger trembled on the trigger.

No.

She'd made a promise to herself. Any killing she did would only be in self-defence. Until she caught up with Caesar, that is.

Instead she lowered the pistol and put a bullet in the man's lower thigh just above the kneecap, enough to put him out of action but without shattering any bone or cartilage. It would hurt like hell, evident in the way he cried out like an injured animal, but he'd walk again, and that was her intention. A sly grin spread across her lips as she backed away. Back when she was still Caesar's number one, the modus operandi had been stealth kills, tactical assassinations – what they called in the business 'forced accidents' – yet she'd always been a crack shot and it was good to know she could still put a bullet exactly where she intended.

Leaving the customs officer writhing in pain, she stuffed the pistol down the back of her jeans and set off, running at speed now, the heightened, in-the-moment excitement of the last few minutes turning sour as she remembered she was late to meet her contact. She gasped out a silent prayer while she raced through the busy streets, promising the cosmos anything it wanted if it kept him there. Because without him she had nothing. Quite literally. Not only had she no lead, but without a phone or money, and with her passport and visa confiscated, she had no way of getting home. She'd been speaking the truth when she told Lars she was prepared for this being a one-way trip, but that didn't mean she had to give in before she'd started.

Past the metro station, she took the next right down 3rd Bimeh Street and slowed. This was the street. She could see the sign for the Mizo Café up ahead, where she'd arranged to meet Baraz Bayat (she peered into a parked car to check the time on the dashboard) forty-five minutes ago.

Shitting hell.

She made her way along the street, still on high alert, ready in case the third customs officer showed up but with her focus now on getting to the café. A gentle breeze coming down from nearby Mount Tochal in the north made the city heat bearable, and for the first time since she'd left the airport she allowed herself to slow down and take heed of this new country in which she found herself.

It was her first time in Iran (first and last, she'd promised Spook) and she was surprised, and not a little humbled, at how modern and welcoming she found the city. The disparity between outward perceptions and internal truths had been at the forefront of her mind recently, and she was angry at herself for being so close-minded where Iran was concerned. She'd expected a dour landscape of sand and rubble, with a snarl on every lip and a Kalashnikov on every shoulder. Instead she was met with wide streets filled with brightly coloured storefronts, and a young, eager populace who practically buzzed with verve and opportunity.

But wasn't that always the way, she wondered, getting closer to the cafeteria to see it was a modern warehouse space (not the poky shisha establishment she'd imagined) – one invariably formed an opinion of a country based on the actions of its rulers rather than the civilians. As far as she was concerned, all governments were bad news, it just depended on how close you stood. And yes, it was true some were better than others (in terms of their human rights policies, for instance), but in her experience no government in the world had clean hands. She'd carried out hits for enough of them to know that much.

The Mizo Cafeteria was an open-plan establishment, done out like a factory canteen, with raw concrete walls and weathered steel girders holding up a pointed glass ceiling. The only concession to tradition were two large Persian rugs lying across the raised seating areas at the front and rear. Other than those, the café wouldn't have looked out of place in the trendier parts of New York or London.

Stepping further inside, Acid moved over to the canteen-style counter and examined the selection of cakes and drinks on offer. A cold beer would go down well right about now, but of course that was out of the question even if she had money. She leaned against the cold counter top and tried to look inconspicuous as she scoped out the room, eyes snapping from face to face. She was the only westerner in here, but with her colouring, her Italian blood, she didn't look too out of place. Although, she had about ten years on the clientele, all of them in their early twenties and chatting animatedly. It was a cool atmosphere to find herself in after the stress of the last few hours. But she didn't see Bayat.

Bollocks.

All she'd had to go on was a small headshot photo of the journalist Spook had found online, but since having her things confiscated she didn't even have that. She followed the perimeter of the canteen to where stairs led up to a raised mezzanine level. Grabbing the handrail, she hauled herself up and poked her head around the side. There were four tables on this level and two of them were occupied. But a cursory glance told her they were too young, and neither of the males had beards like she remembered from the photo. Besides, they all looked too happy, too carefree to be the battle-worn journalist Sofia Swann had described. She was ready to do one more circuit of the place when her eyes fell on the entrance where she saw the third customs officer – the young one who'd interviewed her – striding into the main hall.

Acid faltered, unsure whether to duck behind a pillar or

remain still lest the movement alert him of her presence. A second went by. She didn't move. Didn't blink. Not taking her eyes off the man, she began to walk backwards, feeling for the handrail as she watched him disappear underneath the mezzanine level. With her hand on the pistol in her waistband, she descended the few steps to ground level. At the bottom of the steps she paused, casting her attention left and right around the room. He was nowhere in sight, but her best guess was he'd checked the ground floor and was now on his way up the stairs on the opposite side of the upper level. If she was really lucky he might have cleared the building entirely. She gave it another beat before moving around the side of the stairwell, and straight into his path.

"Ah shit."

They locked eyes, both frozen in time, unsure what to do. Her fingers tightened on the pistol handle but she held off. A stray bullet or two here and there'd be civilian casualties. Fatalities, even. Too risky. The man knew it too but she couldn't guarantee he'd hold onto that opinion if things got desperate. The last time they'd been this close they were sitting across the desk from one another and he was holding the success or failure of her mission in his hands. If only he hadn't been so bloody cautious, she'd have been on her merry way and none of this would be necessary for either of them. She swallowed on a dry throat as her heart beat a staccato rhythm in her chest, everything fading away except for the man in front of her. He didn't blink. Nerves showing in the fine lines around his eyes.

A second went by.

And another.

Acid held onto the pistol for dear life. Ready to draw. Ready to kill.

No one moved.

Then, as if choreographed, they burst into action at the same time, him running forwards as she side-stepped around a table and dragged it across his path, putting it between them. As he cried out in frustration, she skidded around the edge of the room.

But out of the corner of her eye she saw him vault the table and pull the pistol from its holster.

"Stop or I shoot."

She was heading for the main exit, ready to take her chances out on the street when a hand grabbed at her forearm.

"This way, quickly."

She snapped her attention towards the source of the voice to see a stout man a few inches shorter than her. He was wearing western clothes but had the bushy, salt and pepper beard of an old-school Iranian. He glared at her with small, intense eyes.

"Bayat?" she asked.

"Follow me. I know a better way. Come."

CHAPTER 8

With a pressure pulsing behind her eyes, Acid followed her new acquaintance through the back of the cafeteria. Throwing open a thin plywood door, Bayat glanced back over her shoulder.

"He's coming. Quickly."

He pulled her into a short corridor with three doors leading off it, and they ran all the way to the last one which opened out into a cloakroom. Coats and bags were hung up along one wall with a bank of lockers opposite, and there, in the opposite corner of the room, was a thick wooden door with a bar-lock across the middle. An emergency exit. As they hurried across to it, the gruff shouts of the customs officer echoed down the corridor behind them. He was closing in – and here, out of sight from the diners, he'd have a clear shot.

The old journalist smashed his hand down on the bar-lock, but it didn't budge. Stepping back, he tried a second time but the result was the same.

"Here, let me try."

Barging him out the way, Acid gave the lock-bar all she had, but bounced off it the same way Bayat had done. They were trapped, cornered. Except being cornered was something she knew all about. Something she could deal with.

"Wait, what are you doing?"

Bayat's voice reverberated through her head as she strode back the way they'd come – but she only heard it superficially. Her awareness had already shifted from macro to micro. Her mind was now clear of thought as instinct and rage stepped up to lead the fight, fuelled by her manic bat energy.

The second the customs officer was through the door, she grabbed his right arm with both hands and slamming it against the side of the locker unit, forcing the elbow back against itself. Before the man even knew what had hit him, she'd snapped his arm and followed this up by smashing the hardest part of her frontal cranium into the bridge of his nose. The impact had her see stars but she didn't miss a beat. As the man shrieked in pain, raising his one good arm to his face, she caught him with a heavy punch to the abdomen before stamping down on the side of his knee. He crumpled to the floor, wailing in agony, and she reached down and unclipped his pistol – another HP – from its holster.

Slipping it down the back of her jeans alongside the first one, she glanced up at Bayat, now standing open-mouthed by the door. "He's the last of the men who were following me," she told him. "We should be clear out the front. Let's go."

Without a second glance to the incapacitated young officer, Acid marched back the way they'd come, making sure she pulled her t-shirt and jacket over the pistol handles as she reached the main dining hall. In spite of the adrenaline fizzing through her system, she had no sense of disorientation like she so often did of late in these sorts of situations. There had been a time, of course, when she could kill three men before breakfast without losing her stride – or her appetite – but ever since her unceremonious departure from Annihilation Pest Control (and why not face it, the wheels of her sanity were coming off even before then), she'd allowed things to affect her too deeply. The word amongst her ex-colleagues had been she couldn't handle the lifestyle anymore, and that the real reason she'd jumped ship was because she'd gone soft. Some days even she wondered if that might be true. Yet right now all she felt was excited, and alive, and ready for more.

"That was extremely impressive," Bayat said, catching up with her as she marched out through the main canteen. "You took him down like he was nothing, like he was a little girl."

"Hey," Acid snapped, hitting him with a viciously arched eyebrow. "Careful what you say about little girls."

Bayat grinned. The relief on his face took ten years off him. "Fair enough. I take your point. Follow me."

They left Mizo Cafeteria and took a right at the end of the road, back onto the main strip. Without speaking, Acid followed Bayat's brisk pace down a narrow street between an ice cream shop and a pharmacy. There were a lot of ice cream shops and pharmacies, she noticed. Pain relief, then dessert. A winning combination.

"Where are we heading?" she asked, once the commotion was behind them.

"My apartment," Bayat wheezed, slowing his pace. "It will take us about an hour on foot, but it is safer than public transport. We shall stick to the back streets."

"You think they might still be after me? More of them?"

"I am not sure," he replied, squinting down the street before letting out a soft chuckle. "It seems you make enemies quicker than I do."

She blew out a long breath. "Yes. Trouble does have a way of finding me."

As they left the threat further behind, an easier air fell between them. At the end of the street they paused before crossing over another main road and continuing down an almost identical back street on the opposite side. Acid glanced over her shoulder, but there was no one following them.

"Thanks for waiting, by the way," she said. "I would have been screwed if you hadn't."

"I take it from the uniform that man was from border control?"

"Customs, yeah. I had decent enough papers, or so I thought. But hadn't counted on them being so stringent with the checks. Coming here in the midst of a pandemic was probably a stupid idea."

"Coming here at all was a stupid idea."

She turned to see Bayat's face was serious. "I don't know, I like it. Lots of young people. Not the sort of stuffy religious place I was expecting."

"On the surface perhaps," Bayat replied, followed by a deep sigh. "But there is still a lot of tension in my country. Tell me, how did you escape airport security if they flagged your papers?"

She shrugged. "I've gotten out of worst situations. I trust Sofia filled you in about me?"

They got to the end of the next street and Bayat halted, peering down both sides before taking a right and beckoning for her to follow. "She told me you saved her life. That you are a brave woman."

"Is that all?"

"She also told me you were once a paid killer, named Acid Vanilla. Is this correct?"

"That is still my name." She held out her hand. "Pleased to meet you."

Bayat stared at her outstretched palm with worried eyes. "Sorry, do you mind if we don't. I—"

"Oh, sure, of course," she said, wiping her hand down the side of her jeans. "I can't get the hang of this new way of being."

"These are strange times indeed, Ms Vanilla."

"Acid will do. Sofia tells me you're a brave man yourself. 'A one man crusade to take down ISIL', is how she put it."

The question was met with another sigh. "I wish I was braver," he said quietly. "But you must realise, I am not a popular man in the region. I have made a lot of enemies over the years. Especially recently."

"For speaking out about the regime?"

"And about Heydari. He is the man you are looking for, yes?"

"Cyrus Heydari." She said the name slowly, giving the 'Hey' part the same guttural inflection Bayat had. "So he's as bad as everyone says?"

Bayat chuckled humourlessly. "Oh yes. Once a degenerate businessman and petty criminal, he has left his thuggish ways behind to pursue bigger dreams. He now rubs shoulders with kings and insurgents alike. He can be a charismatic man, but don't be fooled. He is a dangerous mix of brains and ambition, with a strong desire for power at any cost. Many say he is gearing up for a place in government, but those in the know suspect that is simply a cover."

"Oh? For what?"

"Like I say, he has ties with many organisations. Firstly with Al Qaeda, then ISIL and other Shi'ite militia groups, as well as friendships with the ruling Al Mualla family in Umm Al Quwain and the Al Nuaimi family in Ajman. He knows a lot of powerful people, as well as those ready and willing to spill blood for their cause."

"I thought ISIS – ISIL – were no more?"

"They were, but many people in the Islamic Republic believe they are once more on the rise. Their ideology and socioeconomic fault lines run deep in this region. The rumours speak of Cyrus Heydari gearing up to re-establish the Caliphate in his own unique way."

"I see. Well he sounds like a lot of fun."

"But don't get me wrong," Bayat continued, shaking his head with a weary sadness. "It is all about money for Heydari."

"It usually is."

He squinted up at her. "You believe you can kill him?"

"Is that what Sofia told you, that I was coming here to kill him?"

"She said he was harbouring someone you had been pursuing, but she also intimated you were quite the powerhouse, and if I helped you find him you might help me too. Help all of Iran."

Acid turned the words over in her head before answering. This was exactly what she'd been afraid of, getting caught up in other people's battles. If the last two years had taught her anything, it was that a slip in her focus could send her spiralling not only into the depths of her own unsettled psyche but into far more trouble than she needed. After Spain she'd promised herself she'd keep it simple. She had one mission, one reason to be here – to kill Beowulf Caesar. There would be no more messing around. No more distractions. So whilst she was aware Cyrus Heydari was likely to be an obstacle (and if that was the case, she'd deal with him), she wasn't ready to make any promises. She couldn't save everyone and she certainly wasn't a hero.

She glanced at Bayat still waiting for her reply. "I'll see what I can do," she said. "But you know where I can find him?"

"Heydari was once a son of Tehran and lived over on the eastern side of the city, but in the last few years he has made a lot of money and has moved away. My sources tell me he now lives near to Shiraz in the south of the country. He has built himself a palace compound out in the desert, a stronghold of sorts."

"Is it far?"

"Over ten hours by car."

"Oh." The enormity of her mission hit her like a punch to the guts. "But you can take me there?"

Bayat stopped and fixed her dead in the eyes. A strange expression fell over his face, as though he wanted to say something but was fighting against it. In the end he nodded, his smile solemn.

"Yes, I can take you there. Come, my apartment is around the next block. I shall make coffee and we can talk some more."

CHAPTER 9

"**D**id you know the first assassins were a sect of Shia Islam?" Baraz Bayat asked the question as he shuffled into the lounge carrying two small glasses filled with black liquid. "They were followers of Hassan-i-Sabbah, the founder of the Nizari Isma'ili state."

Acid accepted the glass with both hands. The coffee was steaming hot and smelt like sugary earth. She placed it on the table in front of her. "I think I read something once. A long time ago. Something to do with being paid in hashish?"

The journalist shook his head as he eased himself down on the chair next to hers. "Not quite. Historians now believe this was simply a vicious slander put around by Sabbah's enemies. He would never have had any dealings with drugs. Unlike the tribal leaders of today. You know a large amount of Heydari's fortune came from heroin?" He shook his head as he stared into his coffee. "It is a terrible business. But no, the word originates from our word *Asasiyyun*, which is what Sabbah named his disciples. In English it means... umm... those faithful to the foundation of Islam."

"Interesting. But forgive me, I didn't come here for a history lesson."

"Then why did you come?" Bayat asked, his manner prickly. "If not to kill Heydari? I am confused."

"As I touched on before, the man working with Heydari is my old mentor. Someone I need to find. He betrayed me. Took from me."

Bayat picked up his coffee and blew on it before taking a sip. "So you have come here seeking revenge?"

"Something like that. Can you help me find him?"

"I'm not sure," Bayat replied. "Maybe I now think this is the wrong idea. It is a big ask. A lot of travelling and worry and I do not know if I can."

"But you said—"

"Yes, but the more I think, I worry. But I can get you a passport. We could leave now. I have people who—"

"What the hell?" Acid sat back in her seat to better take him in. He seemed like he was a sweaty man at the best of times but now it was running off him. Being safely in his own home she'd have expected him to have calmed down, yet he seemed more nervous than he had in the street. "I was told you could take me to Heydari? Give me his whereabouts, at least."

He sighed and thumbed a raised knot in the grain of the table. "I can do. But I wonder if you might reconsider. It is exceptionally dangerous. My friend, he is a good forger, we could be there in—"

"No," Acid snapped, getting to her feet. "No way. I appreciate I might have picked the worst possible time to do this, and that it's dangerous, but I have to follow it through. I have to find Beowulf Caesar. With or without your help."

The old man sagged his shoulders and sipped more of his coffee. The droplets hung in his moustache. "Fine. I understand."

"And you'll take me to Heydari's fortress… palace… whatever it is?"

He nodded but didn't look at her. "I will."

Acid remained staring at him a few seconds, trying to get a better read on him. Sofia had spoken of a man filled with fire and vitriol, desperate to take down the old order and expose the plague at the heart of the Islamic Republic. Yet the man in front of her was cowed and broken. Unable to move without looking pained.

"Can I use your bathroom?" she asked.

He raised his head. "Yes, of course. It is through the kitchen and along the short landing. The only door you'll see."

"Thank you. I'm going to freshen up." She tilted her head to one side. "Listen, Bayat – don't worry. I've got no delusions about what I'm getting into, but I can handle myself. Believe me. And if I have to, I will kill Cyrus Heydari. So we both win."

The man forced a smile, masked somewhat by his bushy beard and moustache. "I hope you're right. But think about my offer. Please. It may be the best decision."

With a non-committal nod, she placed her coffee down – glad she'd managed to swerve drinking it – and followed her host's directions towards the bathroom. The door was hanging ajar as she reached the end of the landing and she pushed it open to reveal an unremarkable room. A toilet bowl, a sink, a grimy shower stall, all done out in light blue porcelain. It wasn't the nicest bathroom she'd ever used, and the low-watt bulb didn't help, but bleach was the overriding smell and that was something at least.

At the sink she used the heel of her hand to wipe at the streaked mirror on the wall.

Woah.

She'd looked better. Daily 10K runs and the booze respite had helped bring a certain glow back to her skin, but a long-haul flight followed by a night in a holding cell had negated most of that good work. She shook her head, glaring at her reflection and catching herself before the words formed in her head.

Getting too old for this.

Thirty-six next birthday, and here she was still stuck in the past, chasing shadows and demons, obsessed (let's face it, regardless of what she might tell herself, obsessed was the right word) with finding the man who'd betrayed her.

In the mirror her right eye twitched.

For so long Beowulf Caesar had been her teacher and mentor, not to mention her closest friend. It frustrated and angered her to the core to realise she still had feelings for him, no matter how fucked up and conflicted those feelings were. She remembered reading once how children who suffered abuse by a parent often blamed themselves. Something about cognitive dissonance and the subconscious not being able to see the parent as anything other than a loving caregiver. It was all terribly sad and messed up, but maybe the same applied here. She'd seen Caesar twice since he'd killed her poor mother – since he'd put the hit out on her – and both times she'd faltered, unable to pull the trigger.

What did that say about her? Was she implicit in her own misery, or just plain soft like they all said? More importantly, would she be able to pull the trigger this time?

She twisted on the faucet and held her hands under the tap for as long as it took to realise it wasn't going to get much hotter than lukewarm. After splashing water on her face, she pulled her hair back into a ponytail and considered her reflection once again. Not much better.

Well, shitting hell.

Maybe Bayat was right. She'd chosen to do this at the worst possible time. Going anywhere in a global crisis was crazy (Spook had certainly stressed this on more than one occasion), but to travel to Iran of all places, with its known troubles and paranoia against the West – this was pushing it, even for her. All this, of course, before she even factored in that Caesar was being guarded by an incredibly dangerous and incendiary individual. A man she knew little about other than whenever anyone mentioned his name an air of abject terror washed over them.

She didn't take her eyes off her reflection as she let out a long sigh. If Bayat could indeed get her a passport and safe passage home, then perhaps she should take him up on the offer. Caesar was in the wind and Annihilation Pest Control all but finished, so the threat was over. Maybe she should leave her pain behind and move on. At the very least pick up the hunt when life and foreign air travel got back to normal.

Normal.

Jesus, what was that like again?

Because even as she was considering all this, she could sense it inside of her. The knotted gremlin of chaos rising up in her belly, nourished by revenge and hate. Hate for Caesar, hate for herself too, but also hate for the life she found herself in – constantly swinging from one extreme to the other. A restless, disordered existence driven by a powerful force she couldn't control. As her awareness spread to this deeper part of her, she already knew the gremlin wasn't going anywhere. Not until this was over. If she left now it would eat her alive.

"Thanks for the offer, Bayat," she announced, as she returned to the front room where Bayat was bent over his phone. "But I need to do this."

He jumped at the sound of her voice and shoved the phone into his pocket. "You are back. Fresh now?"

"I don't suppose you can get me one of those?" she asked him, gesturing at his pocket. "A burner phone, so we can keep in contact. If my mission goes to plan and I make it out the other side, I will need your help getting back to London."

"Yes, of course. We can get one before we set off to Shiraz."

"How will we get there? Do you have a car?"

Bayat frowned, looking towards the window. "Yes. We can leave in the morning."

"Oh? Because I was thinking it'd be good to get going soon. If we leave now, with rest stops and such, we should arrive near Heydari's base tomorrow evening. That'll give me the cover of night and—"

"No. We cannot. We shall leave at first light."

Acid narrowed her eyes at the old journalist. An odd demeanour had descended over him. He fidgeted with his hands, unsettled.

"Is everything all right?" she asked.

"Yes, of course." He got to his feet and walked over to the window, looking out into the night sky. "I very much hope you achieve what you're here for, Acid. I see you have a real fire in you. I used to have this too. Once."

Not taking her eyes off him, she moved over to the wall. "From what I heard, you still have it."

"Sofia Swann is a good journalist. She has the fire in her too. We met at the height of the last Gulf War, did she tell you this?" Acid shook her head – he didn't see, but the question was rhetorical. "I was impressed by her energy, her bravery. I saw in her… how you say… a kindred spirit. But not anymore." His head sagged as he raised one hand to the window.

"What is it, Bayat?" she asked, as the bats whispered caution across her consciousness. "You're beginning to worry me."

"I am not the same journalist Sofia met back then," he said, his voice croaky. "I am not even the same man. I am nothing. A coward. A traitor to my cause."

Acid frowned, about to press him to explain further when there was a loud banging on the front door of the apartment. Bayat spun around, his dark complexion drawn and ashen.

She stepped towards him. "What did you do, Bayat?"

"I am so sorry," he cried, over more banging and yelling. "But you told them about me, about Heydari, why you were here in my country. You shouldn't have done this."

"What the fuck did you do?" she roared, through gritted teeth, pulling the pistols from out of her jeans.

Before he could respond the front door was smashed open and four men wearing army fatigues and black face coverings burst into the room. Acid had the nines raised ready, but she was no match for the four assault rifles already pointed at her head (Kalashnikovs, by the looks of it – so she wasn't entirely wrong before). Notwithstanding the screech of the bats and a forceful surge of manic energy imploring her to open fire, she raised her hands in submission. A searing pain shot through her temples as the masked men moved around the room barking orders at her and Bayat and each other. One of them approached and grabbed the pistols from her before yelling in a gruff accent.

"Knees. Knees."

She assumed the position, placing her hands on her head for good measure as she glared at Bayat who was crying now. Two of the men addressed him in Farsi, gesturing her way as he nodded along with their questions. The weak bastard. She told him as such.

"They got to me first," he called over, as one of the men pushed him to his knees. "What could I do? They would kill me."

"Who are *they*?" she asked.

"I don't…"

"Who are they, Bayat?"

His eyes, wide and unblinking, flitted between the four men, two of them ransacking his apartment, the other two guarding him and Acid, the muzzle of their assault rifles (AKMs she could see now) trained between their eyes. "They're Heydari's foot soldiers. I'm so sorry. I—"

He lurched back as the guard smashed him in the nose with the rifle butt. Blood splattered up the wall to his right.

"Hey, it's me you want," Acid called out. "Leave him. He's done nothing."

At this, one of the men searching the room stopped and marched over to her. He knelt beside her. "You don't get to decide what happens here, bitch," he said. "This man is a coward and an apostate of the Islamic Republic."

"But I did what was asked of me," Bayat cried, raising his hands, begging them. "Please. Leave me alone now. I have done nothing. I have—"

"Shit."

Acid jumped as Bayat's head jerked back and more blood (this time with skull fragments and brain matter) painted the window behind him. Snapping her attention across the room, she saw his executioner was one of the men searching his room. As he lowered his pistol his eyes fell on Acid's and, although they were the only part of his face visible, she could tell he was smiling.

"Enough talking," he growled, pointing the pistol at her. "You. On your feet."

She did as she was told, taking her time as her mind raced with a million options. But it was useless. Three assault rifles and a pistol all pointing at her. She took a deep breath. Held it in her chest. Worked on slowing her heart rate. Times like this it was vital to keep perspective. Panic was as much a killer as a bullet.

"What are you going to do with me?" she asked.

"You'll find out."

The man gestured at the door with the pistol. For a second she hesitated, but instinct told her if she was destined to die at their hands they'd have killed her already, left her to rot with the poor son of a bitch slumped under the window.

"What's going on here?" she asked again.

The man grunted and stepped towards her, grabbing her by the root of her ponytail. "Typical western bitch. Doesn't know when to shut up."

She struggled, but the man held on. "Fine. Jesus. I'll come quietly."

She glanced up at his fierce angry eyes, fighting the impulse to follow up with a suitable snide quip. But before she had chance to say anything else, the man raised his hand and smashed the handle of his pistol into her temple. Her vision sparked with white light and an intense pain shot through her skull. Her next instinct was to run. But her legs had already given way. As she sagged to the ground, the white light swirled into a kaleidoscope of textures and colours. Then, as she hit the deck, it all went black.

CHAPTER 10

Darkness.

A throbbing pressure in her head.

Confusion.

As her cognition eddied back into something like awareness, she sensed the rumble of an engine and movement beneath her. Car tyres on rough terrain. Reaching a shaky arm up to her head, she realised her hands were bound together with plastic zip ties. Dried blood ran down her face and her fingers touched on a laceration over her eye, sore but no longer bleeding. She pushed herself upright, blinking into the blackness as the remembrance of the last few hours hit her like... well, like she'd been pistol-whipped.

"You're alive, then?"

Acid shook her head out, opening her eyes as wide as they'd go to better take in her surroundings. As anticipated, she was in the back of a truck, an old-US army issue vehicle, by the looks of it. The steel flatbed was painted khaki green and a large piece of tarpaulin was stretched across the battered frame overhead.

"You got a name?"

The voice was coming from a young black woman sitting on the wheel arch a few feet away. Her hands too were bound with zip ties, and rested limply in her lap. She sounded to be American, but Acid couldn't place the accent.

"You first," she said, adjusting herself so she was leaning against the side of the truck.

"Me first? *Me first?* What, you don't trust me? You're thinking I'm some sort of spy, placed back here to get information out of you? Because I'm not sure if you're aware, babe, but these dudes ain't too hot on recruiting young western women. At all."

"Jesus, alright. Chill out. I'm just a little disorientated, okay?" Acid sighed and looked up to see the woman eyeing her suspiciously. But as their eyes met, the agitated pout faded into a kind of smile.

"The name's Kendis. Kendis Powell."

"Acid Vanilla."

"Excuse me?"

"I know, it's weird, takes some getting used to."

"Fuck, that your real name?"

"Sort of, yes. It's a long story."

Kendis snorted. "Well, we got a long time, by my reckoning."

"Maybe later. What do you mean, by your reckoning?"

"Do you know what's going on? Why you're here?"

Acid shifted position again so she could lean forward, hitting this Kendis person with a hard stare. She was done with small talk. "Why don't you tell me what you know?"

Kendis chewed on her bottom lip before scooting off the wheel arch and moving over to sit nearer to Acid. "Don't worry," she told her. "I've been tested this morning. No virus."

"I think the virus is the least of our worries, don't you?"

"Well, *now* you're getting it."

Up close she was younger than Acid had first realised, late twenties would be her guess. Notwithstanding the face pack of grime and dirt, her skin was smooth and her eyes fresh and alert. She'd cropped her afro hair short, but the boyish cut deterred little from the serene femininity which exuded from her. This despite the cocksure swagger. Which was probably a front, Acid assumed.

Situations like this, it helped to tap into one's masculine energy. Or better still, one's animalistic, inhuman energy. Back when she first began working for Caesar, they'd called it 'Lady Macbething', in reference to the evil queen's *unsex me here and fill me with direst cruelty* speech.

These days she just called it survival.

"I work for the Peace Corps," Kendis continued. "Been all around the world over the last ten years, been to Iran twice before. This time I was supposed to be helping with the pandemic. Only arrived yesterday and it was one hell of a day. Lots to sort out. After my shift was over, I decided to go for a walk, get some air. Like a dumbass. Next thing I know I've got a sack over my head and I'm being bundled into this truck."

"Where are we heading?" Acid asked her.

"Okay, so my Farsi isn't great so I could only get the gist, but from what I heard from the men upfront, they're delivering us to a guy based down in the south."

"Cyrus Heydari," Acid whispered to herself.

"You know of him?"

"A little. What's your take?"

Kendis raised her eyebrows. "A bad guy. I'd heard talk of him the last time I was here. Motherfucker's got links to every terrorist group in the region, and he's rich too. Heroin, they say. Apparently he's started referring to himself as the New Prince of Islam. Imagine? Some balls on him."

The truck hit rocky ground, throwing the two of them about in the back. Acid tensed her limbs, pushing herself upright as it stabilised. She was already battered and bruised, but in a way it was a good feeling. In the eye of a storm she knew who she was. It was every other part of her life she had trouble with.

"What do you think he wants with us?" she asked, as they settled themselves once again. "Making video nasties, is he?"

Kendis closed her eyes. "Don't say that. But no, I don't think so. Normally, in the past, when these organisations were really into their Jihad, the beheading videos happened fast. A day or two at least before the poor bastards were pushed in front of the world to make their appeals. But from what I hear, people have been missing for months – doctors, volunteers – and no one has seen them anywhere. Not on Al Jazeera, not on the internet, or anywhere. It doesn't add up."

Whilst Kendis had been talking Acid was inspecting her constraints, but decided against trying to break free. For now, at least, it was best to stay put.

"Well," she replied, "I guess we'll find out soon enough." She peered around in the darkness of the truck, searching for anything she might use as a weapon. There was nothing.

"You going to tell me what your deal is?" Kendis asked her.

Acid sighed. "What do you want to know?"

Over the next few minutes, she filled Kendis in, giving her the same version of events she'd given Lars, the doctor at the airport, but now with the added information of how she'd escaped the customs officers and then Bayat's betrayal. When she'd finished, the young woman was staring at her with a look of bemused awe.

"Geez, that's pretty fire. You did all that yourself?"

"Yeah."

"And you're really Special Forces?"

Acid straightened up. "Yes. But don't ask me to say much more. I'm looking for a man called Beowulf Caesar who I believe has been working with Heydari, although I'm not sure the whats or whys of their relationship. He's a bad man as well."

"And you know this guy from old?"

"I do."

Kendis narrowed her eyes. "Who the hell are you? You still haven't told me what the whole Acid Vanilla name is about."

"It was a codename, originally. Now it's the only name I go by. And as far as everything else is concerned, let's leave it at this – I'm Black Ops, that's as much as you need to know. Anything more and it gets messy."

"What, for me? You can tell me but you'd have to kill me kinda vibe?"

"Something along those lines."

Kendis nodded through a pout, but seemed to accept it. Black Ops. It was fast becoming a useful catch-all explanation, Acid realised. One that people acknowledged without question.

"Well shit, sis," Kendis went on. "You sure are a badass, I'll give you that."

"It has been said." She tried for a grin but it felt awkward. "I can handle myself. And my training and experience help me stay alive. You too if you stick close and follow my lead."

"Hell, what have I got to lose?" She let her head roll back so it was resting against the side of the truck bed. "Although I ain't some little pussy, ya know."

"Is that right?"

"Yep. Three older brothers and absentee parents, not to mention my teenage years spent in and around Brentwood. It kind of hardens a person."

"Brentwood? That's DC, right?"

"Sure is. Tough fucking neighbourhood. Makes downtown Tehran seem like Disneyland."

Acid nodded but didn't respond. Kendis certainly talked a good fight, but in her experience there was a world of difference between living a tough life and having to deal with death on an hourly basis. Although, if she'd been in the Peace Corps for a while, she'd no doubt had to deal with her own mortality somewhat. It was just... Acid had promised herself before getting on the plane – no distractions this time. No sidekicks or companions to have to worry about.

She raised her head, listening to the dull rumble of the engine. "Well, if we are heading for Heydari's place, it's a long drive yet. I suggest we try and sleep."

"Sleep? You serious?"

"A good soldier grabs rest when they can. You'll know that."

"I guess, but..." She trailed off as Acid adjusted herself, trying to get comfortable.

"Trust me," she told her, lying down and resting her head on the hard metal floor of the truck. "We need to be rested and ready for when we get to where we're going, don't you think?"

She closed her eyes but, as had been the case ever since she got back from Spain, it didn't take long before thoughts of her old mentor drifted insidiously into her consciousness. He stood there, in her mind's eye, an eager grin cutting across his big face as his hulking form shuddered with mocking laughter before the image changed and the derisive face became her own.

Her eyes snapped open.

This was her own sense of self taunting her, manifested as the one thing – the one person – who still had control over her. And she didn't need a therapist to understand why. Caesar had been her rock for over fifteen years. He'd formed her, cared for her. And yes, some might label this process 'grooming', as Spook was inclined to, but it didn't change anything. It didn't alter the bond they'd once had. Or the way she'd once felt about him.

Though not now. Not anymore.

She was here to kill Caesar. Not to spare him. This was about getting the job done and moving forward. To lay down the last bullet and put this wretched mission of vengeance behind her. And then maybe soon, in the future, she might close her eyes and not see Caesar's face leering at her through the darkness.

Calmer now – or at least, more resolute – she closed her eyes. She already knew sleep was still a long way off, not yet even on the horizon. The silence didn't help. Too much silence sent her spiralling into dark places. Intrusive thoughts and crazy notions collided in her mind as she tried to make sense of the chaos. But one thing she did know for certain, she needed a plan. If this was to be her last mission, she could make peace with that, but she had to stay alive long enough to find Caesar. Cyrus Heydari might not be planning on killing her and her American companion straight away, but from all reports he was a crafty and malevolent man. Whatever he did want them for, it couldn't be good.

CHAPTER 11

Kendis sat bolt upright, already wide awake as the truck came to a stop. Through a small gap in the tarpaulin she could see it was still dark out. She moved over to the side of the truck to get a better view. The blackness of the night had now turned to a dark blue and a soft glow was present on the horizon, the day's sun threatening to show itself. Her guess would be it was around 4 a.m., but it could be earlier. Could be a lot later.

She turned as she heard shuffling from the other side of the truck. The woman, Acid Vanilla, waking up. Kendis watched as she cricked her neck and straightened herself. She was a good-looking woman, with sharp cheekbones and the sort of cat's eyes you knew belonged to someone dangerous but a whole lot of fun. Although, what fun there was to be had at this moment, she wasn't sure.

"What's going on?" Acid whispered.

"We've stopped."

"Yes, I'm aware of that. You hear anything?"

Kendis shook her head but stopped abruptly as the sound of doors opening and then slamming shut reverberated through the truck. Voices drifted through the tarpaulin before it was pulled back to reveal three men, all dressed in army fatigues and with black face coverings. One of them beckoned the women forward as his colleague released and lowered the rear panel.

"Come."

Kendis scooted on her butt towards the opening and the man grabbed at her wrist, hauling her off the truck. She heard commotion behind her and turned to see Acid being dragged out by the hair and giving as good as she got.

"Calm yourself," Acid said, as the men shoved her towards Kendis. They stood shoulder to shoulder.

"Go easy," Kendis whispered out of the corner of her mouth. "Not the time."

She watched the men as they talked, gesticulating wildly over their heads. "What are they saying?" Acid whispered.

"They want to set up camp for the night, get some rest before finishing the journey in daylight."

"Can you ask them how far away we are?"

Kendis did, getting nothing much in response. But a moment later, a fourth man appeared from around the side of the truck, the taller and broader of the four and the one in charge. He strode towards Kendis and pointed a thick finger in her face. "You don't talk. You do as we say."

———

It took the men another twenty minutes to set up camp. Kendis and Acid were propped up against the side of the truck, guarded by one of the men as the others built two makeshift tents out of more army-grade tarpaulin. Once finished, the women were taken at gunpoint and shoved unceremoniously into their sleeping quarters.

"He says we're to get rest and not do anything stupid," Kendis told Acid, after the guard barked instructions. "Says we'll set off again in a few hours."

"Fine," Acid replied, as they both scanned the tent.

Inside it seemed bigger than it did on the outside. The footprint was maybe ten square metres and raised up enough so all five-foot-two of Kendis could stand upright without slouching. There was no groundsheet, just sand and earth, but in one corner the guards had thrown a pile of threadbare blankets and two bottles of water. Hardly the Ritz but it would do, and the water was welcome. She picked one up and twisted off the lid, noisily gulping back a good few mouthfuls.

"Steady on," Acid rasped. "We don't know when we'll get more. Let's try and ration it, okay?"

"Sure, you're right." She screwed the top back on and slumped down on the soft ground. "So what now?"

Acid shrugged, looking about her. She was certainly growing on Kendis. On the surface she appeared to be a typical posh British type – with that husky voice and the way she held herself – yet there was a wicked sarcastic glimmer underneath it all that gave her a real edge. "I suppose we get some rest," she muttered. "What else can we do?"

"Erm, try and escape?"

"How? There's a guard outside with an assault rifle. I imagine they'll be taking it in shifts."

Kendis leaned over and hitched up the side of the tent. "They can't be everywhere. We could slip out, be over the next mountain before they realise we're gone." She watched the strange woman in the darkness. "What is it?"

"I don't know. I understand what you're saying, but then what? We're on the run in the middle of nowhere with no weapons, no supplies…"

"And you just want to lie down and let them deliver us to the meanest sonofabitch the Arab world's ever known? Cos that's how people talk about Heydari. I heard once how he tortured someone to death by lying him down and placing red hot coals all over his body. They burned right through his skin. Into his heart."

Acid didn't flinch. "Yes, I know. He sounds like a real crazy bastard."

"Dude is a madman, pure and simple. Driven by a dual love of money and power. But from what I hear he loves women almost as much. Loves to own them and use them, at least. Shit, some of the stories I've heard, you wouldn't be so flippant."

At this, Acid stepped forward. "I'm not being flippant, sweetie. But there's no point scaring ourselves with rumours, is there? We need to be logical. We need to keep calm." She sat down beside Kendis. "Which is why I suggest we rest. We need to preserve our strength and sanity for when we get to Heydari's palace."

"Sounds to me like you actually want to meet the man."

The English woman shook her head and huffed humourlessly. "Not entirely. But if my mark is staying with Heydari then this is my best way of getting to him."

It was Kendis' turn to shake her head. "You've got big balls, I'll give you that."

"Oh come now, sweetie," Acid scolded. "We can do better than that, can't we? Big balls?"

"Ha. Well ain't you a breath of fresh air? Okay then, what about… ovaries of steel?"

"Hmm. Bit lame. What's that word you lot like?"

Kendis threw up a sharp eyebrow. "You lot?"

"Americans. What is it you say – moxie? I always liked that one. We don't really have an equivalent in England."

"You've sure got a lot of that." Kendis grabbed up one of the blankets and wrapped it around her shoulders. It wasn't cold but she found it weirdly comforting. "What do you think Heydari wants with us?"

She stared at the Brit who gave a shrug of the shoulders. "Best we don't let our imaginations run riot."

"Wow. Good advice. Thanks."

"All I mean is we don't want to get all het up about it before we know what we're dealing with. Facts, not fabrications. Otherwise you just end up fighting monsters in your head. And there's enough monsters out there in the real world to deal with." She settled down next to Kendis. "Tell me, why join the Peace Corps?"

Kendis pulled the blanket tighter around her and took a moment to compose herself. The long version of that story was a messed-up tale, starting in Painesville, Ohio (an actual place) and involving an abusive ex, a short spell in juvey and a whole bunch of wrong turns and dead ends. She opted for the short version.

"I grew up in a military family. First ten years of my life was spent on bases all over the world. Europe, the Middle East, Canada. It was an odd life, but it was all I knew. I always thought I would join up too, maybe Special Forces." She looked Acid up and down and pursed her lips, letting her know she was impressed. "But when I was fourteen my eldest brother, Michael, was killed in Afghanistan."

Acid grimaced. "Ah, shit."

"Yeah. Helmand, two thousand and three. Right after the Taliban resurgence. After that the family fell apart and my goals sort of shifted." She sniffed, no longer wanting to go on with the story. "I decided I wanted to help, rather than kill, people."

At this, Acid snorted softly.

"What is it?" Kendis asked.

"Nothing. I just... well, I'm starting to feel that way myself. After a lot of years. It's a weird feeling."

Kendis sat forward, her head full of questions, eager to know more about this freaky, enigmatic woman in whose company she'd found herself. But before she had a chance to speak, they heard movement outside their tent and a second later one of the guards bustled in under the entrance flap.

Kendis sat upright at the sight of the assault rifle the man waved between her and Acid. He'd removed his face covering, and in the moonlight filtering in behind him she could see he was young. Only a boy, really. But that didn't equate to innocent. It didn't mitigate the cruel sneer on his face, bordering on revulsion, but also lust. Kendis had seen that look before in a man's eye and it wasn't something she'd ever wanted to experience again.

He shoved the gun at them and growled.

"What's he's saying?" Acid asked.

"He wants us to follow him," Kendis replied, getting to her feet but not taking her eyes off the man as he leered at them both greedily.

He spoke in hushed tones, telling them to be quick and to stay quiet. The way he was acting, as if he didn't want his cronies to hear, was another red flag for Kendis. Her heart beat a heavy rhythm against her ribs as the guard herded them out of the tent and into the cool air outside. She glanced at Acid, hoping for some kind of sign that she had it under control. That they were going to be okay. But all she saw was a woman with her head bowed and her hair covering most of her face. The sight of her made Kendis' heart drop into her belly.

Well, shit.

How stupid she'd been. There she was coming to terms with the fact this was going to be a far from restful night, when she should be getting her head around the fact she might not survive the night at all. As the man shoved them forward, all she could think about was her brother and the advice he'd given all those years ago when as a young teenager she'd spoken of her plans to one day travel through South America.

"Kendis," he'd said, "if you ever get kidnapped, try and escape at all costs. The longer they keep you, the more chance there is you'll be killed. And remember, if they take you to one location and then move you to another, chances are you ain't coming back. Ever."

She remembered brushing it off at the time. Her big brother doing what big brothers do. But as his words echoed in her head and sent a shiver down her back, she knew he was right.

Micky was dead, and she wasn't coming back from this.

Ever.

CHAPTER 12

Despite the kid's rifle muzzle stabbing into her kidneys every few steps, Acid slowed her pace to a shuffle as they made their way across the rocky terrain. She was trying to buy some time, come up with a plan, but right now she had nothing. Heydari's young foot soldier continued to bark instructions as they walked on. He seemed nervous and unsure of himself, but she'd seen the look in his eyes – a sinister hunger, which angered and sickened her all at once. Her best guess was he was taking them to the edge of the camp – probably over the other side of the large rock formation a few hundred metres away – where he planned on showing them what he was made of in the worst way possible. After that, she wasn't sure. Execution seemed unlikely after bringing them this far, but the way he was acting, he was clearly working alone and going against orders. It meant he was a loose cannon, unfettered by protocol.

"You all right?" she whispered to Kendis as they hobbled along.

"No. You think he's going to—"

"Oh yes. Absolutely. That's his plan, at least. But don't worry, I'll think of something."

Kendis turned, her eyes wide and startling in the moonlight. "You'll think of something? The fuck does that mean?"

Acid bit her tongue and ignored her companion's remarks. Over the years she'd had to learn to be forgiving of others' reactions in high pressure situations. Or to endure them at least, the better to focus on the task in hand.

In a few more steps they'd be alongside the rocks. She turned and walked backwards a few steps so she could get a better look at the kid. "I take it your friends over there don't know what you're up to?"

The kid raised his chin at her before sniffing back and spitting out a lump of phlegm onto the ground.

"Hey, hello," Acid yelled back towards the tents, now tiny in the distance. "Your friend here is going off script. Hello."

"Shut up," he said, shoving the gun forward. "Turn around. Keep walking."

"Oh, you speak English? Well, you do know you won't get away with this, right? Plus, I read the Koran a while back, I don't remember it promoting this sort of shi—"

"Enough," he said. "This way."

With his aim high, he bustled them around the side of the rocks to where a tall tree stump stuck out of the ground at a slight angle. A quick scan of the area sent an icy spear of energy running down Acid's back. She saw the footprints in the sand, the blood spatter against the rocks, the way the earth had been displaced.

"I see," she said. "Not your first time here."

Without responding, the soldier grabbed her by the neck and pulled her towards him. The action caught her off guard but she regained her fire enough to catch him with a sharp elbow to the cheek as he dragged her over to the tree stump. He cried out, though it wasn't the most punishing of blows and he countered it with a punch to the jaw which sent her dizzy. Without much effort now he was able to thread her arms over the top of the stump and fasten them tight around the other side with a zip tie. The bats screeched across her synapses as she watched him hit Kendis with a vicious backhand before dragging her over and tying her around the other side of the tree. Gnashing her teeth, she yanked at the ties, but the more she pulled the tighter they got.

Once satisfied the two women were constrained, the man placed the rifle down against the side of the rocks and pulled out a six-inch blade from his belt. He sauntered back their way, the thumb of his free hand hooked over the waistband of his fatigues, the other swaying the knife from side to side as if choosing which of them would take the lead.

"Me," Acid said. "Me first."

He nodded as though impressed. "So, you ready for me, baby?" he said, in a terrible American accent. *Bay-bee.* She tensed as he took the knife and sliced through the ties fastening her to the tree.

"Acid, you don't have to do this," Kendis said.

Their eyes met and Acid gave her a look that she hoped was reassuring. "Trust me," she whispered. "It's fine."

Pressing the sharp steel of the knife against her throat – pressing so hard she felt a thin trickle of blood running down the curve of her neck – the man guided Acid nearer to the rocks. Once there, he shoved her against the cold stone, knocking some of the air out of her. Up close he looked even younger. His feeble moustache was moist with sweat and his eyes although mean were alight with an hysterical thirst. Over his shoulder Acid could see Kendis staring at them, as if not wanting to take her eyes from the scene lest it might become real.

"What are you going to do with me?" she asked, breathless and flickering her eyelids for good measure.

It was a risk, she knew that. Most men would see through it and be pissed off. But this grotty prick had such an air of immature unsophistication about him she decided to chance it.

The man stepped back, unsure how to take her as she glanced at the assault rifle, propped against the rock a few feet away.

"Knees," he said, stabbing the knife towards her. "Knees, now."

She stiffened but nodded in acquiescence. "Okay… okay."

He gestured again with the knife and she sank to her knees. She could hear Kendis sobbing. Perhaps for her, but also no doubt because she was about to observe first-hand exactly what she had coming next. Acid leaned her head around the side of the man's body as he fumbled with the flies on his army fatigues. Catching Kendis' eye, she threw her a grim smile, the briefest of nods.

It's going to be okay, kid. Hold it together.

She watched as the man removed his pathetic wrinkled worm from his trousers and smirked down at her.

The poor fucker clearly didn't know who he was dealing with.

An excited grunt fell from his twisted mouth, but before he had chance to fully present himself, Acid shifted up onto one leg and sprang forward. With her hands tied together over her chest she was able to rabbit-punch the pathetic prick in the throat, catching him by surprise. She knew from experience you didn't need much force to crush someone's trachea. With a frustrated, spluttering gasp the man stumbled back, clawing at his neck.

Jumping fully upright, Acid raised her hands high above her head and brought them down against the upper part of her abdomen whilst at the same time yanking her elbows back and apart. Done with enough force and speed this action breaks the locking blade in the zip tie, and once free she smashed a tight fist into the man's face, breaking his nose. In his pain and bewilderment she was able to easily wrestle the knife from his grip and spinning it around she buried it deep into his chest. Perfectly placed. Just below the left clavicle. Straight into his heart. With a guttural grunt he raised his head and an expression of absolute dread washed over him. He opened his mouth to speak but no words came. A second later he slumped to his knees and pitched forward into the dust.

"Fucking yes, my girl," Kendis cried. "You *are* a badass."

"Yes. I did tell you that," Acid replied, as her heart rate returned to something more manageable. She sauntered over to the fallen soldier and rolled him on his back. A foot on his chest assisted her in pulling out the knife. "But enough talk, we need to get out of here."

She moved over to the tree stump and sliced through Kendis' zip ties. Without looking back she grabbed her new companion by the arm, and was in the process of dragging her away when the kid stopped.

"Acid."

"What is it... Oh." As she pivoted around, she shut up. Because she already had the answer. "Bollocks."

Heydari's three other foot soldiers were standing a few feet from the rock formation. Each of them with their weapons raised, fingers twitching eagerly on triggers.

Instinctively Acid raised her hands to her head and beside her Kendis did the same. The two of them exchanged glances. "They must have heard you shouting for help," Kendis whispered.

"You think?"

As she watched, one of the men knelt over the dead soldier to better examine him. He shook his head and the three men began to shout animatedly at each other.

"They're debating what to do with us," Kendis told her, speaking out the corner of her mouth.

"Okay, and what's the general feeling?"

"Two of them want to execute us, but the other, who seems to be the leader, says no..." She trailed off. Acid glanced her way to see her face was screwed up in concentration, listening. "He's talking of the prince, something about him having use for us. He says they should still take us to him."

Acid didn't respond, but it was what she'd been hoping for. If she could get close to Heydari, then she could get close to Caesar.

They walked in silence back to camp, hands still on their heads but with an air of defeat and weariness doubling the length of the journey. Once at the tents, one of the soldiers stood guard whilst the others exchanged words before ushering the two women towards the side of the truck where new zip ties were applied. This time their arms were pulled behind them – impossible to break the ties in this position – and back on the flatbed their ankles and knees were bound as well. No more chances.

As the soldiers secured them, Acid kept her attention on Kendis. She was pleased to see she was now taking the situation in her stride, grunting angrily at the men as they bundled her upright so she was sitting against the side of the truck. She was clearly a tough kid – clever too – perhaps a good ally for what came next. The only problem was, Acid had no idea what the hell they were getting themselves into. The prince had use for them, the soldier had said. Those words didn't fill her with much confidence.

"Well, that could have gone better," she said, sighing as the steel flap at the back of the truck was raised and the tarpaulin fastened back into place. "My fault. I should have kept my mouth shut."

"You were trying stuff, I get it. And it was pretty awesome." Kendis' voice was strained as she shuffled to get comfortable. Beneath them the engine grumbled into life. "The way you took him down with that sucker punch to the throat. *Shee-it*."

In the gloom of the truck, Acid leaned forward to struggle at the ties behind her back. "He was young and inexperienced," she replied. "We were lucky is all."

The truck picked up speed and the uneven terrain rocked them back and forth. Through a small gap in the tarpaulin Acid could see a sliver of the new day's sun appearing over the horizon.

"Let's still try and rest," she told Kendis. "Whatever is waiting for us at the other end, it'll be a lot easier to deal with if we're not so weary."

"Sure, I get ya. But can you sleep like this? These ties are slicing into me."

"Well, try," Acid hissed, shuffling back against her metal bed and closing her eyes. She'd learnt over the years it was important to grab sleep when you could. An hour here, an hour there. It wasn't particularly relaxing or pleasant, but it meant you could continue to do what you were paid for. It kept you alive.

But as the truck trundled onwards, the sleep she assumed was close ebbed away and her busy mind went haywire. Intrusive thoughts flashed across her consciousness as Kendis' words resounded across her recall.

The prince had use for them.

She opened one eye. Kendis looked to be asleep, or was at least resting peacefully.

The prince had *use* for them.

The prince had use for *them.*

She sighed into the darkness.

Well, shit.

Anyway she looked at it, that didn't sound like anything good.

CHAPTER 13

Kendis jolted awake, and as her awareness spread she realised the truck had come to a stop. She leaned against the wheel arch to right herself, grimacing at the pain from where the zip ties gripped the thin skin around her wrists and ankles.

"You okay?"

She glanced over to see her travelling companion was already awake.

"Sure. Fine and dandy." She huffed. "You get some sleep?"

"A little," Acid replied. "Enough. I think we've arrived at our destination."

Kendis shuffled forward on her butt, noticing the bright sun filtering through gaps in the tarpaulin. The air under the cover was close and stuffy, but on seeing the sunshine she realised too how hot it had become.

Shouts came from the front of the truck. Men's voices, speaking fast. Acid glanced over but she shook her head. "Can't pick anything out."

A few seconds went by and then the truck started moving once more, slower now. Kendis imagined them trundling through security gates into the confines of Heydari's fortress, and a few moments later they stopped again, the rear panel was released and the tarpaulin peeled back to reveal a huge courtyard, not dissimilar to what she'd been imagining. In front of her was indeed a high gate (at least ten feet, she'd have guessed), with turreted walls leading off and disappearing beyond her eyeline. Above the walls stood a row of palm trees, their dark green fronds moving gently in the breeze. She shifted closer to the back of the truck as one of the soldiers appeared and beckoned them to get out.

"How do you expect us to move when our legs are tied like this?" Acid snapped. Then, less subtle: "Legs. Untie."

The man growled angrily but clambered aboard. After unsheathing a large knife from his belt, he sliced through the ties on Acid's legs and then Kendis'. The relief on release was tenable yet short-lived as the man grabbed her roughly around the top of her arm and dragged her from the truck. Once she was standing on the sandy earth of the courtyard, she blinked into bright sun, turning to watch as the man clambered back onto the flatbed to get Acid. She struggled more than Kendis had done but was hauled off all the same.

"So here we are," she said with a sigh, as she joined Kendis next to the truck.

Shoulder to shoulder they took in the impressive grounds and the even more impressive building that stood off to one side, a cross between a fortress and a palace and at least three storeys high, with turrets, a tall minaret tower and a gold qubba dome that rose up from the centre. Letting her gaze drift up the building, Kendis saw the main entrance was up on the second level of the palace, accessible by a white marble walkway embellished with gold handrails.

"Move," one of the men grunted, shoving Kendis in the back with the butt of his rifle.

She did as instructed, she and Acid leading the way as the men herded them up the walkway towards the entrance. The doorway was flanked by armed guards wearing the same army fatigues and black face coverings as the men who'd brought them here.

At the top of the walkway the men exchanged a few words, some of which Kendis could pick out. 'Westerners' was one, and something about 'insurance' or 'coverage', but she couldn't get the exact translation. She glanced at Acid, surprised to see she was staring straight ahead with the kind of blank expression any poker player would be proud of.

Kendis had never been into any kind of card games but had started joining in with the nightly poker games on her first assignment in Afghanistan. It passed the time on the long evenings and there was often little else to use her wages on. Not that she'd ended up losing much – if anything she was up – but more so she enjoyed the cut and thrust of the game, the bluffs and double-bluffs. She'd even gotten a name for herself amongst her colleagues as one of the best players on the base.

Ah, man.

Despite the heat, the thought pricked up the fine hairs on her arms and a wave of sadness washed over her. Would she ever see those guys again? Her family? Or was she going to die here, in this ornate Disney-esque palace that seemed too beautiful to be scary, yet from all the stories she'd heard held a monster more beastly and terrifying than anything a film-maker might dream up.

"Come. Now."

She snapped out of it as the guards on either side opened the doors and another rifle butt in the kidneys pushed her forward. In front of her was a wide corridor with a high ceiling and polished wooden floor. Colourful batiks and modern art canvases adorned the walls, whilst small tables had been placed at intervals along its length, each one exhibiting an ornate water jug or a high-sided vase done out in gold leaf and intricate mosaics. The light came from a series of skylights cut into the roof displaying nothing but bright azure blue.

They marched on in silence over to another set of doors where two more soldiers stood guard. As the doors were swung open and the next room revealed, Kendis couldn't help but marvel at the marble Romanesque pillars that ran down the left-hand side. In front of each of the pillars stood more guards, these dressed in the same army fatigues and black masks as before, but carrying large ceremonial swords which rested flatly on their shoulders. There were more doors along the wall and another set of grand double doors at the far end. As they got closer, one of the soldiers veered in front of them and swung these doors open to reveal a circular room adorned floor to ceiling in small black and white tiles. On first glance it looked to Kendis like the Turkish sauna she'd visited in Istanbul, and the sunken bath with gold taps in the centre of the room did little to discourage this notion.

Standing at intervals around the curved walls were small, marble-fronted booths and two doors Over to her right as she looked at the room was a hexagonal plinth around a foot high made of thick marble and with a gold eight-pointed star inlaid in the centre. It looked a lot like an altar, but Kendis promptly pushed that thought from her mind. Probably just somewhere to sit, she told herself. Her attention drifted upwards to the domed roof containing five concentric circles of spotlights and an expensive-looking chandelier hanging from the centre. The soldiers herded them over to the door opposite and two of them moved around the front to stand either side, rifles trained on Kendis and Acid. The third soldier approached the door and knocked.

They waited, Kendis glancing between the three men and then at Acid who was still as straight-faced as before. Yet now, in this light, with the shadows cast from the small spotlights, she seemed more intense than neutral. Her jaw was tight and her full lips pouting enough to accentuate her high cheekbones. Kendis (an empath, she always told people) could feel the energy coming off her. Whatever was going on in that pretty head of hers, she sure seemed ready for it, and once again Kendis was thankful she'd ended up in her company. She might come off a little freaky (it was kind of off-putting the way she peered into the middle distance, as though seeing horrors only she could see), but she was on Kendis' side and she was fierce as hell, and right now that's what mattered.

The soldier was about to knock again when they heard a voice boom from the other side. "Come."

The soldier opened the door and stepped aside, motioning for Kendis and Acid to enter. He remained outside as they walked through the open doorway to find themselves in a huge room that must, on Kendis' reckoning, span the entire east side of the palace. A large banqueting table stood a few feet in front of them, adorned with huge bowls of fruit and the tallest candles she'd ever seen. The fact they didn't look out of place in the room showed how grand it all was. Not her taste, of course – Kendis had been flirting with minimalism a lot these last few years (mostly out of lifestyle choice but also necessity – you had to travel light in her job, be ready to leave at a moment's notice) but she appreciated it was well done. If you liked your interior design bold and brash and turned all the way up to the top, then this would be your showroom.

Two enormous (like, ridiculously big) Persian rugs covered most of the floor, but underneath she could see the same white marble that made up the walls and the ceiling. The other side of the room opened up into a lounge space with two grandiose couches covered in rich, velvet cushions. Along the wall a huge window bigger than the floorplan of her apartment was leaded with ornate diamond patterns, and over in the corner another door, perhaps leading to Heydari's bedroom. The place smelt of incense and spice, like a nice meal had been eaten here recently. It made Kendis' stomach rumble.

As they stood in the doorway taking it all in, she felt a rush of air on her back and heard the door close behind her. She turned around to see the soldiers who'd brought them here had left.

"Something we said," Acid mumbled, narrowing her eyes at the elaborate decoration before the same booming voice as before

– now with a distinct malevolence to its tone – echoed down from the end of the room.

"So you're the ladies who've been giving my men so much trouble." Their eyes shot up the length of the room to where a man – Cyrus Heydari, no doubt – had risen from one of the couches. He raised one hand and brusquely waved them forward. "Come. Let me look at you."

Standing as he was with the bright sun behind him it was hard to make out his features. He looked to be wearing army fatigues, same as his soldiers, but no face covering, and with a long pale blue silk scarf wrapped around him. Kendis noticed wisps of hair haloing his head in the light.

"All a bit dramatic, isn't it?" Acid whispered, leaning into her as they walked on.

Kendis smiled in response, glad of the lift but wondering whether her new friend should be acting so blasé. Any fool could see they were in trouble. As they got closer, the man stepped forward. Up close he wasn't a tall man, five-six at a guess, a little taller than her but about the same as Acid.

"I am Cyrus Heydari," he announced. "The man they call The New Prince of Islam."

Acid let out a gentle snort and Kendis nudged her, but Heydari ignored it.

"What do you want with us?" Acid asked.

Heydari tilted his head from side to side to better take them in, or at least – with his pursed lips and tutting – demonstrate to them what he was doing. He was an odd-looking man, hard to place in years, but likely that was down to the immense amounts of Botox he'd pumped into his face. His eyes were wide and cat-like, and it was hard to say whether he was wearing mascara or just had enviable eyelashes. A trimmed beard (complete with an elaborate fade over his cheeks) and a head of thick hair finished the look, but as Kendis peered on she wondered if it was a hair piece. His whole look sure was unusual, but also disconcerting, and she found it hard not to stare.

"I wanted to meet you straight away," Heydari growled. "To meet the women who killed one of my soldiers. That man had a family, you know. A new wife."

"I did her a favour," Acid muttered under her breath.

"Silence." A sharp backhand caught Acid on the cheek, but she hardly flinched. "You do not talk back to me. You understand? This is my palace. My kingdom."

Acid lowered her head, nodding in compliance.

It didn't make Kendis feel any better. "Please, sir," she started, eyes on the carpet now, trying to hold it together. "I'm – we are – we're civilians. We aren't involved in any conflict. We don't even know why we're here."

"You are a member of the Peace Corps, are you not?"

She lifted her head. "Yes… I…"

"See? I know this. I know everything. And this one here, your brash friend, is a journalist. A journalist who's been asking a lot of questions about me and my associates here in the region." He leaned closer, his face now a few inches from Acid's. "Isn't this correct? Ms Zora Dankworth?"

Confusion furrowed Kendis' brow. She wanted to look at her new companion but fought the impulse. She was Special Forces, after all. Must be an alias.

She braced herself for Acid's inevitable wise-ass response, but it never came. When she still hadn't replied a few seconds later, she tilted her head to take her in. She was staring at her feet, a cowed look on her face.

Well, shit.

She'd expected – hoped for – more from her. Where were those steel ovaries now?

"Why are you asking about me?" Heydari said. "Why are you here in my country?"

Still nothing.

He grabbed Acid by the chin, squeezing her cheeks together and bringing his face so close, the tip of his nose brushed against hers. "Answer me."

"I'm sure the customs officers told you everything I told them," she replied, wriggling free from his clutches.

"They said you knew about those who I associate with."

Acid shrugged. "Just trying to get a bigger picture. You're a mysterious man."

"A mysterious man? Is this a compliment?"

"If you like." She barged into Kendis as she wriggled her torso. "Any chance you might undo these ties? They're cutting into my wrists."

"You want me to release you? Is this wise for me?"

"We aren't going anywhere, are we? Middle of the desert with armed guards at every door." She leaned forward. "You know, I am half Italian – I might be more talkative if I can move my hands."

Kendis raised her head to see Heydari staring incredulously at Acid. But as she looked on, the rage in him seemed to soften. Not much, but it was there.

"Fine. I will allow it."

He reached around his back and pulled out a small knife from his waistband, his grin widening as he held it up to the light before stepping around them and slicing through both sets of zip ties.

"Thanks, much better," Kendis said, bringing her hands around the front and rubbing at her wrists.

Heydari returned the knife to its sheath in his belt. "Now you can talk freely, yes? So talk. What do you want from me? My sources tell me you could be a spy – from the UK or maybe even the USA. People like you are a thorn in my side."

"Absolutely not. I swear to you." Acid lowered her voice. "I just want to write about the region. Tell the story of Iran and the pandemic."

"Pfft. The pandemic." Heydari's tone turned nasty. "A western weapon to undermine my country. Another method of mind control."

"That's not true," Kendis butted in. "Honest. I've seen it with my own eyes. It's rife in the region, getting worse and—"

"No!" Heydari yelled. "It is slowing us down. Slowing me down."

"From what?" she asked, genuine curiosity trumping her fear.

Heydari wagged his finger at her. "You will find out. Soon enough. When we can once again mobilise and move forward. My dream is for the Islamic Republic of Iran to regain full power in the region. Only by doing so can we rise up against the American devils and help our brothers – the oppressed people of Palestine, of Yemen, and Syria. The resistance fighters in Lebanon and Palestine."

Next to her, Acid made a weird whistling noise. It reminded Kendis of the noise her momma would make when her or her brothers were trying her patience.

"Fair enough, I get it. You've got big plans. You want to – what – plan a coup? Take over the country? Go for it. Kendis and I are both impartial. But my question remains. What do you want with us? And if we're such a problem for you, why are we still alive?"

Kendis tensed. It was a good question, but she wasn't sure she wanted to know the answer. Heydari stepped back, wagging the same finger at Acid and letting out a deep laugh.

"You're a feisty one, aren't you? But this is enjoyable. I like feisty people. Though feisty women can be troublesome. The answer to your question will become clear soon enough. For now I just wanted to see you with my own eyes."

Kendis watched the exchange out of the corner of her eye, praying Acid didn't step over the mark but feeling braver in her presence.

"Well, now you've seen me, can we get on with whatever it is we're here for?"

Another laugh erupted from Heydari, but Kendis noticed his chemically taut face hardly moved. The effect on his entire demeanour was even more macabre. He glanced over their heads and shouted an instruction towards the door.

"And I told you, Ms Dankworth," he said, shifting his attention back to Acid. "You will find out in good time. For now my men will show you to your… accommodation."

Kendis jumped as a hand gripped her shoulder. She spun around to see two guards standing behind them.

"Hey, watch it," Acid growled, as one of them grabbed her by the arm and began yanking her away.

"Don't worry, my dears," Heydari called after them. "You will be taken care of. For now get settled and we shall talk again soon."

Kendis made to say something, but before she had a chance she caught Acid's eye and the stern look on her face. Instead she opened her mouth. *What?*

But Acid just shook her head curtly. Not the time.

Heydari's booming laughter followed them through the room as they were led back the way they'd come.

"Keep it together," Acid whispered, as they were bundled through the tiled bathroom. "Seems like he wants to keep us alive, for the time being at least."

But right there was what Kendis was afraid of. Because despite Heydari's strange appearance and jovial manner, she'd heard too many terrible stories and had seen first-hand the fear in people's eyes when they spoke of him. He was the sort of man it was wise not to underestimate. Because those who did… well, they weren't the ones telling the stories.

CHAPTER 14

Acid chewed on her bottom lip as the guards led them down the walkway outside. She was still trying to work out Heydari's angle. Initially she'd thought him pompous and ridiculous, but she wondered if his persona was more orchestrated than he let on. A way to confuse and unsettle people, keep them guessing.

They reached the bottom of the walkway and she cast her gaze over the courtyard, clocking two more armed guards over by the main entrance and a group of soldiers gathered idly around a truck on the far side of the open space. If Caesar was indeed shielded away somewhere in the palace, getting to him would take some doing. But she couldn't think about that now. One thing she'd learned over the years, if you waited until every detail of a plan was watertight you'd never get the job done. That meant there'd been plenty of fuck-ups over the years, and she'd almost gotten herself killed on too many occasions to count, yet it was this ability to live on her wits and take huge risks (fuelled always by her manic bat energy) that meant the young Acid Vanilla had fast become one of the top operatives at Annihilation Pest Control.

She rolled her shoulders back, realising the mere thought of her old boss had her upper body gripped with tension. She'd have to watch that. If he was here, and she had no reason to believe otherwise, it was important to stay calm and detached. She'd seen it happen over the years, people getting too involved in their work, making hits personal for whatever reason. There was no room for emotions here. She'd save those for later. When she could breathe again. If that time ever came.

She glanced over at Kendis as the guards led them under the walkway to the ground floor of the palace. The kid's face was rigid and pensive, her eyes flitting about her. She was a brave woman, Acid knew that already. But everyone had their limits. It was the uncertainty that got you. The not knowing what was going to happen to you. Which was why she always made sure she reined it in whenever her imagination spun away from her. In those moments, she reminded herself of her training and how good her instincts were. The bats – they hadn't let her down yet.

The doorway they arrived at was much less grand than the entrance on the upper level, but still ornately decorated, with a marble frame surrounding the deep mahogany doors complete with black onyx handles. One of the soldiers flanking them stepped forward and removed a key from out of his pocket. With a grunt he unlocked the door and pushed it open, beckoning for them to enter as a wave of airless heat hit them in the face. It smelt like animals. And shit. Actual shit.

Kendis leaned into her. "What is this place?"

Acid was finding it hard to focus after the bright sunshine, but as her eyes became accustomed to the change in light she saw a flight of steps leading down to a lower level and people milling around. She counted seven in total. Three were playing cards around a small table in the middle of the room, whilst the other four were lying or sitting on the barracks-style cots that stood in a row along one wall. All eyes were on them as the soldiers led Acid and Kendis down the step. Acid could see now the people here were all westerners. Their faces were weary and their expressions hollow.

"Zora?"

A man climbing off one of the cots and moving over to them.

"Lars. What are you doing here?"

He shuffled closer, one eye on the guards. When he was close enough, he smiled weakly. "You found Heydari then?"

"Hmm. Not exactly in the same circumstances I was hoping."

Keeping his eyes on the guards, he put an arm around her and guided her away. "Come, best we don't talk yet."

Acid allowed him to guide her away whilst looking over her shoulder for Kendis. Behind her the two guards were backing out of the room. They slammed the door shut before the distinct sound of a key turning in a heavy lock could be heard. Kendis caught her eye and frowned. Acid beckoned her to follow them.

"So what's going on?" she asked, snapping her attention back to Lars. "Oh, shit. Was this my fault? Did they…"

He raised one hand. "They did what they were always going to do."

"What's going on here?"

They walked to the centre of the room as Acid continued to scope out the place. The air quality was bad, like non-existent, and the musky smell invaded her sinuses and made her eyes water. The only light came from two ineffective strip-lights overhead and a row of high windows interspersed along each wall, too high to reach. The rest of the room's inhabitants watched on as Kendis joined them in a triangular huddle.

"They're okay," Lars told the other prisoners. "I met Zora here at the airport. We were contained together. She's a… journalist – is that right?"

"You might as well tell them," she said, turning to the group. "I'm actually an agent with the British Special Forces. I've been watching Heydari and his associates for a while."

The faces around her nodded. But if their spirits were lifted any by the knowledge of a trained agent in their midst, they didn't let it show.

"Well, anyway, hello." She waved her hand around the room,

smiling the sort of half-smile one does at people who you don't know but you want to trust you.

"We shall make full introductions later," Lars said. "But tell me, what happened after the airport?"

After shooting Kendis a glance, Acid filled him in, as much as needed at least. About Bayat's betrayal, and death, being bundled into the truck with Kendis. About killing one of Heydari's foot soldiers.

"Impressive," Lars said, looking at Kendis. "But you both have been through a lot. Would you like to rest for a while? There are plenty of beds."

"That'd be good." Kendis sighed. "I guess we're here now. How long have you been here?"

"Myself, a few days," Lars told her, guiding them over to the row of cots. "But some of the prisoners have been here weeks. Months, even."

"What does he want with us all?" Acid asked.

They got to the cots and Kendis sat down on the end of one as Lars turned to meet Acid's eye. "We can talk later. For now rest is important. You've had a stressful few days."

"Ever the doctor, right?"

"I suppose. But this is my curse too. Why I believe Cyrus Heydari had his men bring me here."

"Oh?" She was about to sit down herself but her interest was piqued. "Why do you say that?"

Lars looked about him and was preparing to answer when a loud roar came from the back of the room. Like the sound of a wild animal waking up. They all turned to the source of the noise as Acid noticed for the first time the small room – more of a cabin – that had been built in the far corner with a corrugated iron roof and two plywood doors standing side by side along its front.

"Toilets?"

Lars twisted his mouth to one side. "Yes and no. One of the doors leads to a makeshift bathroom – a basin, a hole in the ground. The other door is the sleeping quarters of Heydari's prize prisoner."

Acid raised her head to take in the weird structure. "Prize prisoner? What's the story?"

"He calls himself Orcus. He was here long before I arrived. For months, they say. He stays in that room most of the time and has food and supplies taken in for him. He is a strange man. Very angry. It is him that I—"

"Wait." She cut him off. "Orcus. I've heard that name before." She racked her brain. *Orcus.* Was it a codename? The name of an old mission? Someone from her past? She cricked her neck to one side as a memory came to her. "Orcus. Wasn't he…?"

"That's right," a familiar voice thundered over her shoulder. "The Roman god of the underworld."

She spun around, her voice catching in her throat as a large man strode towards her. "You."

Beowulf Caesar raised his arms out to his sides. "Hello, Acid. How's tricks?"

CHAPTER 15

"You dirty fucking bastard!"

Caesar was expecting the reaction and stepped to one side as she swung wildly with her fist. He was at least a foot taller than her but she still managed to catch him on the side of the neck with a punishing blow.

"I'm going to kill you."

She came again, but this time he was able to grab her fist in his palm. He pushed her away. "Calm it down, you crazy mare."

Despite his bravado, Caesar had been dreading this moment. He knew it was coming, of course, it was inevitable (she was Acid Vanilla after all, his number one, his protégé), but to see her up close, with such hatred in her eyes all for him, it sent weird emotions going off that troubled him. It didn't help he'd been feeling like complete shit all day. But, hell, every day since that putrid prick Heydari had betrayed him he'd felt the same. To lock him up like a dog – with a bunch of whining civilians to boot – that was not on.

Not on at all.

Especially as he believed he'd well and truly landed on his feet meeting Heydari. With the backing of someone like him, who had so much sway in the region, he could have gotten Annihilation back on its feet in a month. And in return he'd promised that his new band of killers would help Heydari remove those in his way without getting his hands dirty. Caesar loved a good symbiotic relationship and this was as good as they came. The way he'd sold it to Heydari (or thought he had, at least) was he'd take all the pressure off the New Prince of Islam, allow him to focus on his out-facing persona – to gain power not only over his enemies but also over the hearts and minds of his people. That was how you won. How you became truly powerful.

Only, Caesar hadn't counted on the paranoid goat-botherer – with his rictus face and ridiculously tweezered eyebrows – being quite so power hungry. Yet he had to admit, he only had himself to blame. When you associated yourself with nefarious and despotic crackpots, you couldn't get too angry when they acted nefarious and despotic. He knew he should have been watching his back. The only problem was he was so preoccupied with this bloody woman standing in front of him still gnashing her teeth, that he hadn't seen Heydari's betrayal coming.

Acid bleeding Vanilla.

She'd taken everything from him. Ruined him. And here she was still with the audacity to think he was in the wrong. Although, the more he took her in, he couldn't help but wonder why he'd been so wary for the last year. Sure, once she'd been a deadly force, his best operative by a country mile, but to see her now, bedraggled and weary, with her pretty face sagging from the weight of all she carried, she looked pathetic. Not a threat.

It didn't stop her lashing out at him again though.

"You rotten bastard."

Her eyes were alert, burning with the same intense cruelty he'd noticed all those years ago. But she was also panting, out of breath, and was already backing down. She no longer had the resolve or the vitality to back up her murderous rage.

"You aren't the only one who's been dealt a shitty hand recently," he replied. "I'm not sure if you've been keeping score, my dear, but you've fucking well wiped out my entire workforce.

Every bleeding one of them. Left me a broken man. And for what?"

"You know what," she grunted, her voice unrecognisable from her usual husky drawl. "It was you who made this personal."

"It was always personal, me and you. But don't forget, it was me who made you who you are, Acid. Don't forget all I did for you. I know you're pissed off, but I am too, all right?"

"I've been waiting a long time for this."

"Oh, give the histrionics a rest, will you? You ain't Liam bleeding Neeson. This is me you're talking to." He raised his palms to her. "Look, we're in the same boat here, kid. Over the proverbial barrel, as it were. Prisoners. So like it or not, we might have to work together."

Acid bristled, possibly readying herself for another attack. "Are you fucking joking me?"

"No. I'm not." Over her head he noticed the Norwegian doc (Larson or something) staring at him. He threw him a curt nod. "I know things, about Heydari, about why we're all here."

"Go on then," she said. "Talk." Her face remained fierce but he noticed the muscles in her jaw had relaxed.

He kept his hands raised. "I will, but first let's call a truce. For the time being, at least. You know what they say, sweetie – the enemy of my enemy is—"

"Don't. I don't want to hear it."

He nodded. "Fair enough. But will you please cool it for a minute?"

Without taking his eyes off her, he lowered his arms.

"Tell me what you know," she said.

A scan of the room told him everyone had stopped whatever they were doing and were waiting on him to speak.

Pissing fucksticks.

Not what he needed.

He closed his eyes, composing himself as much as possible but also trying to buy time. He had to play this just right.

"Not here," he told her. "Not in front of everyone. Just me and you."

"Zora?" the doc interjected, as if he'd just found his voice. "What's going on? You know this man? He's the one who you—"

"That's right. The man who's been working with Heydari. Who Heydari has been protecting. Which is why I can't help thinking this is all bullshit."

"Oh, don't be fucking ridiculous, Acid," Caesar bawled. "Do you really think I'd spend more than one night on that rickety bed in this piss-stained stable if I didn't have to?"

"Why is he calling you this name?" the Norwegian asked. "Acid?"

"That's her name, doc. Acid Vanilla. She used to work for me."

He noticed Acid's right eye twitch.

"Is this correct?" the doc asked her.

"In a way." She didn't turn around. "Zora Dankworth is the name on my passport, but it's not who I am. Apologies, I didn't mean to involve you – or anyone – in my shit."

The doctor looked confused. "But you are Special Forces?"

"Special Forces?" Caesar repeated. "Special bleeding Forces, are you having a fucking *giraffe*? That what you told him?"

He knew he was pushing it, so soon after she'd calmed down, but it was such a ridiculous concept to him he couldn't help it. To say it had been a shitty year was a considerable understatement – he took moments of delight where he could.

"I did what I needed to. Like always."

And there she was.

It had taken a while to get there, but he could see the old Acid now. She was there in the way she tilted her head to one side with her hands on her hips. There in that vicious pout of hers (albeit muted presently without access to make-up). As he watched, she twisted her mouth to one side, no doubt poised to say something derisive and devastating in equal measures.

Bloody hell, he'd missed her.

But then her head dropped and her shoulders sagged as she

turned to the doctor. "I'm sorry. I know it's all rather confusing," she murmured. "I'll explain later."

"Blimey," Caesar huffed. "That all you got – *I'll explain later*? There was me thinking – hoping – you might still be a force to reckon with."

She looked back at him with furrowed brows. "Hoping?"

"Don't get me wrong, when I first poked my impressive bonce out of my room and saw you were here I was somewhat shocked – and yes, a little perturbed, shall we say. I mean, you have murdered six of my associates over the last two years." He ran his gaze over the assembled crowd, making sure they all heard. "But then the old grey cells started twitching, genius as I am, I began to wonder if you being here might be fateful. Someone wily and shrewd. Willing to do whatever was needed."

Acid raised her chin and sniffed. "You want me to help you?"

"I want us to help each other. Because like it or not, working together is our best chance of getting out of here." He held up a large finger, changing tack as he wagged it in the air. "You know, they all said Berlin wasn't a one-off. Said you'd gone soft. But I didn't believe them. Not my Acid Vanilla, I said. She was the best. When she put her mind to something she wouldn't let anyone or anything get in her way."

"That's still the case."

"Is it?"

"I came looking for you. To kill you. I've found you, haven't I?"

Caesar laughed, looking about him for effect. "But at what cost? For pity's sake, kiddo. You're in a stuffy old stable full of bleeding do-gooders and wet blankets. At the disposal of that mad prick upstairs."

"What do you mean?"

"Oh, don't you know? Fucking hell, you're gonna shit when you find out."

"Find out what?"

He opened his mouth to answer but paused, choosing to toy

with her some more. Over her head he'd spotted two of Heydari's soldiers entering with the daily rations. Two large trays contained a selection of flatbreads and bowls of thin stew, alongside a bag of bottled water. One per prisoner. Same as every pissing day.

"Ah. Here we are," he called. "Lunch. We can talk more later."

He walked back to his room, knowing the soldiers would deliver his own meagre meal to him. For now he'd said enough. Acid might not be as robust or vivacious as she once was, but he could still play her the same way. He'd seen it in her eyes, the way they burned with curiosity as he dangled each morsel of information, holding it just out of reach.

Hook, line and bleeding sinker.

But why be surprised? He'd made her. She was his creation. Dr Frankenstein's downfall was he never realised the power in what he'd created until it was too late. But that was not the case here. From day one he'd known exactly what he was doing, which buttons to press, which way to push and pull. It was because of him she'd become the best in the industry and the deadliest killer on anyone's books. She might have gone rogue, decided she was more suited to a pissy civilian life than what he'd offered, but he didn't believe she'd lost it entirely. He saw it in her even now. She could still be the best. They'd hurt each other in many different ways, she hated him and perhaps with good cause, but she was his best ticket out of here. He just had to sell it to her the right way.

He raised one hand in the air, waving back at her. "Come see me when you've eaten, Acid. I'll be in my quarters."

CHAPTER 16

Caesar waited until he'd closed the door behind him and had moved into the centre of the room before letting out a gasping sigh. An incredible weariness overcame him, the stress of holding it together just now all but breaking him in two. Moving over to his woefully inadequate bed, he sank down onto the thin mattress. The old springs creaked under his weight. Despite the torment of the last few months, the weight he'd lost, he was still a big man. But his bones ached and he could sense his mind unravelling day by day. Like always, he'd talked a good talk out there, but seeing Acid up close had knocked him sideways. Not least for the fact she looked so different these days – older, but with a darkness to her that troubled him. It was as if she was a mirror, reflecting back his own deficiencies. Neither of them were the people they once were.

Acid had been a raging ball of hate back when they first met, but so full of untapped potential. He'd given her the big sell – telling her how influential he was, what he could do for her – but the truth was he'd been finding his feet just as much, still excavating the diamond in the rough that was to become the indomitable persona of Beowulf Caesar.

He eased himself back against the raw brick wall and snorted derisively at himself. These last months, sitting in this shadowy, dusty room with only his memories for company, he'd had time for plenty of soul-searching (although perhaps soul-searching was the wrong term, seeing as by definition it implied one had a soul to search). Over the years he'd put up so many walls, assembled so many layers to his personality, he had no idea where his true centre was. With the beauty of hindsight he wondered if this was the reason why he'd focused on outward achievements over the last decade. Power, money, success. He'd aimed for the top and he'd damn well got there. For a few golden years Annihilation Pest Control was arguably the best in the world at what it did. Caesar's clients were world leaders, not only in their chosen career paths (organised crime, drug trafficking, guns, you name it), but some were *actual* world leaders – politicians, presidents, government officials.

Yes, it was safe to say Boyd Chapman had come a long way from the shy, uncertain little boy from East London who'd grown up without a mother and little input from the abusive drunk he had for an old man. The abuse only exacerbated after he found the young Boyd trying on his dead mother's dresses.

He groaned and punched the mattress as if somehow this action would smash the memories out of his head. It never worked. Though now of course there were the days he woke up confused and dozy, unable to focus on anything, not even the past if he wanted to. He wasn't sure which was worse – remembering or forgetting.

"Pissing shit."

He had it all and she'd taken it from him. That malicious, selfish… He sighed. Inwardly cursed himself.

Words.

They were just words.

Things he thought he should think. Because deep down he knew the truth – he couldn't hate her. He wanted to. Hell, it would have been so much easier if he did. He rewound the last fifteen minutes in his head, picturing himself pouncing on her, his big hands around her throat. Catching her unarmed and off guard, a simple squeeze might have done it. Yet, even in this macabre visualisation the sassy bitch was grinning, winking at him the way she did whenever they got into a messy situation – just before she did something equally crazy and impressive that got them out of danger.

He sighed again. Louder. More pointedly. But maybe this really was fate. Acid could help him. They could help each other.

A knock on the door brought him back to the present. "Food."

He got himself upright as the door swung open.

"What are we eating today then, chef?" he asked, as the guard shuffled in with a tray. "Lobster Thermidor? Braised calf cheeks?"

The guard frowned and shoved the tray at him. "Here."

"Oh, brown piss water again. Marvellous." He leaned forward and gestured for him to place it down on the end of the bed. "I do hope it tastes as bland as ever."

The young soldier did as he was told before backing out of the room. At the door he shot over a sharp look, his face distorted in a tight sneer. Caesar caught it but didn't respond. He'd experienced the same look many times over the years. Not so much since he became the feared leader of a deadly team of assassins, but still on occasion, and especially from those less comfortable with his sexuality and lifestyle choices.

But fuck them.

Fuck them all to hell.

"Off you trot then," he said. "*Sweetie.*"

The guard shook his head and was about to close the door when the drippy doctor appeared, poking his head nervously into the room.

Caesar sighed. "What is it now?"

The guard departed and the doctor (it was Larson, wasn't it?) shuffled into the room.

"I have more for you," he said, and held up his hand to reveal the small white vial in his palm. "This is the last of the current batch. I've asked the guards to acquire more and stressed the importance."

Caesar held out his hands but the doctor hesitated in the doorway, keeping his distance. That bloody virus. "Throw it," he told him, cupping his hands together in front of his chest and catching the small plastic cylinder.

"How are you feeling?"

"Fine, Larson. As always."

The doctor kept on looking at him with the same pained expression. Like someone had just dropped a rotten fart in his presence. "You'll have to make those last."

"Yes, yes, fuck off."

He turned away and placed the vial on the small set of drawers standing in the corner. Except for the flimsy bed it was the only other piece of furniture in the room.

"You know one of our new arrivals well then?"

He closed his eyes and sucked back a deep dramatic breath. Did not want to get into this. Not with this muppet. "Oh yes, we go way back. Lovely girl."

"So you are military too?"

He sat back on the bed. "My dear boy, were you not privy to my little display of derision when you mentioned Special Forces back there?"

"Yes. But I do not understand. She said—"

"Best you take it up with her, Larson."

The doctor winced. "My name is Lars."

He glared at Caesar, but Caesar shrugged it off. *Whatever.*

"Does she know?" the doctor asked. "About you and—"

"No. And you keep that to yourself if you know what's good for you. Capiche? Didn't you take the Hippocratic oath?"

"Of course, I would never..." He trailed off, looking at his feet now. "I will leave you."

"Probably for the best." He watched as the timid Norwegian pivoted awkwardly and made for the door.

"Wait."

"Yes?"

Caesar blew out a sigh. "Thank you." The words felt foreign and bitter in his mouth and his voice cracked as he spoke. *Pathetic prick.* He coughed quickly to cover his unease. "Mind how you go. I'll see ya later."

The doctor gave a brief nod of acknowledgement then exited the room, closing the door silently behind him.

Caesar waited a second or two for the weird energy to subside before he got to his feet. He marched over to the chest of drawers – swaying somewhat as he went but putting it down to a rush of blood to the head – and grabbed up the bottle of pills. He thumbed off the lid before shaking two out into his palm. His rationed bottle of water lay on the end of his bed but he chose to swallow them dry, working them down his throat with gulps of air.

Pills ingested, he slid open the top drawer to reveal a small leather pouch and two porcelain tiles he'd removed from the floor. He scooped up the contents and carried them over to the bed, lowering himself to kneel beside it. His knees and back hurt and the whole act was draining, but at six-six and still weighing in excess of two hundred and seventy pounds everything he did in this cramped prison cell of a room was draining. He'd been nimbler in his younger days, of course, back when he still carried out hits himself. But in recent years, the last two especially, his old bones had been seizing up.

He tipped out the remaining pills onto one of the tiles, sixteen in total. After returning four of them to the bottle and shoving the cap back on, he picked up the second piece of tile and placed it down on top, grinding the pills into a fine powder. Satisfied with his handiwork, he gathered the powder into a mound with the heel of his hands and slid the whole lot into the leather pouch. Holding it in his palm to feel the weight, it was lighter than he'd hoped but probably enough to have a decent effect.

He smiled to himself, delighting in the craziness of the situation, the bitter irony of it all. Acid had come here to kill him, yet her very presence might be his saving grace. And this pouch of powder right here, gathered together as a final get-out clause, might now serve him in a much better way. All he had to do was get Acid to trust him.

He let out a bitter laugh which hurt his insides. "Easy as pissing pie."

CHAPTER 17

Acid was slurping down the dregs of her soup as Lars joined her and Kendis at the table in the middle of the room.

"It is not great, is it?" Lars said, smiling at what must have been a disgusted expression on her face. "I'm afraid most meals consist of the same."

"What were you doing in there?" she asked, placing her bowl down and fixing him with a hard stare. She liked Lars, but right now she had no patience for bullshit and small talk.

Lars stuck out his bottom lip. "I am a doctor. I believe this is why Cyrus Heydari wanted me brought here. I was only doing my rounds. I check on all the prisoners on rotation. Once a day. That is all."

"So he does want to keep us alive. For now."

"Oh, yes. When I first arrived I was tasked with examining each of the prisoners. I inform the guards of any medicine required and Heydari makes sure they get it for us."

"Careful there, doc," Acid said. "Sounds like a nasty case of Stockholm Syndrome. Any pills for that?"

Lars frowned. "Please don't misunderstand me. I do not want to be here. And you know as much as anyone my feelings about

Cyrus Heydari. But my first responsibility is for the health of the other people here. There was another doctor before me who carried out these duties, but he was old and had underlying health problems. Unfortunately he succumbed to the virus."

He glanced around the room, taking in the other prisoners. "Heydari heard I had experience fighting the pandemic, so he has me monitor his men. Make sure they are all healthy. Are you both feeling okay?"

"Oh yeah," Acid said, spinning the bowl in front of her. "Hunky dory."

"Please let me know if you need anything. Or if you feel ill in any way."

Acid sat back in her seat. There was something about the way Lars was speaking, the words he used, they were too regimented. Like he was reading from a script. She nodded at Caesar's cabin. "And is he okay?"

The corner of his mouth twitched. It was so brief, so miniscule a movement, most people would have missed it, but not Acid. She'd trained herself over the years to notice the slightest of tells. Knowing when someone was lying could save your life. It had done. Many times.

"Yes. He is fine. Angry and petulant and rather scary, but the same as always." He raised his eyebrows at her. "I have not been administering to him long, of course. But you must know more than I, yes?"

"I was just asking her the same thing." Kendis leaned over the table towards Lars. "About how she knew that guy. And all the stuff he mentioned. But I'm getting nowhere."

Acid sighed and raised the bowl to her lips. It was empty, they all knew it was empty, but she needed time to compose herself. Truth was, seeing Caesar up close just now had rattled the living shit out of her, and not because she was surprised or scared or even angry to see him up close. Any of those emotions would have been expected. Easier to deal with. Because the thing that was bothering her – sending her thoughts spiralling into dark, confusing places – was that the overriding emotion she'd felt was relief. After everything that malevolent bastard had done, she'd found herself glad to see him.

But maybe it made sense. She had been so lost the last two years, trying to fit into the safe, civilian world in which she found herself. Then suddenly there he was, standing in front of her, perhaps the only person in her life who truly understood her. Spook did her best, of course, but she'd never be able to fully appreciate what sixteen years in the killing business did to a person. Even The Dullahan, himself an ex-assassin and a hard-nosed one at that, had come from a different era, with a different set of principles. Plus he'd always been freelance so could never appreciate the rush of working so closely with someone like Caesar, who could get the absolute best out of you and had your back one hundred percent. He'd taken the young Alice Vandella's chaotic rage and moulded it into something beautiful. Something valuable too. If Acid Vanilla was here at all it was because of Beowulf Caesar.

But wasn't that true in so many ways?

She glanced up into the expectant faces of Lars and Kendis and almost choked on a ball of emotion. They both looked so kind and innocent staring back at her it was too much. She sniffed, focusing her attention on the empty bowl in front of her. "What do you want to know?"

"Who are you?" Kendis asked. "The big dude thought the idea of you being Special Forces was a huge joke."

She closed her eyes. "My name's Acid Vanilla, okay? That's the name I go by. And yes, I did work for him. Doing bad things." Her eyes sprang open as a kaleidoscope of macabre images flashed in front of her face. Bloody torsos. Cold, dead eyes. Her greatest hits as part of Caesar's crew. She looked at her hands to avoid the stares from her companions burning into her forehead.

"Orcus. This is the man you were looking for?" Lars asked her.

"Yes. Though that was just a cover. His name is Beowulf Caesar."

"You appear close. Like you have known each other forever. Like family, even."

Acid sighed. "It's complicated. Very complicated. He was good to me. Once. And yes we were close. But my life with him got too much. I had to get out."

"And he didn't like that?"

"You could say that." She looked up and fixed them with a hard stare. "I've told you as much as I can. Please don't ask me to say anything more. Suffice to say he's the reason why I'm here in Iran. The real reason. I'd heard he was working with Heydari. And in turn being shielded from the Americans. And from me."

Lars let out a low grumble. Almost a laugh but not quite. "You heard wrong then."

"How do you mean?"

"The only one being shielded is that coward Heydari. That's why we're here. Why we are still alive."

"Shit." Acid sat back, it all making sense now. "We're human shields."

"But why?" Kendis asked. "What're we shielding him from?"

"Like she says, the Americans mainly." He gestured over to where a man with white hair was lying with his eyes closed on one of the cots. "James over there is a missionary, fluent in Farsi. He overheard the guards a few days ago. There is talk that Heydari's movements are being heavily monitored by the US. We know he is a supremely paranoid man but perhaps this is true. He has made waves in the region of late. Angered a lot of people on both sides of the conflict. Some say he is trying to take over as Supreme Leader, taking on ISIL as well as the West. Which is why he has amassed western civilians here, to avoid air strikes against him."

"Clever of him, I guess," Kendis replied, but a slight shudder undermined her poise. "The army will have heat sensors in their satellites."

The kid was looking Acid's way as she spoke, her voice clipped and tetchy, no doubt angry she'd been lied to.

Acid was about to respond but stopped herself. You couldn't please everyone and she had bigger issues to worry about. Namely her ex-boss, and how the hell she was going to handle the crushing waves of conflicting emotions and powerful urges prickling the hairs on the back of her neck. It reminded her of how she used to feel when she was young, before Jacqueline helped her to define her manic mood swings as 'the bats.' She felt reckless and confused. Didn't know whether she wanted to kill or cry.

But she needed to face him. Properly. Just her and him.

"Back soon," she said, getting to her feet.

"You going to be okay?" Kendis called after her.

"I'll be fine," she yelled back. "We're just going to have a chat. No big deal."

CHAPTER 18

After knocking once, Acid opened the door and stepped inside. The cabin was smaller than it looked from the outside and a lot stuffier than the main space. It stank worse too, although perhaps this was due to its current resident, who was lying on the bed, sweat pouring down his face. From the day she had met Caesar (sat in the visiting wing at Crest Hill, him dressed in a floor-length fur coat) he'd been a hurricane of gregarious malevolence. But she'd loved that about him. He never gave one shit about what anyone thought and often basked in the knowledge his decadent, thuggish campness pissed off all those he intended it to. Seeing him here like this – breathless and sweaty, dressed in a torn canvas shirt and dirty jogging bottoms – it was a real kicker. She still despised the man who had sanctioned her mother's death with every cell in her body, yet her mind seemed to separate these two versions of him. The Caesar she'd met all those years ago still haunted her thoughts. He'd given her an amazing life. It was because of him she was who she was – confident, wise, unapologetic, hard as nails (not to mention sassy and with a wicked sense of humour, if she did say so herself). But that man had also hurt her more than it was possible to hurt someone. The truth was now dawning on her. It was the fact it was him who'd done it to her, rather than *what* he'd done, that hurt so much.

"I was beginning to think you weren't coming." He sat upright and swung his sizeable legs to the floor. "You sitting down?"

She raised her chin. "No thanks." She shut the door and leaned with her back against it.

A heavy atmosphere filled the room as they fixed eyes on each other, both nodding along to a silent narrative only they could hear. A thousand chaotic thoughts clashed across Acid's consciousness. The bats screeched in her head. Told her to grab up the chest of drawers and smash it over the bastard's fat head.

"I fucking hate you," she muttered under her breath.

He rolled his head around his shoulders. "Is that so?"

"Yes."

"Well, that is a shame. I always thought you still loved me, deep down. Which was why you couldn't pull the trigger in Berlin. Why you let me escape the island." He leaned forward, pointing a stubby finger at her. "You know, kid, I didn't want to do any of the bad stuff that happened after you went rogue. But you left me no choice. I had to send a message. People were watching."

"You sent me unarmed to an island, to be hunted like an animal."

"That was Raaz's idea. I had no say in it."

"You could have stopped it. You were still her boss, weren't you?"

"How could I have stopped it? People already suspected I was letting you off the hook. I heard Doris telling Magpie, on more than one occasion, that if it was anyone else I wouldn't have let them live this long." He flicked his head, as if tossing aside a lock of invisible hair. "Perhaps she was right."

She shook her head. "You didn't have to involve my mum."

"Oh, come on. I did you a favour. I read her medical records. She was on her last legs as it was. Didn't know her arse from her elbow. Didn't know who you were. Didn't know who she was, even." He grimaced, theatrically. "Must have been a terrible burden for you."

She tensed, fighting with every part of her not to give anything away – lest he'd know he was getting to her, lest he'd see his words were hitting home. A rage knotted her stomach.

Because he was correct, wasn't he?

In many ways she was glad her mum was dead. The poor woman was sick, scared, locked in an existential nightmare from which there was no escape. The person Louisa Vandella had been died long before Caesar put the call out on her. But that didn't make it right. It didn't excuse him, and it didn't excuse her for feeling that way.

"I hate you," she whispered again.

"Well, you do know what they say, don't you? The opposite of love isn't hate, it's indifference."

"Oh, do fuck off," she replied, as a familiar fizz of rage percolated in her chest. "Yeah, *poor me, I'm indifferent to you*. One can't really spit it with the same kind of venom."

He laughed, the bed rocking under his weight. "There she fucking well is! You know I was getting rather worried. Wondering if you really had gone soft."

"You shouldn't pay too much heed to rumours, Ceez, you know that. Besides, the rest of them were always jealous of me."

"Well, you've pissing well killed them all, haven't you? All except Magpie. Unless…"

"Yeah, she's dead as well."

He nodded. "Fair enough. Bet you enjoyed that one."

"I'm not going to lie."

She cast her gaze around the room. There was nothing here either of them could use as a weapon. With Caesar there was always the possibility of something up his sleeve (sometimes literally), but for now the bats were quiet. There was no threat. "What did you want to talk about?"

"Go on, take the weight off." He gestured once more to the end of the bed. "Don't worry, kiddo, I know you're a veritable ball of seething fury. I know you despise me and want to slice me open. I'm not going to get all sentimental and mushy just because you sit down."

She hesitated a second before walking over and perching on the edge of the small drawer unit in the corner. "I'm fine here. So… talk."

He adjusted himself so he was facing her, elbows resting on his knees. Once settled he looked up and fixed her dead in the eye. "Why the hell couldn't you have just disappeared? After you went all doolally in Paris I wouldn't have looked for you. Not too hard, anyway. You could be living it up right now."

"I did what I did. No point dragging it all up."

He shook his head sadly but didn't take his eyes off her. "Would you do the same thing, given your time again?"

"I don't know. Maybe. Maybe not."

"Well you fucked everything up royally, didn't you? We had it good, Acid. We were on the verge of something wonderful." He smiled and her heart did a somersault. "You knew you were always my girl, my number one. I'd have seen you right, ya know that. But no, you went mental, and for what – that pathetic drip Spook Horrorshitz? What were you thinking?"

"Horowitz." Acid's jaw was rigid with anger, only half of it aimed at Caesar. "She's a good kid. She didn't deserve the hit."

"Why not talk to me about it? We could have sorted something."

She shrugged, stared at the ground. "It all happened so quick. Before I knew it, I'd burnt all my bridges."

"And then some." He looked away, chuckling joylessly to himself. "You've bleeding ruined me, kid. I'm done, you know that? Properly fucking done. Washed up and washed out. Stuck in this stinking place."

She raised her head. "What happened with you and Heydari? I thought you and he were working together on something?"

"Yes, so did I! The dirty fucker did me over."

"How do you mean?"

"He's a madman. Do you know how he got this palace?"

"Bayat – my source – he told me he'd built it himself."

"Not quite. He's done some work over the last few years, fortifying the place, but he actually stole it from a rival that he had skinned alive and placed on a pole outside the gate." He watched for her reaction but she remained stony-faced. "Apparently these stables were once the home for Akhal-teke horses, a rare breed over three thousand years old. Beautiful creatures, they call them golden horses due to their appearance, and only six thousand of them left in the world. But as soon as he took over the place, Heydari had them all slaughtered and fed to his men. Delighted in relaying that little story to me, he did."

Acid folded her arms. "Why are you telling me this?"

"To highlight the fact that Heydari is a loose cannon, someone you underestimate at your peril. Like I did."

"That still doesn't tell me what happened between you and him."

He waved a dismissive hand in the air. "It's a long story. I don't want to go into it now. Suffice to say, things did not work out as planned. So I hope you're happy."

"I've not been happy in a long time."

"Yes, well, makes two of us."

They stared at each other, faces locked and unblinking. In all honesty, Acid had been unhappy for more than a long time – to her it had felt like a lifetime. Because it was. Why not admit it to herself? In spite of everything that had happened, the pain he'd caused her, the trauma, she'd missed the terrible fucker. They were the same. Always had been. She might have even used the term kindred spirits if she was one of *those* sorts of people.

Caesar broke the silence first. "We need to get out of here. And soon," he said, his voice low. "They tell you about what's going on?"

"That we're human shields for Heydari?"

"Something like that, but that's not what I'm concerned about. The fucker's been a naughty boy, has mobilised a lot of smaller insurgent groups into his own militia. He's planning on taking full control over the region."

"Meaning?"

"Meaning the Yanks aren't going to allow him to get that far. While he's detaining this merry band of fuckwits under his house, he might keep the missiles at bay. But if US troops decide to storm the palace, we're both screwed."

Acid sat back. "I might be okay."

"You might. But you might not. What do you tell them when you don't show up on any database? There are not many types of people whose entire history has been wiped. Special Forces perhaps, and people of a more... disreputable bent. That why you told them you were a soldier?"

She shrugged. "Maybe."

"And I'll be fucked, of course. Well and truly. You do know I'm on the CIA's most wanted list now, after that agent friend of yours, Andreas Welles, started singing like a little dickie-bird?"

"Well, you did shoot him."

"In the leg!"

She grinned. "I wondered about that. Was it intentional? To miss, I mean, keep him alive?"

"No. It bloody wasn't." He looked away, a strange expression on his face. "I suppose my aim isn't what it was."

He snorted and chewed on his lip, eyes huge and glazed, lost in a thought that seemed to plague him. When he looked back at her, his face was more serious than she'd ever seen. "I need your help. We really do need to get out of here."

She slid off the unit and walked over to the side of the bed. "If I help you escape, don't you think I'll kill you the first chance I get?"

"Maybe you will. Maybe you won't."

"You are aware the only reason I'm here, in the middle of a bleeding global pandemic, is to kill you?"

Caesar got up from the bed, the mattress groaning beneath him as he made a real ordeal of it. Acid wondered if this was for her benefit. Him playing the role of someone weak and unstable, someone she'd feel sorry for. He glanced at her, a deep frown creasing his big features.

"I can help you," he mumbled, as he steadied himself and stretched out his back. "To get out of Iran, I mean." He shot her a look. Up and down. "You hadn't thought that far?"

A shrug, a sneer, but both were half-baked. "I'd made peace with the idea this could be a suicide mission."

"Shitting hell, Acid. Is your hate that deep? Your vendetta so set in stone?"

"It was."

"And now?"

"You fucked me up. In so many different ways. You have to pay. You have to." She spoke over gritted teeth, fists tight, nails digging into her palms, the only way to hold her emotions in check.

Caesar held her gaze, but with a strange intensity behind his expression. "I didn't want to do what I did, kiddo. Like I said, you left me no choice. And don't forget, you were nothing – had nothing – before I took you under my wing. I gave you the world."

Acid looked down at her hands. "I have to do it," she whispered.

"Well how about you wait until we get out of the country? That do you? Help me escape and I can get us passports. Plus safe voyage home."

She looked up and saw a flash of the old Caesar in his wide grin – cocky, funny, her friend.

"See?' he said. "We need each other. Like always."

"But how can you be sure I won't kill you as soon as you get me my papers? As soon as we get back to the UK?"

"I can't, can I? But I certainly don't want to die here in this dirt pit, in these fucking awful rags." He placed his big hand on her shoulder.

At his touch she recoiled a little, but covered it by saying, "You not enjoying your new look?"

He pulled at his tattered shirt, then rubbed at the grime on his forehead and cheeks. "Are you joking? I look like fucking Brando in Apocalypse Now."

"Colonel Kurtz?" She frowned, a slyness curling the edge of her lips. "You mean the crazy megalomaniac who had to go into hiding after killing people he shouldn't have? Hmm. Although I'd say a Brando comparison is rather generous."

"Fuck off," he said, raising his chin, giving her his profile. "Back in the day I could have given him a run for his money. Could have been a contender." He guffawed loudly, but she ignored him.

"All right," she said, with a sigh. "So what's your plan?"

"I've got something I'm working on, but it's going to take another day or so. All I need to know for now is that you're with me. That you're prepared to escape this pathetic grief hole, by any means necessary. And I mean any means. That you've still got it in you."

"Still got it in me?" She was in his face in a stride, pointing a broken fingernail in his smug face. "You know I should kill you right now, for what you did."

He held his hands up, bloodshot eyes widening. "Oh bloody hell. Go on then. Do it. Do us both a favour."

She held her poise but her hand was shaking. So were his, she noticed. Whether it was from fear or weariness, she wasn't sure. On both counts. "You took it all from me… You—" She stopped herself, looked away, rubbing the heel of her hand under her eye.

"Look, kid, if things had been different…" He trailed off, his voice softer than she'd ever heard it. "I meant it when I said you'd ruined me. Everything I've worked for, gone. Isn't that enough for you? I'm choosing to move past that because I know we're better together. We've always known that, haven't we? We're unstoppable. So what do you say?"

She looked up into the big face looming over her. It wasn't

emotion so much as confusion that had her bottom lip quivering, but either way she shut her mouth quickly lest he spot it. Meeting his eyes, she gave the merest of nods. "Fine."

"Good girl," he whispered, squeezing her shoulder. "Leave me now, let me have a think about the best plan of action. I'll come find you later."

She gave him another nod, firmer this time, more resolute, before silently walking towards the door and easing it open. As she stepped from the room she paused, wondering if she should say what she was thinking. But what would be the point? For the time being it was about survival. She sucked back a deep breath and held it in her chest for a beat, trying to silence the maelstrom of pent-up aggression that had nowhere go. Emotions collided with memories, collided with past traumas both physical and mental. An icy dread spiked her alertness whilst at the same time her insides burned with a fiery anticipation for what was to come. It reminded her of how she'd felt when she first joined Annihilation Pest Control. At once excited, but also scared as hell.

But what was she afraid of?

Caesar?

Heydari?

Death?

Or maybe it was herself she feared. The knowledge that despite the immense amounts of reflection and soul-searching she'd done these last two years, she hadn't stepped too far away from the dark soul she'd always been. She closed the door with a quiet click and walked over to one of the empty cot beds. Right now, any one of those questions was too much for her to deal with. Best thing for it was to stay present and be ready for whatever happened next. Because something told her the situation was going to get a lot worse before it got better.

CHAPTER 19

Caesar peeled open one sticky eyelid as he tried to make sense of what was going on. Light was filtering in from under the door, meaning it was morning, but he hadn't remembered falling asleep. In fact he'd accepted the fact that good night's sleep would once again elude him.

The knocking came again, more abruptly now, and his thoughts turned to Acid. Was this her, come to finish him off? He sat up in bed as the door creaked open to reveal a young guard carrying a tray.

"Ah, breakfast. *Wunderbar,*" Caesar growled, pulling the sweat-drenched shirt away from his torso as the kid shuffled into the cabin. "And what are we having this morning? Yogurt and honey? Figs in syrup?" He raised his head as the tray was dumped on the end of the bed. "Oh, no. Grey watery slop. As per bleeding usual."

The kid didn't understand him. Or was choosing not to. He gestured at the bowl. "You eat."

"Yes, yes." Caesar sighed. "I'll force it down later." He was about to dismiss the youngster when a thought came to him. He sat forward, taking in the guard's weasel-like features. "I wonder if you can help me?" he said, deepening his voice. "I need to speak to Cyrus – Mr Heydari – I have important information for him. Can you take me to him?"

The guard frowned. "Prince?"

"That's right." He pushed the tray of porridge to the far end of the bed and threw back the covers. "Tell him Beowulf Caesar requests an audience. Tell him it's in his best interests…"

"No. No disturb the prince."

"No, but I only—"

"No. I cannot. You stay here. You eat."

Caesar sighed. "Fine, forget it. Piss off."

He sat back and picked at one of his gold teeth with a long fingernail as the weasel shuffled out of the cabin. He gave it a few seconds then lowered his feet onto the floor. The dusty porcelain tiles were cold this morning and he leaned down to put on the battered old pumps they'd supplied him with.

Pumps, indeed. They were a far cry from his beloved Christian Louboutin loafers that were currently languishing in his old flat back in London.

"Oh, Acid," he muttered to himself. "What a bloody carry on."

He got up and walked over to the door. In the space beyond he could hear the chink and scrape of metal utensils on porcelain, the guards administering breakfast rations to the rest of the prisoners. As he eased open the door, a sour stench of milk drifted in, adding an obnoxious new layer to the lingering pong of stale humans and the memory of horse. Two more guards – complete with AKs hanging over their shoulders – were stood next to a food trolley by the entrance, whilst the weasel walked around the room collecting bowls and inspecting the cots. Caesar considered the scene without moving. This could be his chance. Although what he had in mind was risky.

"Oi, mush." He strode out into the main space before he could talk himself out of it. Heading straight for the weasel, he grabbed an arm around his neck. "Come here."

"Goh!"

With a thick arm pressing against his windpipe, the guard's

bark of surprise was somewhat muted, but still loud enough to alert his colleagues.

"Calm down, now," Caesar yelled as they ran over, brandishing their rifles. "Mr Heydari needs me alive, remember. And I need to speak to him. That's all I want. Take me to him?"

The youngster felt so small in his clutches, like a tiny bird. As the other guards tensed behind their rifles, Caesar shifted his hold so he was now gripping the kid's chin with one hand and his forehead with the other. All it would take was a sharp yank in both directions and he'd have served his last bowl of gruel.

Caesar remained still, but every muscle in his body burned with tension as the two guards moved apart, each either side of him and keeping their aim high.

"Let him go."

"Take me to Heydari."

"Let him go!"

One of the guards stepped closer, spittle foaming at the corner of his mouth.

"I'll murder the little streak of piss. Not a problem."

The pressure in the room was intense. Everyone on edge. No one breathing. Caesar held the kid tight, watching out the corner of his eye as one of the guards hung back before side-stepping into his blind side.

Pathetic.

As if he hadn't seen him.

Back in his day Caesar would have called it out immediately, threatened to snap the little weasel's neck if he didn't back off. Although, more than likely he'd have already killed the weakling. A twist and a crack, then shove the body at the approaching guard, grab his rifle in the confusion. It would have been goodnight Vienna for all three guards and he wouldn't have broken a sweat.

Back in his day…

Today however he needed a different approach. He had to be

clever about this. He closed his eyes. Braced himself. So if that meant—

Fucking hell.

A sharp pain across the back of his head smashed him into the moment. He released his grip on the guard and stumbled to one side before another heavy blow across his back sent him to his knees. The pain in his head spread deeper into his awareness but was quickly forgotten as he looked up into the muzzle of an assault rifle, aimed between his eyes.

"Don't shoot. You need me." He lifted his hands as the other guards stepped around to flank their colleague. They spoke quickly to each other in hushed tones before the weasel – clearly feeling brave now with his chums backing him – stepped forward and dragged Caesar to his feet.

"Fine," he said. "If you want to talk with the prince so badly, you'll get your wish. But you'll see what he does with such a foolish and impetuous dog."

"Impetuous dog?" Caesar mused, as they herded him to the door and a rifle was jabbed into his kidney. "Someone fancies themselves as a bit of a poet."

The weasel sneered in response before they shoved him roughly towards the steps leading up to the courtyard. As he was bustled up the stone stairs, Caesar managed to peer over his shoulder. Acid was standing by the wall on the far side of the room. Her face was rigid and her demeanour ice cold, but he noticed the hint of a smile tremble her lips as he shot her a wink. At least, he thought he did. It could have been his imagination. Or a trick of the light.

There had been a lot of that going on recently.

CHAPTER 20

With no more words spoken, the guards led Caesar across the courtyard and hustled him aggressively up the raised walkway towards the main entrance of the palace. Blood had soaked into his shirt from the wound above his ear, sticking the thin cloth to his skin.

"I can walk on my own," he said, as they got to the double doors of the entrance hall and the weasel kid grabbed his upper arm. "I'm not going to run off. Where the hell would I go?"

He eyeballed the soldiers standing either side of the entrance. They each wore black face coverings but he assumed them to be older and more experienced than his three escorts. It was something about the rigidness of their backs, the arrogance of their stance. The guards flanking him were runts in comparison. Young upstarts from the local village perhaps, hoping to make a name for themselves as part of Heydari's vision.

The soldiers on the door considered Caesar before growling something in Farsi to one of the youngsters.

"We didn't need any of this drama," Caesar interjected. "All I want to do is have a quick chat with your boss. Something I need to discuss with him. It's going to be worth his while."

The kid holding him dug his fingers into his flesh. "You don't talk, devil."

With a grunt of acquiescence, the duty soldiers stepped aside and pushed open the doors. One of them beckoned Caesar forward before holding his palm up to block the path of the two younger guards, leaving him and the weasel to continue the journey.

"Just me and you then, kiddo," he whispered, as the door shut behind them and the young soldier led him across the room. "What's your name, by the way?"

There was no answer. Just a deep huff of anger.

"Well, I hope you know what you're doing. I hear your boss can turn nasty if you piss him off."

"Shut your mouth," came the reply, but Caesar sensed trepidation in the kid's voice He was losing his bottle. Well, good.

"I only asked your name."

"It is Ahmed. Now shut your mouth, dog."

They got to the end of the first room where two more armed guards were standing beside another set of doors. A hurried and breathless exchange took place between Ahmed and one of them. He looked Caesar up and down, then held up a hand for them to wait.

"Seems like a pleasant chap," Caesar whispered, as the guard opened the door and disappeared into the room beyond.

Ahmed didn't answer but Caesar could sense the nervous energy coming off him. He was in over his head and he knew it.

"Don't worry, lad. It's not your fault. You were angry and embarrassed. You had to bring me up here. To show your boss what an *impetuous dog*, I was. You did the right thing." He paused, letting his head rock from side to side before tutting pointedly. "Although, with all that palaver downstairs, a smarter, less hot-headed individual might have, I don't know, construed that I'd attacked you on purpose. Just so you'd bring me up to see the big man."

He glanced down at Ahmed, whose eyes were darting around without blinking, as if experiencing something only he could see.

"You must be punished for your actions," he replied, but his voice was croaky. There was nothing like cold fear to tense up a man's throat and wilt his resolve.

"Tricky one, isn't it?" Caesar went on, digging his claws in deeper. "I doubt your prince would be happy finding out I'd orchestrated this whole meeting. I hope I don't let it slip." He leaned into him, lowering his voice to a conspiring whisper. "I expect you're fond of your cock and balls, aren't you?"

The young soldier stiffened, before a second later the door opened and the guard glared at Caesar. "You. The prince wants to see you."

Caesar turned to Ahmed. "See? Everyone's happy. And no harm done. Well, apart from this bloody great crater in the side of my head, but I'll live." He shrugged the hand off his arm and doffed an invisible cap. "I'll see you later, Ahmed."

He followed the guard into the circular bathroom with the domed ceiling he remembered from his visit to the palace a few weeks previously. Back when he believed he and Heydari would be working together. Before his betrayal.

In the middle of the room was the man himself, lying naked on his front on a marble slab whilst a burly man with a huge beard rubbed oil into his back. He raised his head as Caesar approached.

"Beowulf Caesar," he purred. "I hear you have been causing problems for my men."

"Is this a bad time, old boy?"

"You are becoming a pest," Cyrus said, propping himself up on his elbows to better take him in. "You do know how I handle pests?"

Caesar held his hands up. "I know all about pests, matey. Annihilation *Pest* Control was the best in the business for over a decade. My organisation. My vision." He folded his arms. "Which is why I think you're daft for not wanting to link up. We could do great things together, me and you. With me taking care of any obstacles, you'd have full control of the region in no time. The government, ISIS, whoever, they'd all answer to you. To us."

Heydari smirked. "They already answer to me. But this way perhaps I get the Americans on my side too."

"You think you can trust the Yanks? Do me a bleeding favour. The second they… Ah!" He waved his hand away, tutting loudly. "You're an idiot, you know that?"

"Silence," Heydari told them. "How dare you talk this way. How dare you attack members of the Royal Guard."

"I apologise," he said, rubbing a hand across his face. "But I wasn't being listened to."

"How dare you," Heydari said. "My men know not to bother me with trivialities. It is an important time for me and for the region. A dangerous time as well."

"Indeed," Caesar replied, arching an eyebrow. "Bloody pandemic and all that."

"Nonsense. You know how I feel about these lies. This virus is nothing but a western construction. Designed to undermine us here in the East." His eyes burned with a ferocity Caesar hadn't witnessed before.

"Fair enough. Like I say, I apologise." He held his hands up, bowed his head reverentially. Screw it, he'd even wish the twisted tart *Namas-fucking-te* if he thought it would help. "But I have to speak with you."

"I cannot help you." He grimaced as the huge masseuse pressed an elbow into the small of his back. "You know my position."

"I do. But do you know your enemy's?"

"I have many enemies, Mr Caesar."

"As does anyone worth their salt. I've always said, enemies are a sign you're doing something right. But I've also heard talk in the camp. From those in the know. They're getting closer."

"The Americans?"

He paused, tonguing his gold canine as he watched Heydari's face sag with the realisation.

"That's what I heard," he told him. "Only a few miles outside of Kavar. You need to tighten your defences, old boy."

Heydari fixed Caesar dead in the eyes. "Why are you telling me this?"

"I don't want the Yanks here anymore than you do. Besides, I wondered if a little intel might afford me a few privileges. Or you might even change your mind about what to do with me. You scratch my back, I scratch yours." He nodded at the hairy masseuse. "Although you do look like you've got that covered."

Heydari sat upright, holding onto the towel around his waist as he swung his legs off the side of the marble slab. Apart from on his head and the neatly trimmed beard, he had no body hair at all. All of it removed.

"You think this will happen? To the Prince of Islam? To the great Cyrus Heydari, with my Royal Guard watching over me? Let them come, I say. I fear no man. Not you, not the Americans. Not anyone." His eyes widened as he orated into the curved ceiling. "I don't even understand why you bother me with such details. You know, the CIA and I will shortly be reaching a mutually beneficial agreement. Your concern is not appreciated. And your intel is useless."

Caesar stuck out his bottom lip. "Fair enough, only trying to help." He smiled, clasping his hands together. "Only… No, forget it. I'll be off." He glanced over his shoulder to get the guard's attention.

"Stop. What is it?"

He turned back into the inquisitive stare of his captor.

Got yer.

Hook, line and sinker.

Of course, it helped if the person you were trying to influence was already a crazed despot, warped with syphilis and paranoia, and whose main source of sustenance was super-strength Afghan marijuana and fake news sites.

"It's nothing. Just, if it was me, I might draw my human shield a little closer. A few of them at least, the ones easiest on the eye. I mean, sure, the Americans ain't going to bomb the place with them onsite. But what if the rumours are true? What if they storm the palace? And, sure, you've got this deal you're supposedly brokering with the CIA. But will a bunch of trigger-happy Blacks Ops lads know about that?" He shrugged, stuck out his bottom lip some more – on the verge of over-egging it but not quite. "I don't know, I'd want some better insurance if it was me. Anyway, I'll get back to my cell. Sorry to bother you."

"You are a fascinating man, Beowulf Caesar," Heydari said, pointing a jewelled finger his way. "I am sorry we couldn't have worked together. It would have been fun."

"We could still do it. Say the word."

Heydari shook his head. "No. I made a promise I would see this through. That I would save my heroic brothers. This is God's way. The right thing."

"Well, I suppose I'll be getting off then," he said, as the guard grabbed him by the arm and guided him to the door. "You be careful now. I'm sure you know that what you're doing is best."

He managed a fleeting glance over his shoulder before the guard led him out the room. The last thing he saw as the door closed was Cyrus Heydari staring at the floor, a concerned frown fighting to be seen beneath the neurotoxic protein solidifying his forehead. He looked worried, in deep concentration.

Caesar smiled to himself.

Still got it, old boy.

CHAPTER 21

Kendis was staring, waiting for an answer. "I get it, you can't tell me everything," she added. "But give me something, please. After all we've been through the last few days."

Acid reached up and pressed her thumb into the trapezius muscle on her shoulder. She'd grown stiff sitting around doing nothing. "You really don't want to know," she replied. "It's a long story, full of misery and with no happy ending."

"But you ain't Special Forces?"

She turned away from the kid's expectant face. "No. It was the easiest thing to tell you at the time."

"Sure. I get it. And it did give me hope, I guess. Believing you'd be able to get us out of the mess we were in. Which you did anyway. It was awesome."

"I do know what I'm doing."

Kendis frowned. "How so?"

"I've had training, got experience. You know..." She trailed off, on the verge of spilling, but thinking better of it. "Let just say I can stand up for myself."

It was better this way. She'd overcomplicated far too many relationships over the last few years with her oversharing. If she was going to leave her past behind she had to stop thinking of herself as a killer.

"But you told Lars you were in Iran to kill Heydari. He said it was why he helped you escape. Was that bullshit too?"

They both turned to watch the good doctor, who was on the other side of the stable block speaking with another of the prisoners – from a safe distance, of course, the prescribed two-metre-plus. Not like them. But Acid had enough to worry about without having to watch what she touched and how far she stayed away from people. Over the last seventeen years she'd been shot, blown up, thrown out of a plane, had broken many bones and fractured even more. It'd be damned ironic if a virus was the thing to take her out, but she felt it unlikely.

"None of it is bullshit," she told Kendis. "But I suppose the actual truth is somewhat different to how I sold it you."

"Oh?"

"Please, let's leave it there." She tried on her famous *don't-fuck-with-me* stare, but the streetwise Kendis either didn't catch it or didn't care.

"So you *were* planning on killing Heydari?"

"Not Heydari. Not exactly."

"Ah, you mean… Caesar?"

She was savvy, this one. Acid nodded. "That's right."

"Woah. Crazy shit," she cooed, before falling silent. Her face distorted around her thoughts as she considered the information. "It's weird though. Your whole persona changed when you were with him earlier. But it wasn't like you wanted to kill him."

"What was it like?"

"Hard to describe. Kinda reminded me how I am with my older brothers. Or used to be, at least, when we all lived under the same roof. On the surface you can't stand to be near them, you're full up with indignation, but there's also a sort of mutual respect and love underneath which holds it together. I don't know… Maybe I'm just feeling homesick or some shit."

Acid snorted softly. The kid really was savvy. "Perhaps it is similar," she told her. "We've got a lot of history, Caesar and I. But he fucked me over. Hurt someone I cared about."

"Now he wants you to help him?"

"Yes." She wrinkled up her nose. Was she stupid for even considering being a part of his plan? He'd broken her heart and fucked up her future. Yet, here he was offering her a lifeline. Just like he had all those years ago.

"You trust him?" Kendis asked.

Acid sat up as the door swung open and one of Heydari's guards shoved the big man back into the room. She kept an eye on him as she addressed Kendis. "I don't know. He's a bad man but I know what he's capable of. Plus, he's clever. Very clever. He could help us escape if we're careful. I suppose it's rather like the old proverb of the scorpion and the frog – don't expect people to change their nature, even if it's to their own detriment. Keep that in mind, keep your guard up, you can deal with him. Just about."

She rubbed her cheek into her shoulder, knowing full well she could have been talking about herself.

"He's looking this way," Kendis whispered.

Acid raised her head to see Caesar jutting his chin, meaning for her to come over. His head was still bleeding but he had an air of dominance about him like he always used to. He beckoned her over again and she slid off the cot.

"You be careful," Kendis told her, as she got to her feet.

"Don't worry about me," she replied, hitching her jeans up. "I'm always careful."

Yet as she strode over to him, a million thoughts ran through her mind. Most of them were bloody and violent, involving pain and retribution of the worst kind. Or the best kind, depending on how you looked at it.

He saw her staring at the wound above his ear as she got closer. "Don't worry," he said. "Probably looks worse than it is."

With fists clenched, she held her resolve in check. "I wasn't worried. What was all that about?"

"Not here," he said, eyes flitting around the room. "Come over to my office."

In silence they ambled across the stable floor to the small cabin in the corner of the room. Caesar pushed the door open and stepped aside for Acid to enter. "Ladies first."

She gave him a withering look as she passed by, bracing herself for the caveat, but it never came. Maybe the last two years really had knocked the soul out of him.

"Not sure you'll find any of them around here," she snapped back. It wasn't her finest work but it distracted her from the awkward silence in her heart.

Inside the gloomy cabin it was as stuffy as before but the air was drier now, dusty rather than sticky. It scratched at her parched throat and lips.

"So what's going on?" she asked, watching Caesar as he walked past her and positioned himself on the bed, reclining back against the wall.

He suddenly seemed exhausted and huffed out a deep breath. "I'm not one hundred percent sure as yet. I've cast my bait into the water. Now we pray the paranoid fucker bites." He grinned. "I think he will. You know how I roll, kiddo. And this certainly isn't my first rodeo. Not by a long chalk."

It was true. One of Caesar's many enviable traits that she'd always admired was how easily he could manipulate people without them knowing he was doing it. There was something about that carefully contrived persona of his that made you feel special, like you were his best friend, like he would never lie to you. It was for this reason her stomach muscles were tensed up tight and she hadn't unclenched her fist.

She moved over to the wooden chest in the corner and leaned against the top. "Well, I'm assuming you called me in here to explain further. Or are we going to play I-spy?"

He grimaced as he pushed himself upright. "I spy with my little eye someone with a bad attitude."

"Jesus." She folded her arms. "Do you blame me?"

"Fair enough. Okay, open up the top drawer there."

She frowned, but did as instructed, sliding open the stiff wooden drawer to reveal three empty pill bottles and a black leather pouch covered in a fine powder. She reached in and lifted out the pouch. A black shoe lace was interwoven through holes in the top and tied in a bow, keeping the pouch tightly shut. She undid the knot and peered inside.

"What is this? Cocaine?"

"Deutetrabenazine."

"Are you sick?"

"No. Not at all. When I was first put in here I got talking to Jerry, the old doc who died last month. Poor fucker. Couldn't catch a breath. But we hatched a little plan and he talked Heydari into getting the pills for me, spun him a tale about some diagnosis or other. You see, it's in the clown prince's best interests to keep us alive and well down here. For the foreseeable, at least. So he got his men on the case and they raided a UN supply truck. Easy when you've got most of the region on your payroll. They're anti-psychotics, I think. But they also have the sort of side effects I was after."

Acid chewed on her lip. His voice had taken on a weird tone, as though all the vigour and confidence had left him. She had many questions but raised her head to let him continue.

"I was a bit screwed after Jerry pegged it, but the Norwegian doc took over the reins when he got here, thank Christ. Managed to get me another vial of tablets a few days ago. Enough now for what we need."

"And what are these side effects?"

"Ah, well, a major side effect of Deutetrabenazine is heavy sedation, especially in high doses. Especially mixed with alcohol and other drugs."

Acid weighed the pouch in her palm. It felt light, but there was a lot of powder, relatively speaking. "Okay, so the plan is to drug Heydari. Then what?"

"Not only him. His men too. You see, the good prince believes himself to be a unique and forward-thinking visionary in the world of Islamic insurgents. Which, in other words, means he likes a little drinky-poo now and again. Likes to smoke the old hashish too, inviting his men to join him in said activities. The idea is they'll respect him more, think of him as an inclusive leader. He also believes smoking and drinking together expands their collective mindsets to new possibilities and ways of working. Some guff like that anyway. It's what he told me first night we met. He watches too much conspiracy and New Age shit on YouTube, if you ask me."

"I'm still a little unclear as to what actually happened between you two," she said. "Why did he screw you over?"

He waved the question away. "All in good time, sweetie. That's not important right now. We need to work out how we get this here powder into Heydari's and his men's bloodstream. That's where you come in."

"Oh, I see." Acid threw up an eyebrow. "Go on then, explain to me how I get close enough. Because I'm not planning on getting a rifle butt smashed around my head."

"You won't have to. That's why I got one around mine. I was up there putting the proverbial cat amongst the pigeons just now. All being well, you'll be as close to the clown prince as you'll ever want. Once you are, all you need do is wait until he's entertaining his men, then slip this powder into the wine. He usually has a knees-up on a Wednesday evening. That's tomorrow."

Acid unfolded her arms and gripped the edge of the cabinet. It sounded like a decent enough plan but it had holes. "And if everything goes as easily as you're making out, which I doubt it will, what then?" she asked. "Are you telling me every one of his soldiers is going to be drinking this drugged wine?"

"Not all of them. But most. Once I know you're up there, I'll wait until Wednesday nightfall before putting my part of the plan into action. He'll keep a few men down on patrol, but new recruits mainly. Young lads from the nearby villages, no one with any real experience. It'll be a piece of piss."

"*Piece of piss.*" She threw up both eyebrows. "Confident chat from someone who's not risking their life."

"Come on, Acid. You've still got it. I know you have."

She bit her lip, annoyed at how the limp compliment made her feel. "I don't know, Ceez. It sounds vague and dodgy."

He sat up and swung his legs over the side of the bed. "Are you fucking kidding me? It's the only way. We have to do this. As soon as possible."

"Why?"

"It just is, all right? Trust me." He was leaning forward now, pointing his finger at her in a fit of rage, but she also noticed his hand was shaking. She'd never seen him scared in her life. "You have to help me."

"And if I don't?"

He sat back, throwing his arms up and letting them slap on his knees. "Then we wait around for the Americans to show up. Because that's our best outcome if we do nothing. Only, the second they start asking questions – taking IDs – we're both screwed. And yes, yes, you might be able to talk your way out of it. But if they open the book on Annihilation Pest Control it won't take them long to work out you're involved in some way." He looked sad, but over-the-top sad, like he was play acting. "If I'm subjected to a lengthy interrogation, I might let something slip."

She snorted back a bitter laugh. "I see. So I help you or you'll name names?"

"It's not what I'm saying, kid. But I'm public enemy number one to these people."

"Public enemy number six, last time I heard."

"Oh, fuck off. Doesn't have the same ring to it, does it? I'm on the list. It's bad enough. Shitting piss, I spent two decades in the shadows and the minute you go rogue the whole arse of my organisation falls out."

"You shouldn't have pissed me off. You should have let me leave under my own terms."

"I fucking well might have done!" he yelled, his hand shaking even more. "You never gave me the pissing chance."

She looked away. They were getting nowhere. "I still want you dead," she told him. "I've made peace with that."

"Have you?"

She sniffed before making herself look him dead in the eyes. "Yes."

"Well like I said before, I'll take my chances. I'd rather die outside – a free man, on my own terms – than in this smelly shit pit." He shook his head. "You know, I spent the first twenty years of my life living a lie, trapped in my own skin, doing what others expected of me. And do you know how far that got me? Fucking nowhere. So if you want to put a bullet in me the first opportunity you get, then so be it."

She narrowed her eyes at his words. This was a new tactic for him. "If we do it, we take the others with us."

"Not a bleeding chance. It'll be risky enough just the two of us. Anyone else will slow us down. We'd never make it."

Her mind flitted to Kendis, to Lars too. They were good people, but Caesar was right. With a heavy heart she nodded, thinking of the line she'd given Spook many times over the last two years. *You can't save everyone.*

"All right," she told him. "I'm in."

"Good girl." He leaned back on the bed, grimacing as he did so. "You keep the drugs on you from now on. If my theory is correct, you'll be up there soon enough. When he sends for you, wait until tomorrow evening and then go for it. I can see the light from his suite shining on the courtyard outside the window here. Signal me when it's done, then meet me back here."

"How will we get over the walls?"

He didn't have time to answer – there was a sharp knock on the door. They exchanged concerned glances before it eased open and Lars' gentle face appeared around the side. "Hello," he said. "I came to see if you were okay. Your head. I have dressings."

Caesar rolled his eyes at Acid, but they were done for now. "Fine. Come in, doc," he told him.

With the three of them in the small space, it was cramped and awkward. As the doctor side-stepped into the room to inspect Caesar's head, Acid shuffled behind him towards the door. On reaching it, she paused. Her heart ached with the disorientation of being in Caesar's presence again and the weight of all the unasked questions she still carried with her. Behind her she heard her old boss sucking back sharp, short breaths as Lars tended to his wounds. It was a nasty-looking laceration, painful no doubt, but he seemed to be in a bad way altogether. When people like Caesar – wild, unpredictable, self-obsessed – were injured or backed into a corner, they were always the most dangerous. For now, that was a good thing. She too had been backed into a corner, and like the feral beast she'd been when Caesar had found her all those years ago, she was coming out fighting. It was all she knew. All she had.

So for now she had to trust him. He had a plan and that was more than she had. She stuffed the pouch of powder into the pocket of her jeans. It was on. One way or another she was getting out of here.

CHAPTER 22

Kendis Powell woke with a start and gasped anxiously into the gloom. The only illumination in the stables came from the moonlight filtering in through the small windows high above them. It wasn't enough to see faces, or even outlines of people, but she could hear movement nearby, the creaking of rusty springs as other prisoners turned in their cots.

"You okay?" a voice croaked through the darkness. Acid, in the cot next to hers.

"Yeah, I—" she started, before a sound outside halted her. Gunfire. The staccato crack of automatic rifles maybe a mile or so away. "You hear that?"

"It's been going on for some time," came the reply. "But it's a way off."

Kendis nodded before realising it was futile in the blackness of the room. "I think you're right. Maybe they're advancing though."

"Hmm. If anything they're moving further away. There was a burst of activity a few minutes ago, probably what woke you up, but it's trailing off."

Her voice sounded different. She was whispering, but it was more than that. It sounded like all the high-range, energetic sass that Kendis had begun to enjoy had dissipated. She squinted as her eyes became accustomed, seeing now that Acid was leaning up on one elbow, facing towards her. As Kendis watched, she flicked her head gently to one side, cascading her thick wavy hair over one shoulder.

Damn, even her silhouette looked kind of bad-ass.

Despite the lies and the mystery, Acid's presence in the camp still filled Kendis with confidence. She might not be who she'd said she was, but Kendis had seen her in action. The way she'd taken out that dude ready to rape them both. Special Forces or not, this was someone she wanted nearby.

Yet it was as though the more she knew about Acid, the further she moved away. A part of her wondered if this was how she always was with people, worried that if anyone got too close they might see the real her. It was frustrating, but maybe they weren't so different. One of the reasons Kendis had joined the Peace Corps in the first place was to get away from her old life and who she was, who she'd been. The shared pain of her family's grief had become suffocating after Micky died. She carried that pain with her like all her family did, but she had the added bonus of guilt weighing on her shoulders – that she'd been the one to escape.

"How are you?" she whispered over to Acid, a dumb question, but thinking about Micky never led her anywhere good. She heard an abrupt snort in the darkness before adding, "I know it's stupid to ask – we're all doing shitty as hell, right, it's awful here. But ya know…"

A heavy sigh followed from the cot opposite, and then: "I'm doing okay. I've been lying awake most of the night."

"Tell me about it – these cots…"

"I don't sleep much, not when I'm like this."

Kendis mirrored her, leaning on one elbow and facing her way. "When you're like this?"

Another sigh. "I've got a rare form of bipolar. Manic episodes, you know? It can weirdly be a big help in some situations. But there are downsides too. I often can't sleep, forget to eat, that sort of thing. Plus when the drop comes it can be deathly."

"Right."

"Sorry, you don't need to know all that. Oversharing, there's another downside." Despite the darkness, Kendis wondered if she'd thrown a smile her way. "How are you holding up?"

"Don't know. Guess I'm trying to keep positive. Telling myself we might get out of this if I keep my head down. If we're human shields that means we're safe, doesn't it? No one will attack the palace if we're here."

"You know that for certain? With your military background and experience?"

A tight ball of emotion stuck in her throat. The question was one she'd sensed on the cusp of her awareness ever since she'd discovered why they were here. One she'd been trying her best to ignore.

"I'm not sure," she whispered. The words were lost as off in the distance she heard more gunfire and what might have been a small explosion. A grenade or an IED going off. "Well, it's cool to overshare around me," she added, attempting to change the subject. "You can trust me, I mean. I'm still hella curious as to who you are."

Kendis was certain she sensed the smile from her companion this time, but the response was equally as dismissive.

"I wish I could," Acid said softly. "I think it might do me good to talk to someone about all the shit going on in my head. But no. It's best for you if you stay away from me. Don't get involved. Whenever I get too close to people they end up getting hurt. You're a good kid. Stay alert, stay safe."

"Geez, what's that, a road safety slogan?"

They both snickered in the darkness.

"Damn, you're right," Acid said, with a long, slow sigh. "That was lame as hell, wasn't it? I do need to get a grip."

For a moment the air beyond their prison walls was still and quiet. A glorious silence. Until another explosion rocked some distant target.

Kendis shuffled upright on the cot. "If those are the Americans, they could be coming to save us."

"Yeah. We can hope."

"You don't sound convinced."

"It's not that. It's just… Never mind."

But Kendis couldn't leave it. She had so many questions vying for space in her head. She was going over them, deciding which to ask first, when she heard the sound of metal scraping on metal and the doors to the stable block creaked open. "Shit. Who's that?"

A shaft of light speared down the centre of the room, growing wider as the door opened fully. In the half-light now she saw Acid sit up as two guards, carrying battery-powered lanterns in one hand and pistols in the other, strode into the room. They walked down the row of cots, holding the lanterns high to illuminate the faces of each prisoner. Spotting Acid and Kendis they stopped and whispered gruffly to each other.

"What's going on?" Kendis rasped.

"Keep it cool," Acid shot back. "They're here for me, I think."

"How do you know?"

Before she could answer, one of the guards had reached down and grabbed Acid by the upper arm, yanking her to her feet and pulling her towards the door. Kendis expected more of a fight from her but none came. So when the second guard grabbed at her own arm, she followed suit and got to her feet without resistance.

"Hey, no," Acid told the guards, looking back at Kendis as she was led away. "Not her. Just me. JUST ME."

"Acid. Where are they taking us?" Kendis called over. It was hard to talk with her heart beating so fast. "They're not taking us to…?"

"Don't worry. Let me do the talking. You'll be fine."

The guards bundled them across the floor and up the stone

steps to the courtyard. The fresh night air was almost a relief after the stuffy airless stench of the stable block, but out here the crack of distant gunfire was more apparent.

"Sounds like they're getting closer," Kendis whispered, as they reached the bottom of the walkway leading to the palace entrance. "God bless the US army. They're coming for us."

But as the guards stabbed their pistols into their backs, shoving them forward, she heard Acid sigh.

"Yes," she muttered, under her breath. "That's what I'm afraid of."

CHAPTER 23

The bats nibbled hungrily at Acid's nerves as the guards led them through the sprawling palace towards Cyrus Heydari's suite. Now, standing outside the doors waiting to be called forth, she heard them screeching across her consciousness, angry she'd wasted all opportunities to break away.

Because Caesar was correct. It being night-time the guard cover in the palace was minimal. It wouldn't have taken much for her to spin around and take the escorting guards by surprise. A swift elbow to the neck whilst simultaneously grabbing for a pistol and she'd have put a bullet in both of them before they knew what had happened.

They'd encountered just one other soldier since entering the main entrance hall, a particularly mean-looking man with a thick beard and cruel eyes who was standing guard outside the door of Heydari's main suite. He'd disappeared a few minutes earlier to inform his master of their arrival.

As they waited for his return, Acid took the opportunity to drop her hand in her pocket and feel for the small leather pouch. She held it in her palm, waiting for the right opportunity. When the door opened a moment later and the gruff guard barked at them to come forward, she stealthily shoved her hand down the front of her jeans and slipped the pouch into her knickers. Not the safest or most comfortable place for it, but it was the best she could come up with on the spot. If they were to be searched, she hoped to hell they wouldn't search there.

"What do they want with us?" Kendis rasped, as the escorting guards departed and they were beckoned into Heydari's suite.

The guard moved into the centre of the room without replying and stood to attention next to a huge dining table, his assault rifle drawn and leaning against his shoulder.

"So where is he then?" Kendis asked. "If he wants to see us so bad."

"Cool it, will you?" Acid hissed, but the guard didn't even look their way. "Let's see what happens, okay?"

Whilst they waited, she took some deep breaths. In and out through her nose, working on slowing her heart rate and freeing up her limbs. Without any idea of what was coming next it would be easy for stress and tension to take over, but experience had taught her the importance of maintaining a calm and fluid composition. People – civilians – often thought tough and immoveable was the best way to be in high-pressure situations, but that only got you so far. Plus, the more rigid you were, the less chance you had to alter your behaviour as the situation required it. Survival was about adapting in each moment to what came at you.

It didn't help that Kendis was still acting antsy, huffing loudly and bouncing from one foot to the other.

"Like I said," Acid whispered, leaning into her. "Let me do the talking. We'll be fine, as long as we stay calm."

"But what's going t—"

She shut up as over on the far side of the room a door opened and the self-titled Prince of Islam appeared. The light from the room behind him cast what looked like a halo around his body. It was probably intentional.

"Come, come," he boomed, beckoning them forth with a flick of his wrist. The charming exuberance present on their first encounter had now vanished and in its place was a brusque agitation. "We shall go to my quarters immediately."

Kendis shot Acid a look, wide-eyed and nervous. But fair enough. It didn't sound too good. Her own mind was a whirlwind of conflicting ideas and troubling thoughts. Had Caesar screwed her over? And if so, how had she let him do it so easily?

As if to aptly punctuate the moment, the sound of a muffled explosion came in from outside. Through the large, leaded window Acid could see it too, flashes of fire and unrest. Far away on the horizon, but it was there.

And it had clearly unsettled Heydari.

He raised his head to peer at the guard standing behind them and shouted something in Farsi. The guard nodded curtly and hurried out of the room. The prince watched him go for a second before turning his attention back to Acid and Kendis.

"Please. Quickly." His face was stern, his eyes wide and unblinking. "We must go."

Acid felt Kendis nudging her as they walked into the next room and found themselves in what was clearly Heydari's bedroom. It was brightly lit by three chandeliers, each of them dripping with cut crystal and spaced in a triangle formation over the biggest bed Acid had ever seen. It was so enormous it was almost funny. In fact if it had been any other situation she would have laughed (an ironic sneer, at least). As it was, she just stared open-mouthed.

"Acid," Kendis whispered, with another nudge. "He just told that soldier to put word out that his new... I'm not sure of the exact translation... his new security... was in position. And for whoever it was to back off. You think we're the new security?"

Acid was sure of it. She told Kendis as much. "He's bringing his human shield closer, to stop the Americans breaching the palace."

"Think it will? Stop them, I mean?"

"I'm not sure. But we might not have to worry."

Before Kendis could ask the inevitable, Heydari slammed the

door shut and locked and bolted it. In three strides he was back across the room, looking them up and down and nodding eagerly.

"Wonderful," he growled, with a flick of his overly groomed eyebrows. "My men picked well."

"Hey, we ain't here to… You know…" Kendis said. "Cos if you think I'm just going to let you… For the sake of…"

The words hadn't left her mouth before Heydari was on her, a hand around her throat. "This is always the problem with you people, isn't it? You think you know everything."

At the sight of this, the bat energy drove out the last pocket of drowsiness in Acid's system. She snapped fully alert and ready to act.

"You people?" Kendis repeated, wriggling away from his clutches and stepping away. "What's that mean?"

"You are American, no? You think we are all the same out here. Barbarians. Thugs. Mindless terrorists."

"And you're not?" the kid continued as Acid observed in silence. "Cos I've heard some pretty appalling stories about what you've done to people. Your enemies and your allies. Not to mention local women and children."

Heydari's smile was awkward, forced through what was clearly a wave of rage. "I do what I have to do," he replied, teeth gritted. "In this world the only way you rule is with fear. The only way you get compliance is with the threat of death. But I want good things for my people. I have a dream for the Islamic Republic of Iran."

"And what is this dream?" Acid butted in. "You as supreme leader? Unchallenged? Free to do whatever you want?"

Heydari stepped to her, his voice rising with zeal. "I want peace."

"You don't get peace by killing people. Believe me, I know."

"Oh that's right," he said, wagging a finger at her. "You're the woman who came here looking for my guest of honour. Came to kill him."

She didn't answer, but didn't break eye contact either.

Heydari clapped his hands together with a loud slap. "You will understand more than most. We have to do bad things sometimes if we want to achieve our aims."

From off in the distance, they all heard it – another explosion. Loud enough to wipe the smugness off Heydari's face.

"Getting closer," Kendis whispered.

"Wrong," he said. "The fighting you can hear this evening is not with the western dogs, but pathetic rebel forces from the local towns fighting with my men, resisting the power of the New Prince of Islam. But it is futile. They cannot resist forever."

He closed his eyes and breathed in a long, deliberate breath. When his eyelids flittered open a moment later there was a renewed fire in his eyes, sparkling with a manic intensity Acid recognised all too well. Because she saw it now. He was just another crazy tyrant, twisted and evil. So hell-bent on his quest for power and autonomy he'd forgotten a long time ago what reality looked like.

"But you are correct," he went on. "There is indeed chatter online about an infidel advance – it seems your countries are growing uneasy with my power and support in the region. But with you here they shall stay back. I shall get the word out that there are westerners staying in my quarters and their heat mapping technology will prove it to them."

Kendis glanced at Acid then back to Heydari. "In your quarters?"

"In my quarters. In my bed too, maybe." He grinned at them. "I tell my men, bring me the two prettiest stars of the ranks. Why not enjoy myself if I am to have extra guests? I see they did not disappoint."

"Mother fucker," Kendis rasped, about to step forward, before Acid grabbed her arm.

She raised her usual husky tenor to a voice breathier and more coquettish in tone. "And… you'll look after us?"

It wasn't full Marilyn M. but it was close. The voice she often employed with chauvinistic wankers like Heydari, who were too swollen with ego to realise the ruse.

"But of course I will," he said, the smile returning. "I shall feed you, bathe you in the royal baths, honour you with the same luxuries afforded to me."

"And all we have to do is… be here… with you?"

She tilted her head to one side. Flirting with people whose face you'd rather be stamping on wasn't easy, especially when your entire system was shredded and broken, but if his leering expression was anything to go by she had pulled it off. This despite the bats screaming their distaste across her synapses, telling her to smash his smug face into the nearest wall.

"Hey. Acid," Kendis whispered, leaning in and putting herself in profile to Heydari. "What the fuck?"

She could feel the ire bristling off her, but kept it going. "Don't you worry," she told her, while meeting Heydari's intense eyes with her own. "I believe the prince here is true to his word and will look after us perfectly. I mean we're here now, aren't we, we might as well enjoy ourselves."

"I can't believe what you're saying…"

She squeezed the kid's arm, not taking her eyes off Heydari. "Isn't that right, sir? We can all get on, can't we?"

The prince clapped his hands together and beamed. "Absolutely we can. I knew you would see it my way. Everyone does in the end."

The two women startled as a concealed door opened at the side of the room and two women appeared, dressed in yellow robes with matching al-amira veils. Neither of them showed the slightest bit of emotion as they sashayed over and stood either side of Acid and Kendis.

"It is very early," Heydari said. "You must be tired and also dirty after so long in the stables. My sisters here will get you bathed and changed and then you can rest a while. After this we shall meet again. Get to know each other better, yes? Have some fun."

Kendis snorted, perhaps about to retort, before Acid countered it once more with a firm squeeze of her forearm.

"Sounds wonderful," she said. "Thank you for this opportunity."

Heydari frowned. "You're not how I expected you to be. The deadly assassin, whom the great Beowulf Caesar is so afraid of."

Shit.

Had she overplayed it?

"Well, a girl has to know how to survive," she replied, not missing a beat. "And a big part of that is understanding when to be a lioness – and when to be a pussy cat." Internally she was cringing at her own words, but he seemed to be buying it. She went on. "You see, I'm a survivor. And like you say, if I'm here why not do it in style – have some fun whilst I'm at it. I do like fun." The final flick of her eyebrows, mirroring the way Heydari had done it earlier, was a nice touch, she felt.

"Wonderful," he said, with a broad grin. "I am glad you see this my way." He patted them both gently on the shoulders before nodding at his 'sisters'. The one next to Acid snaked her fingers through her own, holding her hand. "For now rest and we shall talk again soon."

Acid smiled and nodded before being led over to the open doorway. In the room beyond she could see a large sunken bath, full of milky water and surrounded by ornate mosaic tiles of all colours. It looked pleasant enough. But what came after – perhaps not so much. She had to think fast, because right now all she had was a mind muddled with disorder and conflict.

"I hope you know what you're doing," Kendis whispered, as the women led them into the royal bathroom and closed the door behind them.

Acid met her gaze and nodded curtly in response. She hoped so too. Because if Caesar's plan failed, they were both dead. Or at the very least, would wish they were.

CHAPTER 24

The royal bath was deep, and the water hot, and it felt good to be clean after the last few days. Even Kendis – initially reticent to get naked – now looked to be enjoying herself. Her eyes were closed and the frown that had been there since they were snatched from their beds, and perpetuated by Heydari's plans for this evening, had now faded. It was a blessed moment of calm amidst the confusion and chaos. In Acid's life, she took those where she found them.

"Feeling any better?" she asked her, once they were both submerged with only their heads visible.

Kendis opened her eyes and immediately her expression fell, like she'd been caught out. "Not really," she rasped. "I mean, it feels good to get clean, but… I don't know. This is weird."

"Fair enough."

"You ready to tell me what the fuck's going on yet?"

"Jesus, Kendis. I've told you." She sighed, but she knew the kid wasn't going to leave it. "I used to work for Caesar. I met him when I was young, he took me under his wing, gave me a good life. An amazing life."

"So you are close?"

She didn't respond straight away, just kept staring at the tiles opposite. Then she said softly, "I know it sounds cheesy, but for a long time he was all I had."

Jesus.

She heard herself and snapped out of it. "But I still hate him. He might have given me a lot, but he took a lot as well. Too much."

"Oh shit, you mean—"

"No." She cut her off. "God, he's gay. And he wouldn't anyway. Ever. But still, that doesn't excuse what he did."

Kendis leaned forward, eyes darting around at the two women, Heydari's 'sisters', who were sitting on the side of the bath administering soap and towels. She lowered her voice. "And what about Cyrus? Are you here to kill him?"

Acid followed her gaze, alert to any tells on the women's faces, but they remained placid and neutral. Either they were the best poker players in the world, or they didn't speak English.

"If I have to," she replied. "It wasn't part of my original plan. But plans change."

She glanced over her shoulder to see one of the female attendants holding a jug of water up for her. Acid nodded and lay back, letting her pour it over her hair and face. Once done, she brushed the water from her eyes to see the act had elicited a raised eyebrow from Kendis.

Screw it, she didn't have to be self-destructive *all the time*, did she?

The way she saw it – if she was going to die, she'd prefer to do it with clean hair. Plus, she had to make it work with Heydari, and that meant putting on a good show. She'd seen how her feminine wiles had blindsided the egotistical madman just now and – aside from the fact she'd grown tedious of this hackneyed dance many years ago – it seemed being a relatively attractive woman was going to stand her in good stead.

But hadn't Caesar known that already?

As she closed her eyes and let the woman's nimble fingers massage her scalp, her mind drifted back through time, to her early days at Annihilation Pest Control. Even then, as a wide-eyed and cautious eighteen-year-old, she'd been adamant she wouldn't prostitute herself for her work. And she'd meant it. Literally. Other female assassins she'd encountered (older, more experienced) had been more than happy to use their sexuality to get the job done. But not Acid. She thought it gauche and unfair that she'd even be expected to. Besides, the way she saw it, killing someone after sex, when they were at their most vulnerable, was far too easy. She preferred her work to be dangerous and edgy.

She still did.

Of course, that didn't mean she wasn't a fan of sex, because she was. A big fan. Yet for her it wasn't simply about carnal desire or even ego boost. Rather it was one of the only things in life that got her out of her head for a few welcome minutes (a few hours, if she was really lucky) and relieved her of the pain of being who she was.

But, after leaving Crest Hill, she'd vowed to herself it would always be on her own terms. So a big reason why she'd trusted Caesar so readily and wanted to make him proud of her (despite the total head-fuck of what her new job entailed) was he'd made it clear from the start he'd never ask her to use sex to get her mark. Maybe it was because of his own background – or he really was the progressive thinker he made himself out to be – but there was none of the macho, misogynistic bullshit at Annihilation there was at similar organisations she knew of. She would often laugh with Caesar how it was one of the most diverse places to work, that he should even consider a pension scheme. Hell, back in the early days, he even threw Christmas parties for his operatives.

She tilted her head back against the tile surround of the bath and allowed a warm smile to spread across her face. It had been a good place to work. Right up until the point where it wasn't.

"What the—" A torrent of water poured over her head and

shook all the memories out of her. She turned around to scowl at the woman. "Could have given me a bit of warning," she hissed, grabbing a handful of hair at the top of her neck and squeezing out the water.

"Again?" the woman asked, gesturing with the jug.

"I'll do it."

She held her hands out and the woman passed her the jug. Dunking it under the water to refill, she rinsed out the rest of the soapy residue from her hair before standing up, letting a cascade of water rush down her body. The two 'sisters' averted their eyes, with the one nearest her holding her hand out for the jug. Acid hesitated, feeling the weight of it in her grip. One swing and she'd knock the timid woman flying. After that it wouldn't take much to incapacitate the other one before she slipped into Heydari's room and caught him unawares. She could have a pillow over his ridiculous face in less than a minute. Smother the air out of him in less than two.

"Feel better, princess?" Kendis asked, the nasty tone in her voice dissipating Acid's savage urges.

With a sigh, she handed the jug over. A plan had been made and she was going to stick to it. Caesar was a master tactician and a devious bastard to boot. Regardless of what the bats were screaming for her to do to him at every opportunity, he was her best chance of getting out of Iran alive.

"Don't call me that," she told Kendis, as she slipped back under the water. "Ever."

There was still the distinct possibility, of course, that Caesar would kill her as soon as they were clear of Heydari's palace. Yet for some reason she didn't believe he would. She thought of the other times they'd encountered each other since she went rogue. In London after the Cerberix Expo. Berlin. On that horrific island. It was true, she'd not been able to pull the trigger, but on every one of those occasions, the big man – her mentor, the man who'd given her so much – he hadn't even drawn a weapon. She hadn't been able to kill him, but it was the same for him. And yes, he'd sent people to kill her, sent her to that grisly island, but deep down she understood his position. He had a reputation to uphold. And maybe he had been telling the truth earlier. He'd known she'd survive anything thrown at her.

Maybe…

Or maybe she just had the worst kind of Stockholm Syndrome ever and it was like Spook had always said – he'd groomed her, brainwashed her, made her rely on him so much she couldn't help but still need him in some way.

She looked Kendis straight in the eye. "If your dad killed your mum, could you forgive him?"

The expression on her face said she wasn't expecting the question and she flapped her mouth a few times before answering. "I… don't know. Perhaps. It would depend."

"People do, though, don't they? They say you can't truly hate a parent."

"Who says that?"

"I don't know – *they, them* – same people who say everything."

Kendis frowned. "Why you asking?"

"Forget it," she said. "I'm just thinking aloud. I'm overtired."

Bloody hell.

If she wasn't careful she was going to lose herself in a labyrinth of her own making, hunted by the twin minotaurs of doubt and fear. She bit her lip hard in an attempt to get herself out of her head. Because this wasn't a negotiation. That man had killed her mother. So whatever he might say, however comfortable she felt in his presence, however much being with him felt right, she was here for one reason. To kill Beowulf Caesar. To finish this, once and for all.

She got to her feet and hauled herself out of the bath as the meek waiting girl grabbed a large white towel and wrapped it around her.

"Thanks," she said, as Kendis got out too.

They quickly dried themselves and were about to retrieve their clothes when the women stopped them.

"Please," one of them said, gesturing to a second door, opposite the one leading to Heydari's suite. "Rest... umm... new clothes."

Acid glanced over at Kendis who shrugged. So they weren't going back to Heydari. Not yet, at least. But the fact remained she still had the leather pouch of powder concealed in her balled-up knickers.

"Can I get something?" she asked, already heading for the pile of dirty clothes in the corner.

The sisters exchanged anxious looks but Acid was already over there. She grabbed the knickers up into her fist, ensuring the pouch stayed hidden amongst the lacey cloth. She held them up, smiling coyly at the women. "Sorry, bit of a lucky pair. You know how it is."

The atmosphere turned frosty as the sisters tilted their heads to take her in. But she kept her smile on, throwing her arms wide in an expression of innocuous ditsy-ness.

"You don't mind, do you? They are Gucci, so..."

Gucci. The women knew that word. They nodded knowingly and beckoned her forth, opening the door to reveal a room the size of the bathing suite but adorned with drapes and huge velvet cushions covering every inch of the floor. The only light came from an ornately carved, glassless window about the size of an iPhone, high up on the wall facing the door. Through it she could see the black night was now a lighter grey but the sun was yet to rise.

"Looks pleasant," Acid said, taking in the room. It smelt musty but in a good way, as though incense had been burnt recently.

"Looks like a fucking prison cell," Kendis muttered next to her.

"Yes, well," she replied, out the corner of her mouth. "Let's play nice and we might stand a chance of surviving the next few days." Truth was she was beginning to tire of the American's constant jibes. She understood she was scared and anxious, but couldn't she give it a bloody rest? Her bad attitude was stopping Acid from thinking straight. What she wouldn't give right now for...

Ah, bollocks...

Spook.

It was the first time she'd properly considered her since she'd been here. She'd promised to report in when she landed in Iran but hadn't had a chance. That was six days ago. Even though she knew how Acid was – often overlooking other people's concerns (some might call it self-centred, she called it focused) – it was a long time to be incommunicado. The poor kid would be worried sick. Worse than that even. Acid sniffed back and shuddered.

Stop that. Stop it now.

It was a pointless and destructive line of thought. Best left alone.

She scanned the room as the sisters drove them gently inside. "Are those for us?" she asked, seeing the two piles of pastel blue silks that had been placed in the centre of the room.

The sisters scurried past them, scooped up the material, and motioned for Acid and Kendis to drop their towels and hold their arms out to the side. Acid placed her knickers in the corner and did as instructed, but not before throwing Kendis a hard stare and jutting out her chin – her way of telling her to comply. Working fast and in silence, the women dressed them in the silk robes, finishing the look with a thin decorative rope tied around the waist.

Once done, the sisters stepped back and smiled meekly at their handiwork before gathering up the towels and making for the door. "Hey. Wait a minute. Please?" Acid called after them, pushing herself to stay calm. "What happens now?"

The sisters' smiles widened. They patted the air with their hands. "You sit. Rest. Please."

"Tell us what you are going to do with us," Kendis spat, staccato-like.

"They don't know. Leave them." With a long overdue exhale, Acid settled down on one of the cushions and leaned against the wall. "Sit down, kid. We do need some rest."

The sisters backed out of the room, closing the door as they left, but Kendis remained standing as though waiting for something. A second later she raised her finger in the air at the sound of a key turning in a lock.

"And… there we go. It is a fucking prison cell."

"What did you expect?" Acid sighed. "At least its more comfortable. We might get some decent sleep."

"And then what – Heydari summons us into his fucking bed? Or the US troops think *screw it* and invade anyway. You've seen the way his guards are, they're young, impetuous. Probably never seen proper combat before." She was yelling now, leaning down into Acid's face and pointing wildly at the space behind her. "You don't think they're going to get trigger-happy under stress? Cos I've seen it happen. Many times. Jesus, how are you so calm? Aren't you afraid?"

"What good does being afraid do?" Acid shifted her position, lifting a cushion and propping it between her and the wall. "When the time comes I'll be ready, alert. For now I'm going to relax, bide my time. You should too. Trust me."

"Trust you? Trust you?" She was down on her knees in front of her before Acid had chance to straighten herself. "How the hell do you expect me to trust you? All you've done since I met you is lie your ass off."

Acid held her gaze but didn't react. Partly to let Kendis calm herself, but also she had no idea how to respond. She'd spent her whole adult life lying to people. Herself as much as anyone. She'd had to. To stay alive. And that was true for both the job and her own sense of self. It had gotten to the point now where she didn't know what was true and what wasn't.

Kendis was still waiting for an answer. "Look, you've got to believe me," she started, hoping some more helpful words might fall out of her mouth. How she wished for a surge of manic energy. When the bats were in full flight she could babble for England, her sharp mind working a hundred miles per second. But with hardly any sleep since she arrived and no real sustenance except the watery gruel, she was running on fumes. "I'm an ally. I can help you."

"Help me how?"

She closed her eyes and settled herself back against the soft velvet of the cushion. "There's a plan. To get out of here."

"All of us?"

Acid ran her tongue across her top teeth. There was no point getting into this now. "I don't know, but me and you for definite. And soon."

"How?"

Even with her eyes shut she could sense the tension coming off Kendis. "You have to trust me."

"Pfft. Whatever."

Acid opened her eyes. "Trust me, Kendis."

It might have been the message Acid tried to convey with her eyes, it might have been the fact Kendis too was weary – but this time she accepted it. With a deep sigh she settled down, lowering her face onto one of the huge cushions.

"Fine," she huffed. "I hope you know what you're doing."

Acid ran her fingers through her damp hair. She hoped so too. To get her head back in the game she opened the balled-up pair of knickers and slipped them on, replacing the leather pouch inside the crotch. They were uncomfortable, but that was fine, comfort wasn't helpful. Feeling the pouch there whenever she moved would act as a useful reminder for what she had to do. Help keep her focused.

Outside the window early dawn was slowly becoming morning, the dull grey of the sky turning a light pinkish hue as the sun rose on the east side of the palace. Acid's best guess put it at around five, perhaps earlier. Soon the palace would be awake, but for now sleep was her best move. She glanced over at Kendis.

Trust me?

Hell, that might have meant something if she could trust herself. She sank her head into a cushion, sensing the benign veil of sleep was close. All she could do now was keep her cool and watch for opportunities. After that it was down to the gods. The next twelve hours would decide it.

CHAPTER 25

Whilst upstairs Acid attempted sleep, in the stable block below Caesar was already awake and pacing up and down in his room. Given the floor space consisted of only a few square metres, this wasn't the easiest of acts, but he couldn't sleep and he was restless. Although, this agitation wasn't merely due to the implications of his imminent plan, he'd been on edge every night since they'd unceremoniously dumped him in this cramped pit of misery. He managed to grasp an hour of sleep here or there, when tiredness overcame him, but most of the time his mind was too busy and his irritation too prickly and incessant for rest. Besides, being stuck in this smelly arsehole of a prison cell (because let's face it, that's what it was) the days and nights merged together, forming one drab and dismal moment that seemed to stretch on forever. Some might say this was a gift, all things considered, but he didn't see it that way. He'd made a firm promise to himself many years ago to live his life on his own terms. No exceptions. He'd had plenty of time to reflect over the last year and he knew he had to honour that promise.

Back in the late eighties, when he was still finding himself, the young Boyd Chapman had bought himself a stack of second-hand self-help books. Hippy trash, he'd dismiss them as now, but reading about how to manage his thoughts, how to achieve success both internally and externally, how to step into his power as a unique individual, had helped that angry and confused boy from East London back then.

And stepped into his power he had. Once he'd fully accepted himself as he was – gay but ungainly, brutish but brittle, a cynic who yearned to be an optimist – he was at once free to focus on other things. Such as, how to make a lot of money and as fast as possible. Unfortunately, however, he hadn't yet outgrown his environment and that path had led him to petty crime (breaking and entering principally, a few muggings) before falling in with a local face called Benny the Bull who was fast making a name for himself in the East London underworld. The young Boyd was a hired hand at first, but his unwieldy size and uncompromising attitude was soon noticed by the big boss and he was promptly promoted to the Bull's right-hand man. Which meant on any given day he'd be collecting payments, dropping threats to those who were late with payment, or – his favourite task – carrying out said threats.

Taking care of business, they called it.

Then one day Benny took him to one side and asked if he wanted to make some decent money. *Real fuck-you money.* The moniker coming from the fact once you started making that sort of money the answer to any requests asked of you could simply be *fuck you* and it wouldn't matter. Which was how Boyd started in the killing business. He worked as a hitman for Benny the Bull for three years before the poor old sod got taken out by a rival. The story goes they jumped him outside his favourite boozer before driving him bound and gagged to a forest south of Eastbourne, where they fed him to a pack of hungry German Shepherds.

Worst way to go, poor bastard, Caesar always said, when telling the story. *But at least they didn't bring their dogs with them.*

Regardless of his flippant humour – *You had to laugh, didn't you, otherwise you'd bleeding well cry* – he had felt rather discombobulated and rudderless for a while after that. His father hadn't helped. Despite the young Boyd's growing size and fierce temper, the wiry old bastard still beat the living shit out of his only son at every opportunity. The weird part of that story was the young Boyd let him. A part of him felt the beatings were justified. His father had told him on a near daily basis how much of a let-down he was, how he didn't deserve to be happy, how he was against God and nature and that he was glad his mother wasn't here to see what he'd turned out like. It was typical bigoted bullshit, but you hear something every day it has an effect on you. Especially in your formative years.

Then one day, after a particularly nasty onslaught of fists and homophobia, Boyd snapped. Before the old bastard had chance to even raise his fist, he grabbed him around the neck and squeezed all the hate and life out of him. It took his father less than a minute to die, and by the time his body hit the kitchen floor Boyd already felt lighter and freer. It was then he made that promise – he would always feel this free. No one would be his master or controller ever again.

Bloody hell, Ceez.

Back in the stable block he stopped pacing. He hadn't thought about his father in so long. But maybe that was what happened when you found yourself in these situations, the past came back to haunt you. Reflection and restitution, and all that jazz. He sat on the rickety cot bed and rested his back against the wall.

Even now he marvelled at how easy it had been for him to kill his father, both physically and emotionally. But it was how easy it had been to make it look like a suicide that first gave him the idea for how to achieve his goal of first-class freedom. He'd found a piece of rope in the garage, which he tied around the old man's neck before fastening the other end to the wooden washing frame that hung from the ceiling and hoisting the old codger up onto his knees. What most people don't realise is nearly all hanging suicides are done from doorframes or even door handles – if you want to kill yourself enough, you don't need an elaborate kick-the-chair-away moment, you just need to not stand up. The police closed the case in less than a week, gave him their condolences. Easy as pissing pie.

It was whilst feeding pigeons in Soho Square a few days later that he had his Road to Damascus style epiphany. He would use what he'd learned working for Benny, along with this newly realised skill for covering up murder, to make his fortune. *Real fuck-you money.* He'd start his own organisation, assemble a delicious band of elite killers who'd only ever do high-profile jobs for obscene amounts of money. The key being, if they did it correctly, the homicide or murder squads wouldn't ever be involved. There'd not even be a sniff of underhandedness. It was his belief that people would pay a lot of money for that sort of service.

And lo and behold, he was correct.

There was a good ten-year stretch in the Noughties (or the Naughties, as he always thought of that decade, his favourite for obvious reasons) where he and Annihilation Pest Control could do no wrong. Their clients were the crème de la crème of criminality, the top echelons of tech and finance and government, not to mention all the lovely money which came their way from rival drug barons and cartels all hell-bent on killing each other. God bless 'em.

Caesar was a proud man – arrogant, some might say – but he was also fair, and savvy enough to know he couldn't have achieved what he had without the best people around him, his operatives. And Acid Vanilla was the best of them all.

He'd seen it in their first meeting, him assuming the identity of her uncle to get into Crest Hill, and her being such a sulky little mare she'd hardly made eye contact. But there was a fire in her. Her training had been brutal and demoralising, and that was important, intentional. He didn't want to treat her any different from any of his other operatives – a decision made not because she was a teenager, or female, but because he already had a growing soft spot for her. Everyone saw it but he'd played it down. They both did.

The thing was, he saw himself in the young Alice Vandella. They were both raging at what they saw to be an unjust world and tough as nails to boot, yet on the flipside of their outward aggression they could be introspective and poetic when alone. They both loved art and music and – perhaps because of their similar backgrounds, growing up poor with single parents in rough boroughs of London – desired the finer things in life. They were both outcasts from society, prone to bouts of dark contemplation, yet always with a fabulous streak of sarcastic bile bubbling under the surface. It was for all these reasons that Caesar was tougher on her than any of the other assassins in his charge. He pushed her hard, had her take on the real dirty and dangerous jobs, but it was only because he knew she could do it. She was his star pupil, his best operative. His girl.

Fucking hell.

He shook his head angrily, realising a smile had escaped and was now spreading across his rotten chops.

"Bollocking bloody idiot," he muttered to himself. "Get a pissing grip."

She might have been his favourite, his protégé, but she was still the reason he was here, the reason his life was in tatters and his business in ruins. He didn't blame her for being pissed off, but could he let her get away with it? What sort of message did that send?

Hell, did any of it even matter anymore?

It was so complicated. But it always had been with her. Never a dull moment was their mantra, and it was true. The trouble she'd caused him over the years. Yet she always got the job done. Always got her mark. Brought in the big pay checks. Probably why he loved her so much.

"How are you today?"

Caesar looked up to see the Norwegian doctor's pasty face

peering around the door. He'd been so engrossed in his thoughts he'd not heard him knock.

The doctor smiled, a look of surprise in his eyes. "You are feeling well?"

Caesar straightened himself, dropping his smile of a moment ago into a heavy frown. "Not really. What do you want?"

The doctor looked over his shoulder before stepping into the room and closing the door. "I was worried, I saw the light was on, shadows moving. Are you not sleeping well?"

"Can't get off, not on this poxy little bed."

"This is the only issue?"

Caesar sighed. This again. "What else would it be?"

The doctor gave an awkward shrug. "You can talk to me about it. I am a doctor. Maybe I can help."

"No one can help. You know they can't."

"May I?" The doctor sat on the edge of the bed before Caesar could respond. "Did you hear the commotion earlier? The guards came to take away the English woman."

"Acid?"

"Acid, Zora, whoever she is. You are friends, yes?"

Caesar curled his lip but wasn't sure why or for who's benefit. "We were."

"And now?"

"Who the hell knows. But they took her up to Heydari?"

"I think so. And Kendis, the American girl."

"Both of them?" *Shit.* His sneer twisted into a genuine one.

"What do you think he will do to them?"

Caesar held up a finger for him to be quiet, pinching the bridge of his nose with the thumb and forefinger of his other hand as he did so. The American girl too. This wasn't his intention. At all. Acid had mentioned taking this Kendis woman with them in the escape. He'd brushed it aside at the time, but that irked and worried him. The old Acid Vanilla would never have given two hoots about helping a civilian. It was another glaring example of how far apart they'd grown. But maybe having someone's mother murdered would do that to a relationship. He always said killing his father was the best thing he ever did, but he was also self-aware enough (those self-help books still working) to know the notion made him quite the outlier.

"Do you think he will hurt them?" the doctor asked.

"No. He won't get chance," he muttered, waving his hand in dismissal. "Now go. Leave me to rest."

"You sure you don't need—"

"Fucking well piss off, will you? You rancid prick-end."

The outburst was enough to send the man scurrying out the room, but it also made Caesar's head hurt and shot a burning sensation down both arms. He watched the door slowly close itself, waiting for the catch to click before shutting his eyes and resting back against the thin pillow of his bed.

He won't get chance to hurt them.

It was in Acid's hands now. If he could truly trust her after all that had transpired between them these last few years, he was unsure. But she was no fool. And despite what she said, despite the dark cynicism at the root of her soul, she was driven by self-preservation same as everyone. She'd get them out of here, at least. After that he couldn't call it. There was still a strong possibility she'd take him out.

But maybe, deep down, that's what he was counting on.

CHAPTER 26

In the haze of sleep, right before consciousness fully took hold and she remembered who she was – and indeed, *that* she was – Acid's first awareness was of a hand on her ankle. Soft fingers stroking at her skin, drifting up her shin and cupping the curve of her calf.

"Gerrroff," she mumbled, but smiling, aware of a face but not a name, a hot and firm body winding around hers. She saw blond cropped hair, tanned skin, and then those blue sparkling eyes, gazing so intently into hers, telling her everything she needed to know, showing her everything she'd ever wanted. She sighed. "Spitfire, stop it."

She floated back into the doorway of her dreams, but the hand kept going, stroking up her thigh, the gentle tickling sensation rousing her into near wakefulness.

Wait…

Spitfire left, replaced instead with disjointed images and veiled recollections she couldn't get a handle on. She remembered being in another country, being angry, confused, then – somehow – feelings of relief, a mangled version of happiness.

Caesar?

Shit.

Heydari—

She shook herself awake and sat up. Cyrus Heydari's face leered down on her in high definition, his long fingers caressed her inner thigh.

"What the fuck?" She shuffled away from him, but her back hit the wall. "Stop it." She brought her legs up to her chest, feeling for the leather pouch, still in the crotch of her knickers. Beside her Kendis sat bolt upright with a yelp, her eyes widening at the sight of Heydari's other hand on her own leg.

"Jesus, eugh," she huffed, shifting so her legs were up and under her.

"Beautiful ladies, good afternoon." Their apparent distaste at his touch hadn't shaken the self-titled Prince of Islam one bit. He nodded at them knowingly, eyes narrow over a wide grin. "You have bathed and slept well, yes? Ready for the new day."

The women exchanged glances. Acid shot Kendis a tight-lipped smile, hoping it conveyed everything she needed it to but knowing it didn't.

"What time is it?" she asked, feigning grogginess.

"Almost two in the afternoon," Heydari replied. "You have slept for a long time. I came in to see you earlier. You both looked so peaceful, so pretty there in your new outfits, I did not want to disturb you. So beautiful, both of you. Like babies."

"What's your plan for us?" Kendis asked. "I'd like to know."

The prince didn't answer, just kept moving his gaze from her to Acid and back again, nodding and smiling as if pleased with himself. Then he got to his feet and held his hands out to them.

"You are hungry?" he asked, palms outstretched, eager for them to take one each. "Come, I will have my sisters prepare a late lunch for us."

Acid shot Kendis a begrudging look and took hold of his hand, letting him help her to her feet.

"Some food would be good," she told him, not taking her eyes from the tetchy American and speaking pointedly at her. "I think we could *both* do with a decent meal."

"Excellent." Heydari beamed, helping Kendis up too before clapping his hands together. "You will eat well, we shall talk some more."

He opened the door and stepped aside for them. Acid let Kendis shuffle out first before nodding politely at their grinning captor and following on behind. She could feel Heydari's eyes on her arse as she sashayed through the bathroom and gave her hips a little more sway for good measure. Because whilst she didn't like using her sexuality to get the job done, she wasn't an idiot – sometimes these things helped. Especially with self-obsessed men driven by ego and a thirst for power. She'd learnt from experience; a little sass and compliance was the perfect way to disarm (often both metaphorically and actually) a man like the prince.

"Myself, I have been awake since ten," Heydari said, as they got to the door of his suite and he stepped around them to rap his knuckles on the thick wood. "But I wanted to wait. So we could eat together."

Kendis made a noise like a pissed off rattlesnake.

"Thank you," Acid told him, staring at the kid, employing her well-worn *don't-fuck-this-up* look.

A key turned in the lock and the door creaked open to reveal Heydari's majestic suite and some of the most delicious smells Acid had ever encountered. The large dining table on the far side of the room was laid out with a veritable banquet. With a hand resting on the small of her back, Heydari led them to it and Acid cast a greedy eye over the steaming bowls of exotic food. Mounds of yellow fluffy rice draped with shaved almonds and plump sultanas, and hot oily stews packed with tender meat and vegetables. There were also two shallow dishes filled with baklava and deep-fried Iranian funnel cakes, as well as croissants and pain au chocolat. Acid's stomach rumbled with blind joy as Heydari pulled out a chair for her and she sat.

"Please, allow me," he said, gliding over to where Kendis was standing on the other side of the table, and prised the chair from her grasp.

The muscles in Acid's jaw tensed as she watched the mad prince enjoying playing the good host. As though this was the most normal situation in the world and he was just a friendly guy, not someone keeping them captive for his own end. But then, even the worst of them could justify their actions somehow. To themselves, at least. Acid knew that as much as anyone, because she'd done it herself, and she'd been the worst of them.

"Now we shall eat," Heydari bellowed, taking his place at the head of the table as the same two 'sisters' from before arrived with jugs of iced lemon water.

Acid watched as they filled up their gold beakers before placing the jugs down on the table. "Do you always dine in this room?" she asked.

"I do now. Now the Americans are watching me." He leaned across the table, his eyes like slits. "Do you know they now have the technology that if I was out in the open they could slice me in two with a laser from one of their satellites? A laser indeed. Like your Star Wars movies. They are even developing a weapon which can kill people through walls. A sonic death ray."

Out of the corner of her eye she saw Kendis frown. "I'm not sure any of those things are tr—"

A swift kick to the leg shut her up, as did a strong glare. "Sounds like they're rather afraid of you," she told Heydari. "You must be a very powerful man. More than I realised."

He eyed her for a moment, perhaps wondering whether she was playing a game, but his ego got the better of him. "I think maybe I am. Did you hear of me before coming here? Did you know who I was? What I was?"

"Well of course, you're The Prince of Islam, the most powerful man in Iran."

He reached over and picked up a baklava, scattering loose pistachio pieces as he brought it to his side plate. "My power will be a force for good. For change. My dream is to bring peace and unity to the region." He sat back, addressing both women. "When I am through with my plans, insurgents will sit at the same table as authority. ISIS will work alongside the Iranian army. One force working together for the good of my country. It is a hard mission and one I do not undertake lightly, but I believe that only by bringing this harmony to light can Iran present itself fully on the world stage."

"Present itself fully?" Kendis sniffed. "Sounds like a euphemism for war. So that's your real goal, start more wars? Invade other countries?"

"Not at all." Heydari batted the idea away with a swipe of his hand. "But to maintain our autonomy we must stand up for ourselves. To other Arab nations, but to the West also. This is why we need a united front in our country. Why my country needs me."

"I get it," Kendis replied, picking up an orange from the bowl next to her and squeezing it in her grip like a baseball. "And you'll be the leader of this new and improved Iran? Holding power over the insurgents and the army?"

"Of course," he replied, as if anything else would be ridiculous. "It is my dream. My vision. And I will be the one to action it."

Acid reached for the bowl of rice and spooned a large pile onto her plate, topping it off with a thick spoonful of stew. It smelt amazing, spicy and rich and with the hint of cinnamon. It tasted even better. Like an Indian curry but sweeter and more complex. She swallowed down a few more mouthfuls of food, about to thank their host once more for the food – ramp up the demureness – when Kendis piped up again.

"But how do you action that?" she asked him. "By killing your own people? Ruling with fear? Because, believe me, people are only subservient for so long. That's what causes insurgency in the first place."

Heydari smiled, although Acid thought she clocked a noticeable shiver of anger. He wasn't used to a woman talking back to him perhaps, or indeed anyone. "I understand you feel strongly about these matters. But it will not be like this. I am a man of the people. I look after those who fight alongside me. I give them good money, good food, whatever they need. This will only continue and spread as my influence grows."

Acid sipped at her water. "I heard you look after your men well."

"Yes, I do. I believe a happy solider is a good soldier. Do you know who taught me this? Mr Richard Branson. He is a good leader, yes?"

Acid couldn't hold back the eye-roll. "If you say so. But I get it. Treat them well, they stay loyal. I heard you throw quite the party. Bit naughty isn't it, for someone like you?"

"For someone like me?" He was frowning, but more flirtatious now than angry. There was a real energy between them, she could feel it. But of course there was – she'd done this before. "You mean for a prince, or a Muslim man?"

She didn't drop his gaze for a second. "Both, I guess." A mischievous smile curved the edge of her mouth. "I'm not saying it's a bad thing, of course—"

"Do you like the movies?" he cut in.

"Excuse me?"

"Movies, I love them. American movies, yes? Do you like Nick Cage?"

Acid glanced at Kendis. "I can't say I'm a big fan of—"

"I love him. Mr Nicholas Cage. Or Nicholas Coppola, to give him his proper name. Did you know this? He is the nephew of Mr Francis Ford Coppola. Imagine that. And he doesn't even play on the family name. That is the kind of man he is. Very humble."

"Sorry, what's this got to do with anything?" Kendis asked.

The prince shrugged camply. "My favourite Nick Cage movie is Con Air, have seen this? There is a character in this movie called *Cyrus the Virus*. And he likes this name. This character he is nasty and slimy, he thinks the name makes him sound threatening perhaps."

"O-kay," Acid murmured. "So… what?"

"I watch this and I cannot understand it. Why anyone would

want to be seen like this. I would never call myself Cyrus the Virus. Viruses are bad things, are they not? No one likes viruses. Especially not right now, hey?" He laughed haughtily, shaking his head as though his words were the funniest, most erudite thing he'd ever heard. "Of course, you do know this virus – this pandemic, or whatever you call it – it is all made up by the western governments. It is a hoax. A con. A way of controlling you. People fall for it and I laugh.

It was Kendis' turn to glance at Acid. They exchanged frowns but Acid shook her head. *Not worth it.*

Kendis ignored her. "Again, I don't think that's true. I—"

"You ask me why I can do this as a Muslim man. Because I know what I do is for the good of the world. My God does not mind me enjoying the richer things in life, because I do so much good. Or I will do."

"He told you this, did he?" Kendis asked.

Heydari leaned across the table towards her. "My relationship with my God and my religion is my own business. I know how He feels about what I do. Me and my men, we drink together, we laugh together, we… play together." He looked her up and down suggestively. "And for this they offer me their full loyalty. Are ready to die for me if the need arises. Are ready to die for the cause. This is how we create a better world. A better life for the Iranian people."

Acid chewed on her lip. So Caesar was right about Heydari entertaining his men. But he was right about a lot of things. Heydari was as mad as they came. Paranoid and egotistical, sure, but with a glimmer of genuine insanity blazing behind his eyes. She shifted in her seat as the leather pouch made itself known.

"Sounds like a lot fun," she told him.

"Oh, it is. Tonight you shall see. When you attend."

Kendis let the orange fall heavily on her plate. "When we attend?"

"Yes. This evening you will attend to me and my men."

"There it is again. *Attend?*"

"Feed us, make sure we never have an empty glass." He held up a finger. "Don't worry, my men may be full of youth and exuberance but they are also obedient. They don't do anything without my say."

"And what if you say...?"

The prince's smile morphed into a leer as his gaze flitted between the two women. "That will not happen, I assure you. I do not like to share *everything* with my men."

Acid tried to remain calm as a million bat wings beat against her resolve. Her fingers landed on the handle of the silver spoon next to her plate, a deadly weapon in the right hands.

"So I was right," Kendis said, shooting Acid a pyrrhic *told-you-so* glare. "That's why you want us here."

"I want you here as my protection, like I said. But there is no reason why we cannot enjoy each other at the same time." He placed his elbows on the table and steepled his hands together under his chin. "We are all young and beautiful, are we not?"

Acid almost spat a mouthful of rice across the room. Spluttering, she managed to turn it into a cough. "Went down the wrong way," she said, hitting her chest with her fist. "But I think Kendis here is unhappy about our lack of consent to these proceedings."

"Nonsense," he replied, without missing a beat. "You will relish your time here, mark my words. There are many ways we can grow more at ease with one another. I have potions and powders and fine wine here in the palace, as well as some wonderful hashish. I believe if you partake you will find yourself much more... accommodating."

"Well won't that be nice," Acid muttered under her breath, unable to hold it in. "We'll be too out of it to realise what's going on."

She hadn't meant to say it out loud but the prince rounded on her without warning, his unyielding, Botox-packed face somehow morphing into an angry grimace.

"Who are you to become moral with me – Cyrus Heydari, Prince of Islam and soon to be Supreme Leader of the Middle

East? You are a woman who kills for money, are you not? Who prostitutes herself to catch her prey? Who takes innocent lives for a living?"

Across the table Kendis sucked back a sharp gasp, which elicited an impulsive eye-roll from Acid.

Bloody hell, kid.

Surely she'd spelt it out enough for her.

She turned her attention back to Heydari. "That's not exactly true," she said, releasing her grip on the spoon to raise a finger. "I never *prostituted* myself. Ever. And I never took an innocent life."

Heydari smirked. "Innocence is in the eye of the beholder."

"Hmm, don't think so."

"You kill people as a job?" Kendis asked her. "Like a hitman?"

Acid blew out a long breath. "We prefer *assassin*. Or *hired killer*. *Elite killer*, if you want to be picky." She sat back in her chair to better address them both. "But either way, I don't do it anymore. Any of it."

Kendis was still shaking her head when Heydari said, "But this is why you are here in my country, no? To kill Beowulf Caesar? That is why he sought shelter here."

"I have an extremely complicated relationship with that man," she offered. "He hurt me, very much. I wanted him dead."

"And now?"

"Same." She picked up the spoon and moved the meat around on her plate. "It's the only way I can move on with my life."

"Ha," Heydari scoffed, spitting out a mouthful of puff pastry confetti. "You don't sound very convincing, Miss Vanilla. You know, when he told me about you I imagined some terrible, vicious woman. But here you are, demure, beautiful – and with a tortured soul. I can see now." He held his hand to his heart affectedly. "It is a sad sight to behold. But I understand. I don't think we're too different, me and you. We both know loss."

"You've lost people?"

"I've lost my country. I've lost my faith in the people who lead us."

"Right. Back to that are we?" She placed the spoon down and glanced through her hair at Kendis, seeing her face was still crumpled with a perplexed expression. With a deep breath, she raised her head and granted Heydari a smile. "Why don't we talk about you for a while? Please, tell us about how you came to be such a great and powerful man."

A pregnant pause descended over the table as the words hung awkwardly in the air. Acid chewed some more on her lip, angry with herself that she'd overdone it. But then Heydari smiled and reached for his glass.

"Oh my dear," he told her, with a devious wink. "I thought you'd never ask."

CHAPTER 27

For the next two hours – probably longer (Acid had lost track of time after the first hour, as well as most of her will to live) – the self-exclaimed Prince of Islam waxed lyrical about who he was, where he'd come from and his dreams for Iran. He talked of his childhood, his family, his friends growing up, yet the majority of his monologue was directed towards tales of the many foes he'd vanquished over the years. The stories were varied and sounded impressive enough to start with, but as each anecdote fed into the next they grew increasingly far-fetched. After a while Acid surmised he must be making a large proportion of it up, but if she let it show in her face it didn't slow him down. He spoke non-stop as though spurred on by some kind of psychotic drug.

The signs of a manic episode couldn't be more obvious to Acid. She too would find herself babbling uncontrollably, her thought patterns shooting off at odd and unfathomable tangents. Often in her life these lateral thought excursions were valuable, especially when coupled with the bristling sense of invulnerability her condition provided. But there was always a flip side. The bats had got her out of some tough situations over the years, and also got her into just as many.

She turned back to Heydari as he let out a low rumble and, clocking Kendis' concerned expression, realised she'd missed something.

"Sorry, my mind wandered," she offered. "Can you say that again?"

"I was just telling your friend here how beautiful she was," Heydari growled, in a voice rich with depth and baritone, so different to the mid-range whine he'd been employing for most of the last hour. It was as though he was putting on the type of voice that belonged to people he assumed himself to be like (rich, powerful, attractive). "Her skin, it is flawless. But I admit, she doesn't seem to enjoy my compliments."

Kendis wrinkled her nose. "I'm not into skin care and beauty regimes. I'm a soldier. Not a model."

"You are not a soldier," the prince growled, sending a smirk Acid's way. "You work for the Peace Corps, Ms Powell. A big difference."

Kendis jerked upright. "You know—"

"*I know* everything about everyone. No secrets here. And what a pairing we have. A humanitarian and a killer together at my table. Both beautiful, both fiery in their own way. I like this. It makes me hot."

The way he said the word *hot* (breathy and throaty, and like it had three syllables) elicited visceral reactions in both women: another visible shudder from Kendis; Acid doing her best not to throw up. She gripped the edge of her plate as Heydari stood and moved around the table to take position behind Kendis.

"Come now, Ms Powell," he said, placing overly manicured hands on her shoulders. "You are so tense, let me help you relax."

Kendis whimpered as he rubbed at her shoulders, his long fingers stretching down over the top half of her chest.

Her eyes met Acid's. *Do something*, they said.

But she didn't move. She didn't even raise her head. The next few minutes were important. If Caesar's plan was to work, she had to stay on the right side of Heydari. Had to gain his trust.

Through her hair she watched Heydari moving his face down next to Kendis', rubbing his cheek against hers. The kid looked like whatever she may have consumed from Heydari's feast of goodies was about to make a sudden and forceful reappearance.

"Please," Acid said, finding her voice. "Let us retire to our quarters until later. I promise we shall be much more... agreeable once we have digested our food and rested some more."

"You've had enough rest," Heydari purred, rubbing the back of his fingers down Kendis' arm. "Now it is time for us to have some fun."

"I don't want to," Kendis pleaded, squirming away as he moved around the side of her and grabbed her chin. "Stop."

"What you want is not important," Heydari told her, moving her face around, forcing her to look at him. "Let me remind you again, I am Cyrus Heydari, The New Prince of Islam. My men fear and love me in equal measure. Are ready to die for me. Ready to kill for me just as much. So believe me when I say, I always get what I want."

Acid tensed her grip on the plate, assessing how much damage it would cause if she flung it at his neck. But what then? Piss him off, get locked up again? The plan would be over before it started.

"And what about what I want?" Kendis asked, shifting her head from his clutches. "I am a US citizen, a political prisoner. I demand—"

"You demand nothing," Heydari yelled, before calming himself, his voice slipping back into the chocolatey baritone. "Furthermore, my darling, this will be a good experience for you. I am a magnificent lover. Ask the many wives of my fallen foes. They will tell you. Or they would, if they were still alive." He laughed a deep cackling sort of laugh, which unnerved Acid. It was the sound of insanity.

She released the plate from her grip and leaned forward in her seat. She'd made a decision and was about to tell the lascivious prick she'd volunteer herself to him, when Kendis lashed out with a sharp elbow, catching Heydari in the solar plexus and knocking all the air out of him. Acid was on her feet in a second, but before she had chance to get over there he'd righted himself and retaliated with a sharp backhand that caught Kendis unaware.

"Insolent bitch." He followed the young American across the room as she stumbled for the door. She had her hand on the handle but a fierce hammer punch from the prince slammed her to the floor.

"Stop." Acid hurried over and got in between them as Heydari raised his hand for another go. "She's no good to you bruised and battered. Look, she's tired and tetchy, we both are. We didn't know what was going on. But now we do,"—she placed her hand gently on his upper arm—"we can get our heads round it. Properly. We can be what you want us to be. Do what you want us to do. Please, give us another chance and we'll prove to you how accommodating we can be. We'll serve on you. In every way possible. In every way you'd like. Right, Kendis?"

The kid scowled at Acid, her hand holding her face. "Fuck you."

"You disrespectful dog." Heydari tried to launch himself at her but Acid kept hold of his arm.

"Please, my prince. Supreme Leader. Spare her." She was speaking fast, the words falling out of her mouth quicker than her mind could keep up. "She is an American, brainwashed by her media. She doesn't realise what you're trying to do here. But she will. Let me talk to her, convince her. I swear, by this evening we shall both be perfect servants for you. In every way." She moved her face nearer his, ramping up the flirtation as she stroked her finger down his arm. "As you know, I'm a woman of many means and of much experience. You also know I'm someone who appreciates the finer things in life. Good food. Nice drink. Luxurious palace settings." She smiled a mischievous cat-smile, moving her face even closer to his as she whispered, "You must also know by now that power is a massive turn on for me. Brave, unyielding men like you – free thinkers, visionaries. My god, they do… *things* to me. Me and you will get on so well, my prince. But it would be so much more fun if it was the three of us, don't you think? Please, give me an hour or two to talk to her. I'll make her understand that compliance is in her best interest. She will enjoy it once she submits to her new life."

She stopped and looked at Heydari, taking in his intense stare, his face rigid with more than chemicals. They were both doing the same thing, she realised – looking for a tell in the other. Acid held her nerve, employing every technique at her disposal to remain calm and composed. Finally the prince turned and barked something over her shoulder. Acid didn't take her eyes off his, but a moment later a draught of cool air entered the room as the door creaked open.

"Please, escort these two women back to their chamber," he told the young guard who appeared beside them. "They will wait there until this evening, when they will attend to me and my men."

Acid reached down and helped Kendis to her feet, giving her wrist a hard squeeze in the process, which she hoped conveyed the correct message. "It will be our pleasure," she told Heydari. "And we shall look forward to it. Isn't that right, Kendis?"

"Y-yeah, sure." Another squeeze got the stuttered response.

"And she apologises for her outburst. Yes? Yes?"

"Yeah. Sorry," Kendis grumbled at the floor. "Like Acid said, I'm tired and tetchy."

"Then you will join us again in three hours' time," Heydari said. "My sisters will collect you from your quarters and give instructions on how the evening will run. Then, afterwards, we shall try this again." He pointed a finger at Acid, wagging it between her and Kendis. "And please, if you want to see tomorrow, make sure you are a lot more accommodating. Now go."

With a dramatic flourish he strode over to his enormous bed and threw himself petulantly on top. Acid watched on, fighting the impulse twitching at her eyebrow, before the guard nudged them over to the door and she let herself be hustled out of the room.

Three hours.

Three hours until she was back here. Three hours to psyche herself up enough she could pull the plan off, whilst somehow getting Kendis on side. It wouldn't be easy. But then, escaping from the heavily-guarded fortress of an insane despot never was.

CHAPTER 28

I t was well after sundown when the sisters came to collect them. The sky – the only thing visible through the small window in the women's room – having changed from fuchsia pink to midnight blue to dusky black since Heydari's brusque guard had bustled them into the cell-like chamber.

Acid sat upright as the door creaked open and the taller of the two sisters gestured for her to stand.

"Looks like it's party time." She sighed, giving Kendis the look she'd perfected over the past two years, ever since she'd found herself inexplicably intertwined with Spook Horowitz. The expression said *Trust me* but with a strong undercurrent of *Don't you dare fuck this up.*

Kendis shook her head. "Party time? Jesus."

It hadn't been easy to convince her to go along with the plan (especially as it was only the wispiest suggestion of a plan), but the promise of freedom was a strong driver for compliance. And besides, if the drugs – still concealed in the crotch of Acid's knickers – worked the way Caesar had described, then they wouldn't have to spend too long swerving the lecherous prince's advances. If it didn't... well, she'd been eyeing up the pistol in the guard's belt as he escorted them back to the room, she could work with that. It would be a much bloodier way of getting out of here (not to mention foolhardy), yet from the way her imagination had been running riot since Heydari's pitiable display earlier she'd certainly enjoy it. She'd go out with a grin on her face.

"Just keep in mind what I told you," she whispered to Kendis, leaning into her as they got to their feet. "We'll both get through this."

"Yeah, sure. Trust the hired killer. What have I got to lose?"

Acid turned her attention to the doorway, making a point of sticking out her chest as she passed the sisters. "Come along, sweetie," she called over her shoulder to Kendis. "Tits and teeth, let's do this."

The sisters led them through the bathroom to the door of Heydari's suite. Once there, they turned to take in Acid and Kendis, screwing their faces dismissively at their appearance. A quick flourish of hands, nipping the silk robes here and tucking them there, and they seemed satisfied enough. The taller sister signalled their arrival with a firm knock and the sound of movement came from the other side.

Acid stiffened, sensing Kendis doing the same but possibly for different reasons. She had the urge to say something encouraging, give her a reassuring nudge at least, but the sisters were watching them and she thought it best to stay in character. For now she was a humble and compliant servant of the prince. Out of sight from their escorts, she found the American's tight fist hanging a few centimetres from hers and gave it a squeeze. A second later the door opened and the sound of music and laughter – along with the pungent aroma of hashish – spiralled around their heads.

"It's about time," she heard Heydari's voice boom across the room. "Please, show yourselves."

The sisters stepped aside, beckoning the two women forward. Acid shot one of them a cutting side-eye as she followed Kendis into the room.

Rather us than you. Hey, girls?

Illuminated in the glow from soft electric lamps and the flicker

of candles, Heydari's enormous suite appeared even more decadent than it had earlier. Acid now noticed the many exotic orna-
ments and vases on plinths around the room, and the thick
Persian rug covering most of the floor looked to have gold thread
woven into its elaborate design. The table they'd sat around
earlier had been moved to the side of the room and on it stood
four earthenware jugs and the biggest bowl of dates she'd ever
seen. At the back of the table stood twelve bottles of red wine,
unopened and laid out in three rows of four.

"Please, welcome my new waiting girls."

Acid snapped her attention to the source of the voice as Cyrus
Heydari eased himself off a large maroon-leather ottoman stool.
The muted day robes were gone and, in their place, a bright
turquoise tunic complete with a long flowing white cloak. An
elaborate leather belt finished off the look, decked out in turquoise
stones and what appeared to be large diamonds. With a beaming
smile he swaggered over to the two women and got between
them, throwing a heavy arm over their shoulders.

"What do you think, guys?"

Six of Heydari's foot soldiers were reclining on the huge
couches at the far side of the room, each one holding a pipe that
attached to one of three large hookah bowls. Their faces were now
clear of any masks or material covering, but they still wore their
dusty army fatigues. A row of Kalashnikovs were leaning up
against the window and, as Heydari led her and Kendis over to
the couches, Acid noticed each soldier had a handgun tucked into
their waistbands. Because of the hirsute nature of their appearance it made them seem older than they were, but she'd guess
they were in their early twenties. Young and lusty and easily led.
The way Heydari seemed to like them. All of them were well-built
physically, and their thick chests and broad shoulders only exacerbated the intimidating aggressiveness that danced behind their
eyes.

Acid flinched as Heydari moved his hand from her shoulder to
grab at her upper arm, telling the men, "These beautiful western

women are Acid Vanilla and Kendis Powell. They will be waiting on us this evening. And then later… well, they will be waiting on us some more."

The men eyed them greedily, shouting over at them in broken English.

"You talk with me. Yes?"

"Sitting on my lap."

"Beautiful nice."

Acid snorted – she couldn't help herself – triggering Heydari to grip her arm tighter. He leaned in, lowering his voice to an ominous whisper.

"Careful, my dear. From now on you speak when I tell you, abide by my wishes, be at my mercy. In every way. Otherwise you will find out exactly what happens to people who displease me. Do you understand? Both of you?"

Acid gave a brief nod. Kendis let out a breathy, "Yes."

"Good. Now, come with me." He directed them over to the table, his disposition easing as he let go of Acid's arm, waving a limp hand over the wine bottles. "Fill up the jugs with the wine and bring them over to join us. My men are battle-weary, they need nourishment and comfort, some soft warm flesh to snuggle beside." The way he said this last bit – with his nose all crinkled up, like it was a cute thing he was saying – made Acid want to grab up a wine bottle and smash it into his neck. She sucked back a slow, deliberate breath, calming herself as she shifted her stance, feeling the pouch still there in her crotch.

"I don't suppose I could use the bathroom first?" she asked, switching the coquettish act up a few notches and addressing him through her eyelashes. "I haven't been since I got here. I don't want any accidents later."

She placed her hand on his arm as a scowl tried to form across his frozen brow. He shook his head and huffed before turning and walking over to the door. He rapped twice with his ringed fingers, calling out something in Farsi.

"Be quick," he said, as one of the sisters put her head around the door. He snapped his fingers at her and then at Acid before stomping back over to be with his men.

"Bathroom?" Acid asked, and the sister nodded nervously. Taking her by the hand, she led her out into the main bathing suite and around the edge of the sunken bathtub where she was presented with another door. It was smaller and less grand than the door to her own sleeping chamber, and painted white to match the walls, so she hadn't noticed it earlier.

"This is the bathroom? The lavatory?" she asked, pushing at the door. "Oh yes, I see."

Stepping into the room, she squinted as a bright sensor-linked light flickered on. The room was more westernised than she expected – a typical layout of toilet bowl, cistern and sink, complete with a shower cubicle in one corner – but the fact each item was made of gold was pure Heydari. Jarring, but not unexpected. The walls and floor had been done out in tiny black and gold tiles, each one only a few centimetres square but placed in such a way it gave the optical illusion that a vortex had opened up in the middle of each wall and the middle of the floor as well. It was unsettling and weird, just like its owner. And maybe that was the point, she wondered, as she closed the door and hurried over to the toilet where she quickly undressed and sat on the cold seat.

She did need to urinate after all and, as she did, she leaned forward and retrieved the powder from between her legs. Rolling the leather pouch up into her palm she held her fist out in front of her. The dark pouch wasn't totally concealed but, taking stock from different angles, she reckoned she might get away with it. The light in Heydari's suite was dimmer than in here, and she had a plethora of distraction techniques up her sleeve if needed.

She finished up and placed the pouch on the side of the sink as she wiped and got dressed, wrapping the robes around her and checking herself in the large round mirror above the sink. The woman staring back at her looked pensive and worried, but she dismissed any ideas of what that meant – it was just the stark lighting causing her to look that way. Besides, she was now in mission-mode. The plan was set and overthinking off the table. If she survived the next few hours it would be because she let instinct and experience take over.

She turned for the door as the bats screeched across her consciousness.

It was time.

CHAPTER 29

Back in Heydari's suite she was greeted with hearty cheers from his men and a sharp glare from Kendis. At the door she did a little curtsey to more cheers, before heading for the table of drinks. She kept the hand holding the pouch close to her side, swaying her hips like they were deadly weapons to counter any stiffness held in her torso.

"The wily Ms Vanilla has returned," Heydari bellowed from the far side of the room, standing with his arm around one of his men. "You feel better now? Ready for fun times?"

She allowed him a polite nod, followed it up with an impish grin. "Sorry about that," she purred. "A girl needs to make sure she's at her best. But oh yes, I'm ready for you now. All yours."

She positioned herself next to Kendis who was standing at the table with a full jug of wine gripped in both hands. She hadn't taken her stern eyes off Acid since she'd returned. "You get it?" she muttered, out the corner of her mouth.

"Of course," Acid replied through a smile. She cast her eyes over the table. Kendis had filled all four jugs using seven of the wine bottles. Acid knew the powder had to stay relatively concentrated if it was to work the way Caesar had described. So keeping one eye on the festivities taking place across the other side of the room, and putting Kendis between her and them as much as possible, she swiftly administered the powder into two of the jugs. Once done, she dropped the leather pouch onto the stone floor and kicked it under the table. Gulping back a breath – the first one she'd allowed herself since returning from the bathroom – she cast her gaze across the room.

Heydari was watching her.

Shit.

She froze. He raised his head. A wide leer cracked his face and he beckoned her over. "Come talk to me," he called. "I am so lonely over here. We all are."

The knotted muscles across her shoulders relaxed and she hit him with a winning smile, eyes alight with fire and flirtation.

"Coming," she told him. She carried the heavy wine jug over, swirling the liquid as she went to further mix up the potent concoction.

"Who would like some?" she purred, swaying into the space between the couches and offering the jug around.

The men cheered but half-heartedly, already lethargic from the pungent hashish still smoking away in the bubble-pipes. Watched on by Heydari's lustful eye, Acid poured out large measures into each of their metal tankards, smiling sweetly and fluttering her eyelashes as she went. But when she got to the mad host, he held his hand up.

"Not for me."

What?

"What? I mean… I thought you liked wine… the finer things in life?"

He leaned back against the arm of the couch and smiled up at her. "Oh I do, but I also need to stay clear-headed. For the time being, at least."

It took everything she had to remain neutral-faced. "I see. Well, I think it's commendable. And incredibly princely."

He liked this, beaming and nodding as she shot him another flirtatious look. The mission wasn't going to plan, yet she had him right where she needed him. If she could find the right opportunity then—

He beckoned her closer. "Also, I want to remember everything about this evening." He patted the plump velvet cushion beside him. "Join me. We can, how they say, get better acquainted."

"Of course." She lowered herself to perch on the edge of the couch, but Heydari's arm quickly appeared around her waist and pulled her onto his lap.

"There we are, much better," he growled, his hand snaking down her stomach. "Would you like a drink? Either of you?"

Kendis looked like a deer caught in the headlights. "Oh. No, I... don't..."

"I'd love one, please," Acid cut in. "Do you mind?"

She freed herself from his grasp and leaned forward to grab a tankard off the table. As she did she surveyed his men, all of them drinking heartily, oblivious to the power of the intoxicating cocktail. She stood up and, holding the tankard in front of her, poured out a half-measure of wine. It smelt much sweeter than she was used to and was thicker, as though perhaps fortified.

Damnit to hell.

She'd give her right tit for a decent drink right now. Even this syrupy stuff had her soul in raptures. She wanted nothing more than to gulp back the entire tankard and pour herself another one. Resisting the urge, she shifted around to face Heydari, tilting her head back and letting the drink hit her lips but not opening them. She could sense the heady concoction in her sinuses, and her heart raced with the notion that the bitter powder within would be noticeable, yet another scan of the room confirmed to her that none of Heydari's men had noticed. The molasses sweetness of the wine had helped mask the flavour, and some of them were already raising their tankards for Kendis to pour them a second helping. Acid took a deep breath. With the concentration of drugs already in their system, she gave it five minutes maybe less before they started getting messy. Before it would be obvious something was wrong.

"You know, I am a silly man for not thinking of this earlier," he growled, grabbing at Acid and pulling her close. She rested the tankard on her knee as his hand came to rest on the curve of her upper thigh. "It makes perfect sense to have protection close at all times. And with such beautiful protection, I can have my cake and eat it too."

"Beautiful?" She sighed, sinking into his grasp. "Is that so?"

"But of course. You are very beautiful. Especially when you smile. And I will make you smile a lot more." He leaned in conspiringly, his hand squeezing at her hip. "I will make it my mission to tame the deadly Acid Vanilla. And I will succeed. Maybe not straight away, but you are no fool, you will see it is in your best interests for us to be friends."

"Deadly?" she repeated, as he traced his fingers up her inner thigh, resisting the urge to smash her elbow into his face. "Does it bother you, who I am? What I'm capable of?"

He leaned back so she could see his whole face – indicating with his expression how ridiculous he considered this line of enquiry. "Of course not, my dear. It only makes me more excited. Besides, what can you do? You have no weapons. No way of escape."

Acid held her nerve, sizing him up. He was a pumped up, puffed up peacock of a man, but there wasn't much of him. No weapons wasn't an issue. No way of escape? That was up to Caesar.

"Now, now," she scolded playfully, leaning into him. "Is that how to talk to your new friend? I thought we were supposed to be getting better acquainted?"

As his hand stroked up the back of her leg, she ran through her options. Opposite her on the other couch, Kendis was now sitting between two of the soldiers – them offering her their pipe to smoke, shoving tankards of wine under her nose. They were speaking in Farsi but Acid imagined the gist of the conversation, telling the increasingly agitated American to *Chill out*. To *Try it, she might like it*.

She tensed. The men were drinking faster than she'd imagined they would, knocking back their wine like it was water, most now on their second or third tankard. If Heydari noticed them wilting before she had time to act, things could go very bad very fast. It was going to be tight.

"You know, I've been in many scary situations throughout my life," Acid told the prince, shifting around so she could see his face. "Have had to deal with lots of evil people. But I don't think you're so bad. You're a nice man, I think, deep down. A very nice man."

Heydari grinned. "I can be a nice man. When I want to be. To those who deserve my compassion."

"And do I deserve your compassion?"

"We shall have to see."

Their speech had grown rapid and husky and she could feel his hot breath on her cheek. A flitting glance across the room and one of the soldiers was already slumped against Kendis, his head lolling onto her shoulder. Another of the men made to pick up his tankard and slipped off the couch.

"Oops," she said, turning her attention back to Heydari, trying to make light of it. "Somebody can't handle their wine."

Heydari frowned at the soldier, about to say something before Acid placed her hand on his cheek and guided his gaze back to hers.

"Not everyone can be as gracious or as princely as you. Let him enjoy himself." She leaned in closer so her lips were almost brushing against his ear. "Is there somewhere we can go, somewhere more private? I would like to show you how... grateful I am for your generosity. For letting me stay in your wonderful palace."

The prince had pushed his face into her hand, clearly enjoying the feeling of her touch. But when he moved away, his eyes were narrowed. "You want to go somewhere just the two of us?"

She nodded, letting her bottom lip hang open a touch. "I do."

"All at once you seem very accommodating," he said, eyes still searching hers. "Should I be concerned?"

"Not at all. Like I told you, I've had a less than conventional life. Had to deal with a lot of horrible shit over the years. And one thing I've learnt is whatever life throws your way, it's important to make the best of it. To adapt and modify one's behaviour, and even ideals, so as not only to survive but to thrive in whatever situation comes along." She smiled, the picture of serenity. "You've got to understand, I have no interest in the petty morals of civilians. I think we're very similar, me and you. We're both rebels, both visionaries, both survivors. Whilst I was resting I came to a realisation – an epiphany, if you will. Here I am surrounded by splendour, being entertained and looked after by not only a supremely powerful man, but a handsome one to boot. Why not enjoy it?"

She finished up and sat back, breathless for real. It was quite the speech, even for her, and it was all she had. Heydari held her gaze for a second or two longer, but enough time for her to worry that he'd seen through her. But then his shoulders dropped and a mischievous expression cracked his rigid features.

"Where would you like to go?" he asked. "To the royal bedroom?"

"No. Let's go next door. To my chamber," she whispered, speaking even more urgently now as she noticed one of the soldiers was out cold, his head rolled over the back of the couch. She placed her tankard on the table and took Heydari by the hand. "Come on, it's cosy in there. Lots of cushions. Lots of fun. I promise."

She got up and pulled the prince to his feet, dragging him away from his fallen henchmen and out the door. In a furtive glance over her shoulder, she saw all six of the men were now in various states of slumber, and the largest of the four was lying face down in Kendis' lap, making a sound like an adenoidal tiger. Kendis caught Acid's eye and gave her a nod, the fear and anger that had creased her fine features replaced by acceptance and perhaps even admiration.

Nearly there.

The two sisters were both waiting in the next room and got to their feet as they entered. Acid stopped and held her hand up to stop them and Heydari stumbled into her, giggling like a schoolgirl.

So he liked her taking control. Wasn't he in for a treat.

"We want to be alone," Acid snapped, hoping her glare would get the point across the language barrier. "Go to your rooms."

Heydari coughed himself serious and waved the women away, no doubt saying the same thing as she had but in Farsi. Acid waited for the two women to shuffle out of the room before turning back to the prince with an eager shrug of her shoulders.

"Thank god. I don't need those two being all jealous and judgemental."

"Jealous?"

"Come along, they're not really your sisters, are they? I imagine they both hold a torch for the great prince, attending on you all day and night as they do."

Heydari frowned. "No, they really are my sisters. Sanaa and Talisha. We share the same father, at least. They are both older than me. Not my type."

"Right... I see. Well..." She shook her head, getting back into the role and placing a hand on his chest. "Oh god, I want you so bad. Let's go."

They moved across the room to the chamber where Acid and Kendis had spent the last twelve hours, and where she'd told the young American of her plan to get out of here. Freedom. They were so close now she could taste it.

"Step into my lair," she purred, walking backwards as she entered the room.

"With pleasure," he replied, so excited she almost pitied him. The mad Prince of Islam reduced to a small boy in a sweet shop. "Where do you want me?" he asked, already undoing the fastenings on his robes.

"Wait," she said, shoving his hands down by his sides and

grabbing hold of his belt. "I'll take care of that. I insist.'

"You insist, do you?"

"I do."

"Great."

With the belt gripped in her fist she yanked it tight, dispensing a sharp knee to his groin that appeared to paralyse him instantly. She pushed him against the wall and – not letting up – ground her knee into the spongy tissue of his testicles for which he let out a tortured groan of surprise. As she released the pressure, she saw his eyes were open wider than she'd seen them up to now and his expression had shifted from lusty anticipation to something more questioning, as if asking, *Why?* It was funny to her, men always seemed to react the same way to this particular move, as if even in a fight to the death it was the one move too off limits.

Stepping back, she followed up with a punishing right hook that smashed into his cheekbone and knocked all the shock off his face. Before he could even get a grip on what had happened, she was behind him with her arm around his throat. As she squeezed his carotid vein shut, the bats screamed at her to finish him, to snap his hateful neck and have done with it. But for once she resisted. Heydari was a wicked and twisted fucker, but he wasn't her mark. The Americans would deal with him.

She tightened her hold as his body grew limp in her arms. Another second and she let his lifeless body drop to the floor. Removing her sash belt, she knelt and dragged his arms and legs behind his back, hog-tying him the way Caesar had taught her all those years earlier. Once satisfied the mad prince wasn't going anywhere, she ripped a piece of cloth from the bottom of her robe and stuffed it into his mouth. Then she hurried out into the bathroom suite, finding her old clothes still bundled up in the corner of the room where she'd left them. She got dressed promptly, her trusty leather jacket feeling like home as she slipped her arms into the sleeves and pulled it on. Popping the collar up was the final step. Acid Vanilla was back in business, and it was time to get out of here.

CHAPTER 30

The moronic doctor was still standing in the doorway to the cabin as if frozen in time. Why the pissing hell wasn't he doing as instructed?

"What is your problem?" Caesar asked him. "I thought your English was good. Comprenez-vous? Non?"

He sniffed. "I am Norwegian, not French. And yes I do understand, but I am worried this is a mistake."

"Is it? Well fuck me sideways, I didn't realise. Thanks for that, doc. Best bloody well forget it then. I'll just lie here and rot for the rest of my days." The old bed springs groaned beneath him as he sat upright, and his voice dropped to a sinister rasp. "I'm not sure if you remember, but we're being held prisoner by a mad fucking terrorist, used as collateral in a war game with the West. You might enjoy risking your neck as a human shield, but I find it rather unpleasant. Sitting around here is more of a mistake than what I'm planning, I assure you. So, be a good chap and go tell the guard what I've told you to say."

The doctor still didn't move. Caesar's eyes fell on the metal food tray lying on the foot of his bed, wondering how many swings would be needed to take the weak fucker's head off.

"I am just concerned that in your condition – with what we know – it may be a problem for you, and—"

"I told you, I don't want to discuss it." Caesar raised his hand, his finger shaking as he pointed at the timid prick. "I need to get out of here. Now. And this is my only chance. So, please do as I ask."

The doctor tilted his head to one side and sighed pointedly, as if to underline his misgivings. But it only wound Caesar up. The wet streak of piss.

"All right, look," he told him, softening his tone, trying a different tact. "What if I told you I was getting out of this shit pit, tonight, and you could come with me? Think of it, doc. Freedom."

"But at what cost? You know I hate Cyrus Heydari with every bone in my body, but I have devoted my life to helping others. I cannot risk an attack from the Americans if they believe there is unrest in the camp. It will be disastrous. People will die. I beg you, please don't do this."

Caesar swung his legs onto the tiled floor with a derisive snort. "Too late for all that. Plans are afoot." He turned to the window, to the small square of courtyard visible through the glass where a patch of light cast by Heydari's window had recently flashed on and off. "The only question now is will you be a help or a hindrance?"

He grabbed onto the steel bar across the end of the bed for support as he hauled himself to his feet. The doctor flinched as he stepped towards him, but held his ground.

"But, Mr Caesar, you are—"

"Enough. Will you do it?"

The doctor's shoulders sagged and he looked at the floor. "If there is no other way."

"There's no other way. Go now. Say exactly what I told you, word for word. They'll believe you and there'll be no comeback. That's if you really want to stay in this shithole."

"I have to. I am needed."

"Wimp," Caesar muttered to himself, as he staggered over to

the bed. Then, turning to address the doctor. "Quickly then, we haven't got much time."

"Fine. I will go."

He looked to have more to say but thought better of it. With a solemn nod he turned and left the cabin, letting the door swing shut behind him.

Once alone, Caesar eased himself down onto the side of the bed and pulled the thin bed sheets around his shoulders. A dry cough escaped him as he leaned forward, elbows resting on knees and head bowed, assuming the position of a sick and broken man. Through the cabin door and across the sleeping stable block, he could hear the low murmur of voices – the doctor speaking with the soldier on duty. With it being Wednesday, and the night shift, there was only one guard on detail – always the same when Heydari threw his little soirees – but that was why Caesar had planned it this way.

Beneath the cloak of implied sickness he let a sly grin tease at his lips.

Never take your eye off the ball, sweetie.

Not when Annihilation Pest Control operatives were at work.

Of course, by rights, he couldn't class Acid as one of his operatives any longer, yet despite everything she'd done since her departure, all the pain and suffering she'd caused him, all the revenue he'd lost, he still thought of her as his Acid Vanilla. His best work.

She'd called him her mentor, but the truth was she'd taught him just as much, chiefly that you didn't give in, no matter what the situation – or life – threw at you. At her best she was a deadly killing machine, but with a human heart still beating beneath the anger and bile. That was one of the reasons why Caesar had been so drawn to her in those early days. A lot of the people he met in the murder-for-hire business were cold, empathy-less nutjobs. Psychopaths, the criminally insane, or those so muted and warped by trauma and PTSD, their souls had all but vanished. Not her. She could take out a corrupt government official in the morning and be laughing and joking over oysters and champagne a few hours later. It wasn't so much she didn't care about the enormity of what she did, but that she simply saw it as her job. One that she was highly skilled at, paid well for, and provided her the life she wanted. Like Caesar himself, she appreciated the finer things in life, and if she had to kill to get those things, so be it. Life had dealt them both a shitty hand, but they weren't going to let something as boring as circumstance get in their way. They'd aimed for the moon and got so much more besides.

Yet even then at the height of their powers, Caesar knew to keep an eye on the young Acid lest she go too far off the rails. She was so different from all his other operatives. Creative and innovative in her thinking, yet more brutal and unyielding when she put her mind to it than anyone he'd ever worked with. A total wild card. Despite the intensity of her inner rage, she was intelligent and witty and such a deep thinker, constantly trying to understand why things happened, why people were a certain way, why the world was the way it was. It had given him cause for concern even then and was the main reason why he'd come down so hard on her in those early days. All in an attempt to dampen the more rebellious and empathetic aspects of her nature. Compassion and defiance would only ever be obstacles to his vision and he had hoped these troubling facets of Acid's nature had been quashed – she'd often tell him how she cared little for anyone but herself and only strived to be number one. Yet somewhere along the way she'd obviously had a change of heart.

But wasn't that just like the recalcitrant girl?

Bloody hell.

He closed his eyes, smiling at the memories as his heart contracted tightly in his chest. Because he also knew if things were different she would be dead right now. He'd loved her, cared for her, given her the world, and she'd betrayed him. He could see her side of the story, of course, could even imagine himself acting the same way if the circumstances were reversed, but that didn't change anything. You didn't get to do what she'd done and live.

Those were the rules. The problem was, things *were* different. Caesar's situation had changed considerably since Acid had first gone rogue and he'd put a price on her head. He needed her now more than ever. So he'd spare her life. Even if it did make him look soft.

"He is in here, please hurry."

The doc's voice outside the cabin door snapped him back to the present and he huddled under the thin blanket, limbs shaking as the door opened. The doctor entered first, gesturing for the duty guard to follow and pointing at Caesar's shivering form as if to say, *See, I told you.*

"What is it?" the guard asked. "Sick?"

Caesar raised his head to meet the man's eyes. He was one of the ones Heydari had recruited recently. Young boys from the local town who had turned their backs on a life herding mangy goat up on the hillside to join the prince's growing militia.

"Please," Caesar croaked. "Help me. Take me inside to your leader, the prince."

The guard didn't move. Caesar held up his hands, pleading with open palms, displaying to the bewildered kid how lowly and unthreatening he was.

"He may need better treatment than I can provide," the doctor added. "You should help him. He is Heydari's most important prisoner, is he not? Take a closer look at him. See for yourself how ill he is."

The doc was doing well. Better than Caesar had hoped. The guard lifted the Kalashnikov off his shoulder and leant it against the wall before turning around with his hands on his hips.

"Please," the doctor told him. "He needs help."

"Please," croaked Caesar.

Shaking his head, the young soldier stepped forward, perhaps looking to examine Caesar himself.

Only he never got chance.

Pushing himself up off the bed Caesar grabbed him by both shoulders and smashed his thick cranium into his face, making mincemeat of his nose. The kid stumbled backwards as a confused whimpering sound wafted out from somewhere deep inside of him. He might have been a new recruit but he was well trained, and despite the pain erupting through his sinuses he went for his pistol out of instinct. His fingers clawed at the clasp of his belt holster, managing to free the firearm. But unfortunately for him, Caesar had already stepped behind him and had him gripped around the neck and forehead.

"No," the doctor yelled, holding a hand out to him. "Don't do it."

Caesar squeezed on the kid's carotid artery. A few more seconds and he'd be out cold. But where was the fun in that? He grinned manically at the doctor before employing the swift flexion and extension required to sever a person's spinal cord. With a crack of cartilage and a pop of synovial fluid it was done. The doctor turned away as Caesar flung the guard's broken body onto the bed.

"I didn't know doctors were squeamish," he mused, reaching down and prising the pistol – a Russian TT-33 – from the dead guard's hand and stuffing it down the back of his waistband.

"You told me there would be no unnecessary deaths," the doctor snapped.

"Hmm. Define unnecessary."

"He was a young man, his head full of lies. This wasn't his fight."

"Yes, well," Caesar replied, shoving past him on the way to the door. "All's fair in love and war, and all that jazz."

He peered around the side of the door. The other inhabitants of the stable block were all asleep, or pretending to be. He squinted over at the main entrance. There was about an inch gap at the bottom between the door and the dust of the courtyard, and he could see the first light filtering through but nothing else – no shadows, no outlines of feet, no more guards.

"You sure I can't tempt you to come along for the ride, old boy?"

The doctor shook his head, his eyes on the dead kid. "Where will you go?"

"You know where I'm going."

Caesar held onto the doorframe, still peering out into the expanse of the old stable. "I've got a guy who can get me a passport and provide safe passage through Russia and Eastern Europe. But there'll be plenty of people on my trail – the CIA, FBI, Heydari's cronies, a bunch of triads I pissed off in Macau – so we'll see how I get on, I suppose. It doesn't help my case that one of the people helping me escape wants my head on a spike, but I'll take my chances rather than rot away in this dusty pit."

"Acid? She is going too?"

"She is," he replied, but didn't turn around. "Heydari is dead, by the way, just a heads up. I know you don't like killing and whatever, but there you go."

Behind him the doctor sniffed. "There are some deaths I do not mind so much."

"There we go, sweetie, I knew you had it in you." He glanced back over his shoulder, giving the doctor a beaming grin as he caught his eye. "I suppose I'll see you around, old boy. And if anyone asks, you never heard of me, okay? Never saw me." He held two fingers up to his eyes and pointed them at the doctor before letting out a bellowing laugh that sounded more joyous than it felt.

Leaving the cabin behind, he made his way across the room as a gentle knock echoed through from outside. Then, as he got closer, he heard a hushed voice drifting through the gap in the doors.

"Caesar, you there?"

His heart did a backflip. She'd done it. The clever little minx had done it.

But then, he'd never really doubted her.

She was Acid Vanilla.

His best work.

CHAPTER 31

A cid shot Kendis a steely look as she hopped from foot to
foot beside her. "Calm it down, will you? We're nearly
there."

"I don't know why we have to bring this dude with us," she
whispered back. "He's bad news, isn't he? You said it yourself."

Acid's annoyance at the moody American was growing by the
second. She squinted at her in the early dawn light. "Define bad
news."

"Oh I see, like that is it? You both as bad as each other. Villains
in arms."

"No," Acid hit back. "This is purely a symbiotic arrangement.
But sometimes a nefarious past can be a bonus. For you as well.
So keep your head down and your mouth shut and we might all
get out of this in one piece."

She slung the small canvas backpack she'd found in Heydari's
suite over her shoulders and knocked on the door again, this time
easing it open a touch. The fact it was unlocked was a good sign.
Through the gloom she saw the ungainly silhouette of her former
boss bundling towards her.

"Get a move on," she hissed.

As he got closer she saw how unsteady he was on his feet, his face gripped in a painful grimace.

"What happened?" she asked.

"Nothing," he snapped, as he hurried up the few steps and blinked in the morning air. "I'm stiff and weary after being cooped up for so long. What the buggering fuck is she doing here?"

She glanced at Kendis. "She's coming with us."

"No she bloody well isn't."

"Yes. She is." She stepped towards him. "Or you go on your own. See how far you get."

"I see. And what will you do, with no passport or money and no way of getting out of the country?"

"I'd manage. Somehow. Can you say the same?"

"Course I bleeding well can. Don't forget who you're talking to here, missy." He stuck a quivering finger in her face before turning it into a fist and slamming it into his other palm. "This is my plan, which means my rules, and *she* is not coming."

"Hey," Kendis butted in. "None of us are going anywhere unless you two stop bickering." She stepped between them, her eyes blazing as she scoped out the area. "There are no guards around but it doesn't mean they aren't going to come looking for us as soon as they realise we're gone. There have got to be other sentries."

Acid chewed on the inside of her cheek. But the kid was right. She returned her attention back to the big man. "She won't be a burden, I swear. She's a good girl, got ovaries of steel."

Kendis let out a bashful chuckle, but it was quickly drowned out by a loud huff from Caesar.

"Fine," he said. "But Princess Jasmine here is your responsibility."

Kendis glanced down at her blue robes. Then at Acid. "Some of us didn't get a chance to change."

"All right, kid. Not the time." She gave Caesar the nod which he returned.

"Okay, this way."

He was already on the move, heading out of the stable as swiftly as his cumbersome frame allowed. Acid watched him for a moment, her mind racing with possibilities, before Kendis grabbed her by the hand and they followed on behind, tracing a path along the east wall of the palace until they reached the corner. The perimeter wall was a few metres in front of them but standing at least ten foot high. Too high to climb.

"Keep up, girls," Caesar growled, as they caught up with him. "See, there it is, still in position. Little beauty."

He pointed over to where a trailer had been parked up at the foot of the wall, obscured in part by a mound of old barrels. The flatbed of the trailer was only around five feet off the ground but the surrounding wooden sides would provide another foot in height. It meant they had a four-foot scramble to the top of the wall, but with a little effort it was possible.

"You sure of this?" Kendis asked.

The question was widely ignored by her accomplices, Acid and Caesar both letting out silent huffs of annoyance. But her next statement not so much, as she pointed to the opposite corner of the stable block and hissed frantically: "Guard."

Acid turned to where an armed man, dressed in full fatigues and head cover, was patrolling the nearside of the stable block. He hadn't seen them yet, but he was heading their way.

"All right, hang back," Caesar said, herding them back around the corner out of sight. "I'll take care of him."

Sliding a gun from the back of his waistband, he flattened himself against the wall.

"You can't shoot him," Kendis said. "You'll only alert more of them."

"I'm not going to pissing well shoot him," Caesar replied, looking at Acid as he flipped the gun around so the handle was facing outwards. He shook his head conspiringly, but she wondered if the performance was as much for her benefit – letting her know he was carrying. But that was okay. She had a similar

Russian issue TT-33 in her backpack, procured from one of Heydari's snoozing henchmen. Unlike her old boss, however, she was keeping it under wraps. It was Caesar himself who'd taught her to seek the element of surprise, to be resourceful and inventive with her kills.

As the guard appeared around the corner Caesar stepped in his path and smashed the handle of the gun against his temple. At the same time, he grabbed the neck of the guard's rifle with his other hand and twisted it away from him. The shock of being pistol-whipped sent the man flailing into the building and Caesar followed up with two more blows, the second of which made a repellent splintering sound – a fractured eye socket perhaps, if he was lucky. That would have done the job, but as the guard's limp body slumped to the ground Caesar knelt over him and continued with a flurry of savage blows, displaying a side of him Acid had only been privy to on a handful of occasions. When Beowulf Caesar lost it, he really lost it. The expression on his face was chilling, his jaw rigid with emotion and his eyes blazing with hate and fury as he decimated the guard's skull – as though this unknowing man was the embodiment of everyone and everything that had ever wronged him. And now Acid could count herself in that list.

"Hey," she whispered, leaning over his shoulder. "I think he's dead."

Caesar hesitated, the gun raised. He stood upright, considering the bloody pulp at his feet before wiping the handle of his gun on the guard's trousers. "Best to be safe than sorry," he growled, shoving the gun back in his waistband. "Righto, ladies, shall we vacate this festering palace once and for all?"

They followed him over to the trailer and watched as he struggled to even get a leg up onto the flatbed. He was ungainly at the best of times, but Acid had never seen him this unfit and unsteady on his feet. It was just age perhaps, or the fact he'd spent the last ten years with his feet up behind a desk rather than out in the field. "Little help, maybe?"

Acid went to help him but stopped as Kendis whispered, "Wait." She grabbed the sleeve of Acid's jacket. "I'm thinking one of those will make getting over a lot easier."

She pulled her over to the stack of barrels, getting behind one of them and rolling it on its curve, testing the weight. Acid took it from her and did the same. Possibly it was once full of oil or water for the camp – or even that disgusting sweet wine they'd been drinking – but now it was empty.

"Good thinking," she replied.

The two of them rolled it over to the back of the trailer and with a struggle heaved it onto the flatbed, all the while watched by a bemused Caesar.

"Right. Me first," he told them plainly, grabbing the barrel and positioning it in front of him.

Acid sensed Kendis about to respond and shot her a sharp look to head her off. It wasn't the time. Poised and silent, she watched on as her old mentor scrambled up onto the barrel and grabbed wildly for the top of the wall. There was only another foot to clear now, but he still made a song and dance of it, tragic old bastard. It was grim to watch. Finally he got his huge ham-hock thigh over the top and sat astride the wall, casting his gaze over the palace grounds.

"Well, so long, you crazy fucking Arab. I can't say it's been a pleasure." He moved his attention back to Acid. "You did kill the warped fucker, didn't you?"

She chewed on her bottom lip, something inside of her urging her to lie, to tell him what he wanted to hear. "He's not going to be a problem," was all she could manage, and he saw straight through the ambiguous comment.

"Pathetic."

With his face distorted in a mocking sneer, he heaved his other leg over the top of the wall before lowering himself down and dropping with a heavy thud onto the dusty ground.

"You next," Acid told Kendis.

"No. You go."

Acid narrowed her eyes at her. "He won't bite, you know. He's a big softy, really."

The comment only strengthened Kendis' scowl. "Yeah? Tell that to the guard he just pulverised."

"Fine. I'll go. Shift over."

She clambered up onto the barrel and had her hands on top of the wall when she heard shouts behind her. Men's voices.

Shit.

A glance back to the far side of the courtyard revealed two more of Heydari's young foot soldiers looking over and pointing.

"Bollocks, we've been spotted." She leapt at the wall, pulling her body up onto the sharp ledge and swinging both legs over the top. Below her Caesar was holding his arms up, beckoning her to jump, while behind her she heard the distinct crack of an automatic rifle puncturing the calm of the dawn. She pushed off the wall and dropped to the ground. A sharp pain shot up through her heels on impact but she was clear. Caesar grabbed hold to steady her, and they both turned to watch for Kendis. More gunfire punctuated the silence, but it sounded to be a way off, the inexperienced guards perhaps shooting into the air as a warning or to wake up the rest of the men.

"Kendis," Acid called up. "Hurry."

She could see the kid's head visible above the wall, fingers grasping at the raw concrete. "Fuck," she rasped. "I'm stuck."

"What do you mean?"

"I've got my... shit... got my robes... they're caught on the barrel. On the metal rim, or a nail or something."

Acid could hear her grunting with effort. But also the guards, their shouts louder now.

Caesar grabbed at her arm, tugging her back.

"We have to go. Leave her."

"No. We can't."

"Oh, drop the bleeding heart routine. If we stay here, we're dead. Is that what you want?"

Up above them Kendis let go of the wall and turned around.

Acid imagined the trigger-happy soldiers shoving their rifles towards her.

"Kendis, I—"

"Just go. I'm okay," she hissed. Then louder, to the guards. "Don't shoot. Please."

Bloody hell.

Acid froze. Unsure what to do, and angry at herself for hesitating. This wasn't who she was. It wasn't what she did. Acid Vanilla was strong and hard and forthright. She was—

"Acid. Let's go."

She could see Kendis' hands in the air. It was over. They had her.

"I'll come back for you," she yelled, as Caesar pulled her away.

They made for a large mound of rocks running alongside a winding dirt track that led away from the palace. Through the haze of the morning air Acid could make out the outline of a town on the horizon. They'd made it. They were clear. Yet as she glanced up at her old boss, wheezing uncomfortably beside her – the man who'd been her mentor and guide for over sixteen years, who she loved and despised in equal measures, who she'd come here to kill and now had no reason not to – she couldn't help but think her problems were only just beginning.

CHAPTER 32

"Pissing hell. This way, quick." Caesar slid behind the safety of rock cover as a string of bullets traced their path, ricocheting off stone and sending eruptions of dust up from the road. Peering around the edge of the rock formation, he saw one of Heydari's foot soldiers had climbed up on the barrel after Kendis and was unloading a full magazine in their direction. But he was shooting indiscriminately and aiming over their heads from what Caesar could tell, showing his amateurishness. The limp prick.

"Hey, Kendis. I'll come back for you," Caesar mocked, as they continued on along the side of the road, hidden by the rocks. A few more errant shots pinged off the stone in their wake, but no one was giving chase. Not yet, at least.

"Piss off," Acid slurred, as she trudged on ahead of him.

It was brave of her, talking to him like that. Or damn foolish. He slowed his pace and silently slid the pistol out of his waistband, aiming at the base of her neck. One squeeze of the trigger and that would be it.

"Do it if you want," she called back, without turning around. "You'll probably be doing us both a favour. And the world."

"Jesus, you're a bag of laughs, aren't you?" He lowered the gun and shoved it back down his trousers before continuing on, catching up with her as she bent to tie her bootlace. "Still with the Dr Martens, I see? You remember when I bought you your first pair? Harrods, wasn't it? Cherry red in patent leather, if I recall."

She didn't look up. "They weren't *patent* leather."

"Well… anyway." He waited for her to stand before asking, "Did you mean what you said? That I'd be doing you a favour?"

She shrugged. "You know me, Ceez. Typical gloomy goth chick." She continued on her way, leaving him to stare after her.

"And what about me and you?"

"What about me and you?"

He followed, trying to match her pace without losing breath. Not easy in this heat. Not now. "You still want to kill me?"

She spun around, eyes blazing with a ferocity that still had the power to take his breath away. "How dare you," she told him. "How dare you be so fucking flippant about this. That was my mother. The only family I ever had. Do you think I'm happy about how things turned out? I had a bloody good life working for you. I know I had a wobble but I wasn't going to leave. You think I want to be a bloody civilian? Because I don't. My life is fucking mental right now, more than ever before. I don't know who I am from one day to the next. Don't know how to be in this new life. Or even if I want to be. So please, spare me the sarcasm, just this once."

The vitriolic outburst caught him off guard, but he promptly regained his stride, and his rage.

"But you did leave, didn't you?" he hit back. "The second you disobeyed my orders and spared that meddling hacker. Spook Hawkshit, or whatever the bleeding hell her name is. You had a job to do and you fucked it up so badly you put the entire organisation in jeopardy. Made me look like an idiot. An amateur." He looked down to see he was wagging his finger in her face, his whole hand shaking. He rubbed it against his forehead before wiping it on his trousers. "But then, rather than fucking off into the sunset never to be seen again, you came at me. Again and again. I've got every right to put a bullet in your fucking skull right now, missy."

"Well bloody well do it then, you old bastard." She marched towards him, over a foot shorter in height but coming on like a tsunami. "Go on then, *boss*. Do it. I told myself this would be a suicide mission anyway."

They locked eyes, potent energy swirling in the air between them. Neither of them moved. This was not how Caesar had expected this to go.

"They all told me you'd gone soft," he growled. "Raaz, Magpie, the lot of them."

"Yes, well, they all told me the same. Right before I killed them."

He countered the hardness in her eyes with a softness in his voice. "Why did you do it, Acid?"

"Do what?"

"Fuck up everything we had. Everything we'd worked so hard for."

She brushed a hand across her face and let out a deep sigh. "Look, I'm tired, okay? We both are. So, did you mean it, about helping me get back to London?"

"I did. I know someone up in the north. They can get us across the border into Armenia and then up through Georgia. From there another fellow can provide the relevant papers to get us home."

"And after that?"

It was his turn to shrug. "Who fucking knows? You kill me. I kill you. Or we just go our separate ways. Let the proverbial bygones be bygones. I suppose that's up to you."

She closed her eyes, as if in pain. "Yes, I suppose it is. Fine. For now let's get to the nearest village and find a safe place to rest for a few hours. Get some supplies too."

"Sounds like a plan," he replied. "Lead on, Macduff."

She gave him the sort of look a petulant teenager might give an embarrassing parent, but offered no further comeback as she set off walking. Caesar watched her for a few moments, hyper aware of the cold metal of the pistol against the skin on his back. The gun calling to him. He left it there and followed on behind.

CHAPTER 33

Night was drawing in by the time they reached the village and located a few bottles of water and a packet of salt biscuits. Acid had thought the rickety township much nearer when viewed from Heydari's palace, but without any other landmarks with which to measure relative distance the mind played tricks (hell, didn't it always). Their journey had also been made slower by the blazing unforgiving sun and the fact Caesar still seemed unsteady on his feet. Now, holed up in a derelict shack on the edge of the small village, with what appeared to be grenade damage up one wall and bullet holes peppering the hessian window shades, they could at last rest.

Acid sat cross-legged on the cracked tile floor and opened the packet of crackers. Shoving her whole hand in the box, she grabbed a palmful before throwing it into Caesar's eager waiting hands and crunching a couple of the salty biscuits. After a day of no food they tasted like prized sourdough. Without any money they'd stolen the meagre supplies from a grocery shack on the other side of the town, which again had taken longer and been more arduous than it should have as they tried to stay out of sight of locals. Cyrus Heydari was more of a crackpot egotist than the all-powerful ruler he made out, but he still had a strong hold over the region.

So why hadn't she killed the twisted bastard when she had the chance?

Things would be a lot easier right now if she had done. But then, she could say the same thing about Caesar.

Why the hell was he still alive?

The question had been echoing around her head for hours. Both of them had been in survival mode for most of the day, preserving energy by staying silent and keeping their heads down, so she'd been alone with her thoughts. And true to form, those thoughts had been chaotic and confusing and conflicted as hell. Then there were the bats, returning with gusto. An ever screeching pressure beating against her nervous system, pushing the needle on her mania further into the red.

She watched her old boss as he leant against the wall and munched noisily on a fistful of crackers, thinking back to all the times she'd vowed to kill him over the last two years.

Had she ever meant it?

Really?

Raaz, Magpie and the Sinister Sisters she couldn't care less about, but she'd killed Davros and Spitfire too and they were her friends (more than friends in Spitfire's case). What had happened to the fire and rage that spurred her on to kill them? Where was her crushing obsession for vengeance when she needed it the most? Why was this time so different?

But she knew the answer, didn't she?

Because they were right.

All of them.

She had gone soft.

She had one job to do – one last job – and she couldn't do it. She couldn't avenge her poor mum.

How terribly, terribly pathetic.

"Jesus bastard Christ. You look like you don't know whether to get a haircut or take a shit."

She raised her head to see Caesar staring at her, speaking through a mouthful of crackers.

"Come on, sweetie, cheer up. We're safe. For now."

"Are we?"

"Safe as we can be." He held his hands up. "We're in agreement, yes? No more of this revenge nonsense. We both fucked up. But it's done with. In the past. We need each other, Acid. You know it's true."

"You can definitely guarantee safe passage back to England?"

He rolled his eyes dramatically. "Yes. I've told you I can. But that's not what I meant. We need each other on a deeper level. We always have. I know I hurt you and I shouldn't have involved your mum. So listen, I'm only going to say this once – and it's the first time I've said it since I was a teenager – but I'm sorry."

She swallowed, searching her memory for a time she'd heard him apologise. She couldn't remember any. *Never explain, never apologise*, that was his motto. And now here he was, this once powerful and still vindictive man, feared the world over, saying he was sorry. But then, he'd never been anything but Caesar to her. The man who saved her from a life of low-rent boyfriends and supermarket checkout jobs. She'd always been clever, but the sort of girls who spent their formative years in homes for the psychologically dangerous didn't get decent jobs or nice husbands. They didn't get anything.

And he'd saved her.

Given her the world.

Plus, he'd always had her back. Stuck up for her whenever she needed it – to Raaz, Magpie, whoever. She knew he cared about her. But what he'd done… Could she…? Would she forgive him?

"Bleeding ball sacks, the face on you," he wheezed, easing himself down to the floor. "If looks could kill I'd be dead already. Look, if you want to do it then, here, take this rotten Russian piece and get done with it. I'm sick of looking over my shoulder, to be honest." He slid the gun across the tiles at her before closing his eyes and letting his huge head loll back against the raw plaster of the wall. He looked exhausted.

Acid eyed the gun but didn't flinch. "You don't seem yourself," she said. "What's wrong?"

His eyes snapped open, face distorted in shock. "Fuck off. I'm just tired. Sick of all this bullshit. Worrying about where you're going to pop up next. It's gone on long enough, kiddo. So do it. Or don't. But if you don't, lets pissing well put it to bed and move on with our lives."

She considered his words. He was right. It had gone on long enough. And here she was, still not able to pull the trigger. Or not wanting to. All the chaos she'd caused, all the people who'd been hurt, and for what? Caesar was still alive and she was more confused and fucked up than ever. She thought of Spook, of Vinh, even Danny – all the people who'd almost died being in her orbit.

"Do you think Kendis will be okay? And Lars?" The words were out of her mouth before she realised who she was talking to. She lowered her head. "They won't be made to pay for our escape?"

Caesar shrugged. "Why do you care? They're simple pawns in a much bigger game, my dear."

She shook her head as she twisted the top off a bottle of water. It was a typical thing for him to say, but it was also something she'd have said herself only a few years earlier. Before she'd left his side. Before she'd gone soft. Because what else would you call it? She was no longer that same cold, callous killer, ready to obliterate anyone in her path at the drop of a hat. It wasn't like she could put her finger on when or why, but somewhere along the way something had switched inside her and she didn't have a clue how to turn it off. But it ached and it was confusing, and some days it was all she could do to keep going.

"Bollocks, I'd kill for a drink," Caesar said with a sigh, as though reading her own thoughts.

She placed the water bottle down and reached for the strap of the backpack she'd been carrying. Dragging it towards her, she unzipped it. "Funny you should say that," she told him, pulling out the two bottles of wine she'd appropriated from Heydari's suite. She didn't have a corkscrew, but being cheap plonk both had screw tops. Small mercies.

Caesar's eyes lit up as she rolled one over to him, and he snatched it up with more sprightliness than he'd displayed the previous three days combined. "You little beauty," he said, twisting off the lid.

Acid opened the second bottle and they drank in silence. The wine was indeed sickly and thick, like bad port, but the alcohol burn in her throat and sinuses was apparent, and for now that was all she needed.

Caesar broke the silence first. "Do you remember Argentina?"

"What, Mateo and Matias?"

"Mateo and Matias," he repeated, wistfully. "The lovely Ferrari brothers. What a couple of crazy fuckers they were. Spiteful buggers with it."

"Not after we'd finished with them." She drank, remembering the job. One of her first partnered with Caesar, back when he was still working in the field. A hands-on leader. The best kind. Before he got power and money hungry, not to mention fat and lazy. She laughed. "You skinned one of them, didn't you?"

"Matias, yes. But only his back." He lifted his shoulders comically. "Not my fault, he wouldn't give us the whereabouts on his brother. Who was the client then? I forget."

"Someone high up in their government. We had to make it look like a hit from a rival cartel. The Koala Krew. Something like that."

Caesar nodded. "Kolla Krew. That was it," he said, lifting the bottle to his lips.

Acid raised her chin as she watched him. "Don't worry. I'm not going to kill you. Not here."

"Meaning?"

She pointed at him. "Your hand. It's shaking."

"Oh, that." He brought the bottle down to his lap. "A trapped nerve in the old shoulder. Doesn't hurt, just annoying." He glared at her, a grin cracking his face. "I'm not scared of you, sweetie. Never have been, never will be."

"Right. That why you've been hiding out in Iran for the past few months?"

"Don't flatter yourself. I came here because I believed the clown prince would help me get things back on track. The plan was agreed. I'd work for him for a few months. Then, with his backing, bring my new vision into fruition – the Nomadic Assassins Network."

Acid rolled her eyes and glugged back a mouthful of wine. He'd been going on about that even before her abrupt exit from the organisation. "So what happened? The Great Showman Beowulf Caesar failed to sell him on the idea? Surely not."

He sneered. "You met the odd little fucker, with his plastic face and messiah complex. Turned out he's got his own agenda going on. Thinks he's some sort of saviour to his people. Plus he's loaded up to the eyeballs, so not as driven by money as I was hoping."

"I see. And what does drive him?"

"Oh, that's a long story."

"We've got all night."

He waved the idea away. "Do you remember what happened with the Ferrari Brothers, after Mateo caught up with us?"

"I remember he wasn't happy."

"He almost took your head off. He was about to until I took him out – with an expertly placed bullet, if I recall, right between those big brown eyes of his. You're welcome."

With a snort she took another drink. She remembered all right. Remembered being terrified, the sharp blade at her throat, the knee pressed against the small of her back. She'd thought her time had come. Dead at twenty-two. No life at all. She also remembered the intense wave of relief as Caesar appeared and without missing a beat blew Mateo's brains out the back of his head.

"I'd have handled him. Somehow."

It was Caesar's turn to snort. "I saved your bloody life. And not for the last time, I might add."

"Piss off. When else?"

"Belfast. Washington. Remember?"

She did. But didn't let on. Instead she swallowed back more wine. It tasted better with every mouthful, and with every mouthful this miserable, messed-up situation seemed more and more normal.

But really it was normal. For her, at least. She was back in the field, outgunned but not outplayed, with her mentor by her side. Take away her mum's murder, and the blinkered revenge mission she'd been on the last two years, and it was a typical day at the office.

"I'll give you Belfast and Argentina," she muttered. "But Washington is pushing it."

"There have been other times."

"Whatever."

They drank in silence before Acid sat up at the sound of male voices nearby. With her breath frozen in her chest, she leaned into the source of the sound, listening but not able to pick out anything except a low rumble.

"What is it?" Caesar asked, but she held her hand up for him to be quiet.

Staying low, she crab-walked over to the window. From here the voices were more distinct but they were speaking Farsi. She raised her head up to the window, peering out through one of the bullet holes in the hessian cover to see four men standing across the street from her. A thin local man wearing ragged clothes had his back to her and was surrounded by three much larger men, all dressed in familiar combat fatigues and black face coverings.

Bollocks.

As the local man gesticulated wildly with bony arms, she assessed the threat. Each of Heydari's foot soldiers was carrying an assault rifle at waist height and had pistols holstered in their belts. The one standing closest to her also had three US-issue M67 grenades strapped to his torso. She remained at the window, her only movement coming from the hand she waved in the air behind her, informing Caesar to stay down, to keep quiet. A second passed. And another. The soldiers were shaking their heads, looking as if they were ready to move on. But then the local man turned around. And with great confidence pointed straight at their building.

Shit.

CHAPTER 34

Acid grabbed up Caesar's pistol and was over to him in two strides. Heaving him up to a standing position, she shoved the gun into his hand before rushing to the backpack and pulling out her own TT-33.

"Where did you get that?" Caesar rasped, as she held it up.

"Where do you think?" she said, sliding along the wall until she reached an open doorway with a thin corridor beyond. "You see. I could have killed you at any point in the last fourteen hours. But I didn't. Now follow me."

They moved along the corridor, past two internal doors that faced each other half-way along, towards a wooden backdoor at the far end. Acid yanked at the handle. It was locked. She barged against the door with her shoulder. Booted the lock. It didn't budge.

"Here, let me try," Caesar growled, grabbing her by the shoulder and pulling her back. He went at it the same as her, shoving all his weight against it before smashing a heavy foot down on the handle. The result was the same. "Pissing fuck."

The sound of boots crunching on broken tiles snapped their attention back to the front room. Caesar glared at Acid, his face stern. He gestured to the two internal doors and moving back up the corridor they took one each, Acid leaning on the handle and silently easing hers open as Caesar did the same on the one opposite. As the soldiers' footsteps echoed through the empty front room, the pair slid into their respective foxholes to wait.

Acid checked her weapon. She had no experience with these Russian handguns and the last thing she needed right now was a hang fire or a dud load. She checked the mag and cocked one into the chamber before looking up into the unblinking eyes of her old mentor standing across from her ten feet away. From his position he had a better view of the front room and, as she watched with her breath tight in her chest, he peered around the doorframe, risking a quick glance before whipping himself back against the wall. Catching her eye he held three fingers up and then both hands, miming holding a rifle to his chest.

Three of them. All in shooting position.

She noticed the trapped nerve was still playing up, his hands shaking worse than ever. But maybe fear was playing some part in it. This was the first real action the old man had seen in some time. She hoped he could handle himself, could still fire a decent shot. Either way they'd find out soon enough.

As she moved backwards into the room Acid's boot heel hit something heavy, and with a furtive glance behind her she saw it was an old wooden chest. It wasn't big enough to hide behind but it could provide some cover, give her a split-second perhaps. In these situations that was often all one needed. Shifting with quiet stealth around the back of the chest, she lifted the lid and positioned herself on one knee behind it with the TT-33 held in both hands, aimed at the doorway.

A second went by.

She saw the muzzle of the first rifle as it aimed from room to room, followed by its owner, a tall, broad-shouldered man. The black scarf wound around his whole head meant only a sliver of his eyes could be seen. She pressed her finger against the trigger. If she played this wrong she was dead. She might take one of them, but the other two would blow her insides out before she switched her aim. The bats screeched as the first soldier stepped into the room.

Their eyes locked.

Time stopped.

A loud crack permeated the silence as the soldier's head jerked back in a cloud of red mist. Acid had fired first, but only by a breath. She ducked as a hail of his bullets pock-marked the wall behind her. Hitting the deck, she squeezed off three more rounds, zipping them up the next man as he bounded into the room. But this time her aim was off and the shot wasn't fatal. The soldier yelled, stumbling into the wall, but lacing the room with a heavy onslaught of bullets that sent her scuttling back behind the chest, where she pressed herself against the ground, trying to disappear.

This was not good.

Not good at all.

The bats' screeches grew louder and more all-encompassing as plasterboard and dust shattered off the walls and ceiling. She gripped tight to the handle of the TT-33 but there was no way she could risk exposing herself to take a shot. The incessant rat-a-tat of the sub-machine gun continued, shaking the room, shaking Acid's resolve too. This was it. She was dead. She knew it. He was going to—

Huh?

She jolted her attention back to the moment as a deeper sonic crack disrupted the staccato trill of automatic fire. She heard shouting. Another gunshot.

Then there was silence.

Keeping her head down she remained in her hiding spot behind the chest. Was he waiting for her to show herself? Playing with her? Or perhaps he was here to capture not kill – gearing up to take her back to Heydari where her real fate would begin, something nastier and much more painful. Her troubled mind raced with images and ideas, useless, intrusive thoughts fogging her judgement, igniting a rage inside of her and making her want to scream. To rage at the light. At the bats. At her own stupidity. At the—

"He's dead, sweetie," a voice purred a few inches from her ear. "They all are."

She raised her head over the side of the chest to see the two men slumped against the wall on adjacent sides of the room. Blood and brain matter arced across the plasterboard.

"There's another in the far room with half his head missing," Caesar added with a wink, holding out his hand. "I'd call that four."

"What?" She grabbed his big hand and heaved herself to her feet. "There were three of them."

"No. Four times. That I've saved your life."

"Oh, do shut up."

He laughed, but why wouldn't he? The way she'd said it was pithy. Playful, even. Like nothing had changed between them. And maybe it hadn't. Caesar was the only person she'd ever met who she could one hundred percent relate to. He understood her more than anyone else. They came from the same place emotionally and spiritually (even geographically, give or take a few Tube stops). It felt good to have him in her corner again. She felt, well… comfortable. Safe.

And that made her hate herself even more.

Conflicted?

That word didn't even begin to describe the torment going on between her ears.

"We should get going," Caesar said, moving to a small window on the back wall and peering out. "If the locals are talking, we aren't safe here."

Acid shoved the pistol into her waistband, no point hiding it now. "You think there'll be more of them?"

He turned from the window. "I know there wi— Oh, pissing hell."

Acid followed his gaze towards the soldier slumped against the wall. He wasn't dead. Not quite. He looked up at them with red, mocking eyes as his hand fell open, releasing a round metal object that rolled into the centre of the room.

"Grenade," Caesar roared.

Grabbing Acid by the arm, he yanked her out of the room. They pushed off against the corridor wall bursting through into the front room and making for the door. Acid counted in her head, reckoning they had about three seconds before the place went up. The bat chorus was deafening as she ran across the room. All she could see was the rectangle of light standing against the dark walls. She gritted her teeth. Leaned into the run. Looking up, she saw Caesar was already through the door. She burst into the street after him as a loud boom ripped through the building and a whoosh of blast air sent her diving into the dirt. She covered her head with her arms as rubble rained down on her followed by something large and heavy. She figured a piece of timber at first, a chunk of doorframe perhaps, but then it moved and she realised it was an arm. Caesar, leaning over the top of her. Protecting her.

"Get off me," she said, once the last of the debris had fallen.

With a grunt he lifted himself off her and she propped herself up onto her elbows to take in the shack. If it was run down before, you could now class it as decimated. Half the front wall remained but the rest was rubble.

"See?" Caesar yelled at the local man still watching from across the street, the one who'd given them up. "That's what happens when you get involved with that freak. Now piss off, you snivelling scrote."

The old man considered them with sad eyes, before lowering his head and shuffling away. They waited until he'd disappeared around a corner then got to their feet and brushed themselves down.

"Bastards," Caesar growled. "Think they can get the better of us? Not a bleeding chance. Not with us on the same team."

He had a point, but something was bothering Acid. "What did you mean back then, about there being more of them?"

"Don't you think there will be?"

"Possibly, but it was the way you said it, like you knew something I didn't." She glared at him the longer he took to answer. "What is it, Caesar? Tell me."

He wouldn't look at her, instead running his tongue over one of his gold canines the way he always did when considering his options.

"Fine," he said. "Let's find somewhere we can lie low first, then I'll explain. But I'll be honest with you, sweetie, you aren't going to like it."

CHAPTER 35

Despite the frustration and anger tearing at her insides Acid held her tongue, biding her time until she knew they were safe. But once new shelter was found (another run-down shack, this time on the outskirts of the village away from any other buildings), she didn't hold back.

"Go on then," she said. "Tell me what's going on. Shit. I knew there was more to this. I should have thought. I—"

"Calm it down, kiddo." Caesar sighed, shuffling over to a battered sofa, the only piece of furniture in the room, and easing himself down on it. "It's not like that."

"No? What is it like?"

He met her eye, tonguing at his gold canines some more as he considered her. "The thing is," he began, his voice uncharacteristically quiet, "I wasn't just a human shield for Heydari."

She crossed her arms and leaned one shoulder against the wall. "I thought that's why he had us all there?"

"That's why you were there, and the others. But like I told you, I thought me and the clown prince there were going to work together, be partners. But the snide bastard double-crossed me." He sat forward, rubbing at his palm with the thumb of his other hand. "I let it slip, you see, about the Yanks being on my case. Idiot that I am. It turns out Cyrus isn't as daft as he looks."

"I don't get it. What are you saying? If you weren't there to protect him, why was he keeping you prisoner?"

"The fucker's been trying to make a deal with the CIA. He's requested they release six prisoners – ISIS militants – in return for handing me over. I was a bargaining tool."

Acid frowned, the implications whirling around in her brain. "And the CIA were going for this?"

"Apparently. They've been finalising it for the last few weeks."

"So… what? Where does that leave us?"

Caesar puffed out his cheeks. "No change. We just have to watch our backs. He's got a lot at stake, he won't want to lose his main play – yours truly."

Acid let her hands drop to her sides as a nasty feeling bubbled in her guts. "But if he does lose you he's got nothing to trade. What does that mean for Kendis and the others?"

Caesar raised his eyebrows in apparent acknowledgement of her dawning realisation. "Well that's the thing, isn't it? Without me I imagine he's going to use the remaining prisoners as leverage. Release the ISIS lot or I start cutting off heads, sort of thing."

"You think he will?"

"Oh yes. Don't let the playboy lifestyle and whimsical demeanour fool you. He's an evil fucker when he wants to be. One reason why I thought we'd work perfect together." He grinned at her, but even he couldn't make it land. Not with the white-hot rage surging through her system.

"You fucking bastard," she hissed. "You knew this would happen. You've put a death sentence on Kendis and Lars and all the others."

"Oh piss off."

"They're innocent."

"Are they? Like I said to you back in London, there are no innocent people, not in this world. Come on, Acid, we have to look after number one. I thought I'd drummed that into you enough. We are what matters. Me and you. Together we can get out of this rotten country and back to Blighty. Back to freedom."

"They're going to die. Because of you. Because of me." She whipped the pistol out of her waistband and had it pressed against his skull before she even knew what she was doing.

But it was right.

The bats said it was right.

The time had come to do what she should have done the second she saw him.

"You evil shit. You don't deserve to live. All you do is destroy people."

She twisted the muzzle of the pistol into his skin, focusing on the sweat pouring off his brow. Anything to distract herself from the knowledge she could be talking about herself right now.

"I can't let the Americans get their hands on me," he growled. "Neither of us can."

"But you lied to me. As soon as the Americans realise you've gone, what's to stop them storming the palace? They won't know Kendis is in the main building. She could be at real risk. And Lars, he jeopardised everything to help me. He's helped you too, hasn't he?"

Caesar huffed out a contemptuous sigh. "Like I say, all's fair—"

"Oh shut up," she hissed. "You know, I used to look up to you so much. I thought you were amazing. A proper gentleman, with ideals and vision. But look at you – you're nothing but a coward. Shaking where you sit. A self-centred deserter with nothing to back up your pathetic arrogance. I may have gone soft, but you've gotten old, and greedy."

He hadn't flinched once as she ground the end of the gun into the fleshy furrows between his eyebrows. Now his mouth drooped into a bitter sneer.

"All those people in the stable block, they knew the risks. Doctors Across Borders? The Peace Corps? I'm sorry, kiddo, but you make your bed… It's shitty, I know, but it's the way it is. Dog eat dog and all that."

A surge of righteous indignation spiralled through her body, but it was aimed at herself as much as him. She'd saved his life at the expensive of everyone else. She felt her eyes filling up but didn't dare blink in case a rogue tear fell and exposed her. Her finger quivered on the trigger.

Fucking hell.

What was wrong with her? Why couldn't she do it?

Caesar stared up at her. "I had no choice," he rasped.

"There's always a choice, Ceez. That's what I've realised over the last few years. And you *chose* to fuck everyone over. Like always. Well it's time to pay for what you've done." She adjusted her grip on the pistol. "This has to happen."

"Go on then," he said. "Do it. If it has to happen I'd rather it was here than in some CIA black site."

The words took her by surprise and she hesitated. "But it wouldn't be like that, would it? Because you'd make a deal. You've got a lot of shit on a lot of important people – you'd wriggle out of it, same way you always do."

"Not anymore. I don't have time."

"Time? What are you talking about?"

His eyes fell closed. "I'm dying, Acid."

The muscles in her arm loosened, but she kept the gun raised. "We're all fucking dying. Since when has that made any difference?"

He blew out a sigh as he looked up at her. "Huntingdon's disease. You wondered why I had those tablets you used on Heydari. They were for me. I persuaded him to get them for me whilst he held me captive. I've got to say, that was a stupid bloody move on his part."

"Right. Well…" She shifted her hand on the gun, its grip slipping beneath her damp palm. "So we get you some more pills, you'll be fine."

"I wish it was that easy. I've been taking them for the last couple of years, but they only curb the outward symptoms, the shakes, the unsteadiness." He held his hands up to show her, both of them trembling now. "There is no trapped nerve. It's a neurological condition caused by the Huntington's. Horrible fucking disease, one of those slow debilitating bastards."

Acid opened her mouth to speak but found herself lost for words. She dropped her arm by her side and sank onto the couch beside him. They both stared at the wall in front of them for what seemed like forever.

"How long have you got?" she asked, when the silence threatened to consume them.

He sniffed. "About five years, if I'm lucky. And careful with my lifestyle. Which I don't plan on being."

"Shit."

"You said it, kid." He laughed, but there was little humour behind it. "It's weird, I always knew there was a strong possibility I'd get it. It's genetic, you see. My old mum died of it when I was young. I could have had a test, but I chose not to. Been like the Sword of bastard Damocles hanging over my head my entire life. But in a way it's what drove me as well. There's nothing like the grim reaper looming in the background to spur you on, to not waste a second. But now, here we are."

"Yes. Here we are," Acid whispered. "I don't know what to say. I was so ready to kill you. A part of me still wants to – needs to. I need closure, but… not like this. Fuck…"

"You're probably going to say I took that away from you too." He nudged her arm. "You'd be right, I suppose. Believe me, a bullet from you would be a blessing compared to what I've got coming. I really thought that was it back in Berlin, you know. You should have done it then."

"I know I bloody well should have. I've been telling myself that for the last eighteen months. But, you know… I've gone soft, haven't I?"

"You were always soft on me, hot stuff. But I can't say I was much different where you were concerned." He barked a cough into the room before sucking back a deep breath and speaking through the exhale. "Yes. It's been quite the ride. Never wanted it to end like this though. Going out in a whimper. But, you know, swings and roundabouts. At least I'm still Adonis-like. Leave a good-looking corpse and all that."

She snorted. "I'm glad you've kept your sick sense of humour."

"What can you do? We like it that way. Don't we, sweetie?"

She couldn't help but smile, though she turned to the wall as she did.

"You know the German's have a word for it?" he continued. "*Witzelsucht.* Means 'wit sickness'. A compulsion to crack jokes most people find offensive. Got a nice ring to it, I think."

Acid's smile grew but she still couldn't find any words. None of the right ones, at least. All she managed was a whispered, "Bloody hell."

"I know. It's a bit of a head mangler, isn't it? For what it's worth though, cookie, I am sorry for how things turned out. I never wanted me and you to break up. You were my number one. And I do care for you."

"Despite putting a price on my head?"

He nudged into her. "Despite putting a price on your head."

"And sending me to that bloody island?"

"I told you, that was Raaz's doing. I couldn't tell her no, could I? But I wasn't happy about it. Why do you think I kicked her off the chopper?"

"Come off it. For me?"

"Well… and she was getting too big for her boots. Meddling mare. Listen, kid, I was angry as hell, but I never wanted it to play out like this. Not after I'd calmed down. Shit happens, I know that. Especially when people like me and you are involved. Creative, incendiary types. But what could I do? I was already on the back foot with everyone. Everyone you hadn't killed, at least. I mean, bloody hell, Acid, you wiped them all out. Davros, Magpie… Spitfire even. That one must have hurt."

She bit her lip. "I don't think about it. I was blinded by fury at the time. A lot more than I am now. I guess the rage faded somewhere along the way."

"I've missed you these last few years. You were my girl."

"Spook thinks you groomed me."

"Spook can fuck off. I made you."

"Isn't that the same thing?"

"Pfft. Who knows." He relaxed into the couch, letting his head roll onto the back cushion. "Would you change anything?"

Bloody hell.

That was the question, wasn't it?

She'd considered it often since leaving Annihilation, but hadn't come up with a proper answer. Sitting here now, with Caesar beside her, she could probably say she wouldn't. Because if she did, who would she be now? She shook her head, hoping it might disperse the confusing thoughts. It was enough to send anyone crazy.

"It's shit, isn't it?" she whispered.

"Yes, my dear, it most certainly is shit. But can you see now why I couldn't risk another second in captivity? I have to die the way I lived my life. Free. Away from the constraints of iron bars or laws or other people's morals."

Acid understood. It didn't make her feel any better though. Kendis had shown herself to be annoying as hell, but she didn't deserve to die. Plus, she'd told her she'd come back for her.

"So we leave Kendis and the others at the mercy of the crazy prince while we leg it over the border?"

"Pretty much. No other options, are there? Unless you're seriously considering storming the palace to rescue them." He laughed, but when she didn't respond he twisted around to ogle her. His face told her everything she needed to know about his feelings towards that idea.

"It could work," she said.

"No, it bleeding well could not," he spluttered. "I mean, I

always loved your plucky never-say-die attitude, Acid, but not when it borders on suicide."

She turned away. He was speaking the truth. It was insane to think the two of them could take on Heydari and his soldiers. If only she'd killed him when she had chance. But as always, that was on her. She'd hesitated when she should have been forthright. Faltered in the face of death.

Wilting back onto the couch, she let the pistol flop onto her lap. Maybe she should still do it, put a bullet through Caesar's head and then her own. Put them both out of their misery.

She sighed. "You're right. It's a stupid idea. I've not got it in me."

Caesar twisted around, arching an eyebrow at her. "Hey, kid, that's not what I said."

She scowled. "What do you mean?"

"Don't get me wrong, it's a stupid idea – a fucking ridiculous one – but you not having it in you? No. That's not true."

"It's what you keep saying. What everyone said – Davros, Spitfire, Magpie – that I've gone soft. And you're right. They were right. I'm soft as shit. Useless. You know, I almost didn't have it in me to kill Magpie. The person I hated most of all. I mean, I'd have happily killed the sour-faced harpy back when I was still working for you."

Caesar chuckled. "Yes, and I probably would have allowed it. She was rather a joyless tit, wasn't she? Face like a slapped arse. But you're dead wrong, sweetie. That was only trash talk. Me trying to wind you up. Unnerve you. You're Acid Vanilla, kid. You might not be the deadliest female assassin in the world anymore, but you're still the most dangerous bitch I've ever met. And I'm counting myself in that. You've always been hard as nails and a top tactician, and as far as I can see nothing's changed." He leaned into her, lowering his voice conspiringly. "You haven't gone soft, Acid. It's much worse than that. You've grown a fucking conscience."

"Eugh. You think?"

"I know it, kid. But doesn't mean you aren't still a force to be reckoned with. Even with sissy civilian morals you can still get the job done. Any job. If you put your mind to it."

The words sent a prickle of electricity rippling down her arms and legs. She'd told herself the same thing many times over the last few months, but it always felt like she was forcing the matter, engaging in the sort of New Age self-talk crap which never worked. But to hear it coming from her old mentor, it offered renewed vigour.

She looked at him. "Are you talking yourself into this? You saying we go for it?"

"It really could be suicide."

"I know. But that's still closure."

He chuckled silently. "One way of looking at it."

"So you'll help me – to rescue Kendis and the others?"

He looked away and shook his head at something only he could see. "On one condition."

"Go on."

"I'm doing this as one last hurrah. A bit of a giggle. Okay? I am *not* doing it because I care one iota about those pathetic fuckers in that smelly old stable. Not even the Norwegian doctor. So please, do not frame it as such. Ever."

"Fair enough, you heartless bastard."

He raised his hands in the air. "Pissing fuck, what the hell am I doing? You know I'm not the man I was, don't you? Look at me. Whatever goes down, I'll give it my best, but it's going to be you doing most of the heavy lifting."

"I understand." She got to her feet and held out her hand. "So are we doing this?"

He puffed out his cheeks. "I suppose it will be rather enjoyable to work alongside my old protégé one last time. Plus, the prospect of seeing Heydari's ridiculous head on a spike does get me excited." He took her hand and she helped him to his feet. "So yes, Acid, my dear, I suppose we are bloody well doing this."

CHAPTER 36

"I am asking you one last time," Cyrus yelled in his sister's face. "Was it you?"

Talisha stared up at him with brown, oval eyes. For once she didn't look half-asleep or disinterested. But there was nothing like holding a knife to someone's throat to get their attention.

"Of course it was not us," she hissed, looking to Sanaa for back up. "We would not betray you. You are our prince, our brother. Our leader."

Cyrus could see the reflection of his face in her dilated pupils. Dilated because she was afraid, but that was exactly what he wanted. Scared people told no lies. Not to him, the rightful Prince of Islam. Not with his reputation. He released his grip on her hair and lowered the knife. It had left a red pressure line of broken blood vessels across her throat.

He sheaved the knife but returned to his sister with an angry wagging finger. "So who was it told them of my situation?"

It was bad enough that miserable woman had doped his men and left him tied up like an animal for his sisters to find. But to hear this now, with everything else going on, it made his blood fizzle with an intense rage the like of which he'd never experienced. It wasn't fair. He'd worked so hard.

"All we know is the American troops are close. Readying themselves to seize the palace." Sanaa's eyes darted between him and her sister as she spoke. "We must assume they have had word that you no longer have the same leverage. And no shield close. But this is clearly impossible, unless—" She swallowed, dipping her head as Cyrus held his hand up to her.

"Enough."

He'd suspected there was a rat in the palace for some time. You didn't get to be who he was, where he was, without some detractors. Someone had tipped the Americans off. But if it wasn't his sisters, then who? He turned to the window, making a tight fist with both hands as he looked out over the palace courtyard.

Damn them all to hell.

It simply wasn't fair. He'd worked so hard for this. Despite his lowly upbringing he'd always thought of himself as a real visionary, a man blessed not only with a ruthless mentality and a cunning intellect, but someone who was artistic and thoughtful too. In his mind he was the perfect candidate to take Iran, and even Islam, into the modern age. He had a huge library, stacked floor to ceiling with books on war, on strategy, on self-mastery. He'd read each one more than once, watched countless videos on YouTube on how to be a good leader, how to be confident, how to get respect, how to give amazing speeches that inspired people. He'd done the work, done the reading, and now, finally, he was reaping the rewards. He wasn't going to let them take that away from him. Not today. Not by these American devils. His vision for the region was strong and unyielding, the same way he was. He would die before he surrendered.

"I worry it is worse than we thought, my lord," Talisha whispered, not meeting his eye as he turned from the window to acknowledge her.

"Go on."

"We have intercepted an encrypted message stating you have chemical weapons in the palace. And that you are readying them to use on neighbouring townships. This is what the Americans believe."

"What?" Cyrus barked, his anger taking physical form as it bristled down his arms and up his spine. "This is nonsense. I love my people, I would not do this to them. I am a modern leader. A prince. These infidels put me in the same ring with butchers like Gaddafi and Hussein. But they know what they're doing, don't they?" He walked over to them, wringing his hands together to stop him from hitting something. "They are controlling the narrative for the world stage. Telling these lies about me so they can ruin my vision, my plans, and all the while be seen as the good guys. But I will not allow it. You see it, don't you?"

The sisters gulped audibly. "See what, my brother?" Talisha asked.

"They want to paint a picture of me as a crazy tyrant, holed up in his palace of riches whilst his people suffer around him. At his own hands."

The anger surging around his body intensified as his sisters both looked at the floor. Why didn't they look him in the eye? Did they believe these falsehoods themselves? Cyrus ground his teeth, unsure what to do with so much rage burning under his skin.

"You think I am crazy?" he asked, before catching himself and taking a deep breath, working on keeping his tone deep and his voice steady. Like an authoritative leader should sound. "You really think I'm crazy?"

The sisters exchanged glances. "Of course not," Sanaa told him. "You are an amazing man, my lord, we all know this. But perhaps it is time we put down our weapons and surrendered. Accept peace. True peace. We do not want to die."

"No one will die except for those dogs," he shouted into the domed ceiling, before lowering his head to take them in. "Sisters, please. You must have faith in me. We have done too much good work here to let them take it from us."

"What good work?" Talisha asked, a tinge of annoyance in her voice. "You sit around and drink and smoke hashish.

You hurt those who talk against you, and shield yourself with western prisoners. But for what end, my brother? I love you, but I do not understand you. What are we fighting for?"

"For our country. For our region. For... for... acknowledgement. For people to see us and know we are important. That we have created a better life for ourselves. You want to be the daughters of a poor goat-herder all your lives? Or the sisters of a prince?"

Talisha and Sanaa looked at each other as if working out how to respond. It just riled him further. He'd thought they understood him, but no one did. No one had the clarity of vision like he did. No one.

He marched over to the door of his suite and swung it open, surprised to see his three most trusted soldiers standing in the corner, muttering to themselves. He glared at them until they noticed him and shut up immediately.

Khak da saret.

He'd expected them to be standing to attention, weapons drawn and ready for action. Did they not understand the urgency of the moment, or their great honour to be serving a man such as he?

"Face me," he yelled. "What is this?"

The men did as they were ordered, positioning themselves shoulder to shoulder along the wall. "We are worried, my prince," one of them stammered. "We have heard the Americans are on their way."

"Yes. And we must be ready."

"But we are not prepared. We do not have the weapons or the men—"

"How dare you," Cyrus snapped. "How dare you undermine me. I have told you we shall be ready. If they come here we shall face them and we shall win. We will not let these devils control how the world sees us. You will protect your prince. Understood?"

The young men nodded and raised their machine guns higher. "Yes."

"Yes, what?"

"Yes, Prince Heydari, Supreme Leader, Prince of Islam, Lord of Arabia," they all barked at once.

"Good. Now, you…" He pointed at the guard on the right. "Gather all my men together, wherever they may be – at home, in the field, on manoeuvres, resting. Tell them to return to the palace immediately and be ready to fight."

"Yes, my lord."

The guard turned and hurried away as Cyrus turned his attention to the remaining soldiers. "You and you. Go to the stable and bring the remaining prisoners to my suite. All of them. Then I want you to call Abu Qadar on his encrypted line."

The men's eyes grew wide. "Abu Qadar?" they whispered in unison.

"Yes. It is time to call in that favour. Now, go."

The men filtered out of the room and Cyrus shut the door after them. Once alone, he closed his eyes, telling himself all would be fine. This was a small setback but nothing he couldn't handle. He had the men, he had the firepower. And really, he mused as he headed back to his warm bed, if the Americans were coming for him, it meant he was doing something right. No one got to be a world leader by playing it safe or towing the line. He was a rebel, a fighter, and a man of tactical brilliance. They would learn. They all would. Cyrus Heydari wasn't done yet.

CHAPTER 37

I t was approaching nightfall as Caesar and Acid neared Heydari's sprawling compound. Half a mile from the front entrance they found a row of bushy cypress trees and settled down to take stock and wait for night to fall.

"Almost there." Caesar sighed, leaning against the sturdiest-looking tree and wiping his forearm across his brow. "Do you have any water left?"

Acid held up her bottle and tipped it upside down. "All out."

"Bugger. Me too."

It had been a long hot day, but they'd purposefully taken their time getting here, approaching in a wide arc and staying clear of any and all settlements lest they be spotted by Heydari's scouts. The baking sun had been oppressive in its heat and whenever they'd happened upon a shaded area they'd stopped for a while to rest and consume food and water, both agreeing it was important to stay refreshed and rejuvenated for what came next. That was the story they both adhered to, at least, but it was clear to anyone that without the pills his condition was getting worse. He was growing more and more unsteady on his feet and the shakes were becoming uncontrollable. He needed the rest.

Acid had kept shtum regarding everything they'd talked about last night, and he was glad of that. Whether she felt awkward, unsure what to say, or just didn't care, he wasn't certain, but he'd done enough wallowing over the last year or so to last him a lifetime (even if it was to be a pitifully shortened one). So whilst he might have responded to the idea with his typical dour cynicism, deep down he relished the chance to work with her one last time. It was an imprudent and hazardous mission, of course, and the plans she'd come up with so far were so full of holes you could see through them, but it took his mind off the inevitable and he was grateful of that.

Besides, if this was going to be a one-way trip, at least he'd go out fighting, with a gun in his hand, Acid by his side. Not a bad way to go, all things considered. Better than the bleeding alternative. Beowulf Caesar had grown up as a gay man amidst the first killer pandemic of modern times, and had watched many of his friends waste away as victims of that awful disease. He wasn't looking forward to a similar fate at the hands of his own debilitating sickness. Suicide had been on his mind a lot over the last few years – especially once his organisation was ruined – but he couldn't bring himself to do it. He was still adamant he'd die as he lived, on his own terms, yet the actuality of taking control of his fate, of swallowing a bullet – no, his ego wouldn't allow it.

He watched Acid as she settled down against a tree and untied the jacket from around her waist. That stinking leather jacket. She noticed him watching and held her arms out. *What?*

He looked away through the trees. "We'll be safe here until nightfall," he told her. "If you still want to do this."

"We have to."

He rubbed his back against the tree, trying to scratch a particularly hard to reach spot under his right shoulder blade. "What's the plan if they don't go for it?" he asked.

"I don't know. We blast our way in."

An unwitting grin spread across his face. But the girl had that effect on him. Anyone who held such forthright *fuck-it-let's-see-what-happens* attitude was all right in Caesar's book. He'd met many people who purported to hold such an outlook over the years, especially in his line of work, but he found with most of them it was simply a pose. They'd tell you they didn't give a shit whilst looking over their shoulder for reassurance or a way out. But not her. Half of the time he couldn't tell whether she was brilliant or crazy, but the truth, like any real genius, was she was both. Wild and unpredictable, but she always got the job done. Every single time. It was why, even back when he was seething with rage – calling her every name under the sun and demanding her head on a silver platter – another part of him (the part he was only now willing to acknowledge) suspected she'd overcome any attack that came her way. He hadn't counted on her wiping out his entire workforce and leaving him in tatters, but, hell, you had to give the girl her dues.

And what the pissing fuck did it matter now anyway?

He shifted closer to where she was sitting, field-stripping her pistol, and eased himself down alongside her. His leg muscles ached with fatigue and the misery of his affliction, but after a few attempts he found a position that wasn't agony.

She watched him without reaction. "Are you going to cope with this?" she asked, and closed one eye to peer down the barrel of the 33.

"Piss off."

She lowered the barrel to look at him. "I'm serious, Ceez. I know we were both full of it last night, but we'd had a drink and… you know… there was a lot of emotion going on. But now, with a day to consider it, is this a good idea?"

"No, of course it's not a good idea. That's what I've been trying to tell you. But whenever has that stopped us?" He sat forward, shoving his pathetic quivering hands under his legs out of sight and fixed her with a hard stare. "Listen, kid. Whatever this is, I don't like it. Not one bleeding bit."

She frowned. "What are you talking about?"

"I'm talking about you. Second-guessing yourself. Being all cautious and thoughtful. That's not the Acid Vanilla I know."

She looked away. But he could tell from her profile he'd hit a nerve. The way she chewed on her bottom lip as she reassembled the pistol. In the dusk light, with the sun all but disappeared over the horizon, she looked tired. But not in a physical sense so much as a spiritual one. She was worn out. Battered by life.

But who the pissing hell wasn't?

"I suppose I have been questioning myself a lot lately," she said softly, and sniffed. "Ever since I left Annihilation if I'm honest." She looked across at him as if waiting for a response. But he had none to give, so she sniffed again and went on. "I'm finding it hard to understand who I am away from my old life. Away from… everything. You."

She said it with a shrug of her shoulder, but he grinned. "Well, I am bleeding well wonderful."

"You can be," she said, and laughed through a gasp. "When you're not being an absolute fucking bastard."

"A man has to eat, girly. You messed up my whole operation. Made me look bad. I had to retaliate." He tilted his head to catch her eye. "But I thought we'd got over that?"

"Yeah, well. Some things are hard to get over." She glared at him, her eyes alight. "I can't believe you're fucking dying."

He sighed. "That makes two of us. But you got your wish. Think of it that way."

"I wanted to kill you. I didn't want you to die."

Her eyes glimmered in the fading light with a rawness he hadn't seen from her in years. He wasn't sure how he felt about seeing it now, but he understood all too well what she was saying. Blind indignation only got a person so far. When those emotions faded, reason kicked in. Sometimes that was a bad thing, sometimes it wasn't. He'd hurt her terribly, she'd hurt him too, but they'd also given each other so much more.

"Well, sweetie, I don't like seeing you like this. It's fucking pathetic, for starters. Making me depressed looking at you. So listen, I want you to promise me, if you survive this you work on getting yourself back together. Do whatever it takes, but don't lose sight of who you are. Fair enough you don't want to be an assassin anymore, but that doesn't mean you have to be a wet fart for the rest of your days. Because you, young lady, are a fucking whirlwind. You've got a shotgun soul, Acid. And that's fine. Go with it. It's who you are. Sounds to me the reason for all this bullshit and misery is you not accepting that. It's okay to be a bit messy, a bit angry at life, and to not fit into anyone else's box of what 'good' or 'bad' means. Like I told you all those years ago, kid – there is no good or bad. Just different shades of grey."

She clicked the magazine back into the pistol and swiped the back of her hand across her nose. "Jesus, Ceez, you ever thought of becoming a life coach?"

"Don't mock it. I'm a fucking genius. You know that."

"Do I?"

He held her gaze long enough that she couldn't help but let a wonky half-smile escape across her lips. It had been a long time since he'd seen that smile and he was surprised at how it made him feel. He was about to respond, but stopped himself as she got to her feet and brushed the sand from her jeans.

"Thanks," she said, as she peered through the trees at Heydari's palace.

"What for?"

"The pep talk. You're right, I do need to accept who I am, what I am. Then perhaps I can work out how that person fits into the normal world."

He shook his head, bracing his palm against the tree trunk to push himself to his feet. "There you go again, overcomplicating it. There is no normal world, toots. Not for people like us, at least. But that's okay because you've got more sass and brains than most of the dullards in this rotten world put together. You don't need to mould yourself for normality. You need to make this *normal* world fit around you."

She looked at him, eyes still narrow. "How the hell do I do that?"

"I don't bloody well know. But therein lies the adventure, my dear."

"Cryptic bastard," she muttered, but he could tell by her face the words had landed. She couldn't keep anything from him for long.

"Right, then," he said, raising his head to the sky. "I'd say it's nightfall in anyone's book. Most of Heydari's guards will be inside the palace now, keeping guard. Time to go to work." He placed a hand on Acid's shoulder, half to stop it from shaking, half because it felt like the right thing to do. "Ready?"

She met his eye and nodded. "Ready."

"That's my girl," he growled, giving her shoulder a squeeze. "Let's show these cretins how we do things at Annihilation Pest Control."

CHAPTER 38

Acid could see no sign of life as they approached the high gates of the palace compound.

"Do you have to dig the muzzle quite so hard into my damn kidneys?" Caesar grumbled, as she shoved him forward, one hand gripping his upper arm, the other on the pistol in his back.

"Shut up and stay in character," she whispered, out the corner of her mouth. "We're almost there."

Up close, the palace walls looked even higher and the thick wooden gate even more impenetrable. She gave Caesar the nod before reaching up and banging the heel of her fist against the wood.

"Hey. I have a gift for the prince. Someone he'll want to see. Open the gates."

They waited. Nothing. The bats nibbled at her nerve endings. Caesar twisted around to her and stuck out his bottom lip.

With a frown she approached the door again, slamming her fist down harder. "Hello? I have returned Mr Heydari's number one prisoner. I want my reward." Caesar side-eyed her but she shrugged. "Worth a try."

She gave it a beat, and was about to knock again, when she heard voices on the other side.

"Who is this?" a gruff voice called out. "What is it you want?"

"I have tracked down an escaped prisoner for Mr Heydari," she replied. "The one they call Caesar. The big man with no hair. He is very important to your leader. He will want him returned. Open up."

Caesar shot her a sharp look as he mouthed 'big' and 'no hair' with mock annoyance. She gave him a camp shrug before the door shook and they heard the sound of metal against metal. Acid tensed, watching as Caesar's hand slipped behind his back to grab the TT-33 in his waistband. She kept her own piece pressed against his midriff as the door creaked open and a man's head appeared. He wore the black headdress the same as all Heydari's men, but he'd removed the part covering his nose and mouth so his whole face was visible.

"You are prisoner too?" he asked. His light green eyes sparkled in the moonlight and, despite the assault rifle he had gripped at waist height, he appeared boyish and uncertain of himself. Like a kid playing at being a soldier. All of Heydari's men seemed around the same age – late teens to early twenties and not much older. Young kids with no prospects, easily brainwashed with the promise of a just cause and a cool uniform. But wasn't it always the way?

"I was staying with the prince," she told him. "In his suite. In his bed."

"Oh?" He looked her up and down, his face unflinching but his eyes giving him away. In the low light from the moon his cheeks flushed red as his gaze fell on her chest, before flicking quickly back to meet her eyes.

"That's right." She smiled her sweetest smile, like butter wouldn't melt. "But I was kidnapped by this man, an enemy of your leader. He took me but I managed to apprehend him and steal his gun." She held up the piece to show him, feeling Caesar's arm shaking as she did.

The guard's young face sagged, no doubt with the weight of this unexpected responsibility on his shoulders. What to do? Acid kept her smile in place as a maelstrom of manic bat energy sought to knock her off course. It was a risk, this approach. If the guard was privy to the details of their escape, all was lost. But from the blank look on his face she surmised her instincts had been correct. The mad prince didn't want any of his men knowing he'd been duped and hog-tied.

"What is going on?" another voice grunted, before a taller man appeared. This one was wearing full face covering and his eyes were close together and mean-looking. He glared at Acid and Caesar and raised his rifle to his chest. "What do you want?"

The first guard turned his head to address him, speaking rapidly and gesturing at the two of them as he did. Acid gripped Caesar's arm tighter, steadying him. They didn't look at each other. Two guards were what they were expecting at this time of night, but it would have been a whole lot easier if the second had been as hesitant as the first. The new, taller, bolder guard opened the door wide before shoving his smaller accomplice to one side and stepping forward. "You bring a prisoner for Mr Heydari?"

Acid held her ground. "That's correct. And I'd like to deliver him myself."

The guard sneered, heavy on the disdain (it was always a good sneer, she thought, if you could clock it from the eyes alone). But then he beckoned for them to enter, aiming his rifle at her as they stepped through the gate, and barking orders to his colleague, who hurried over and prised the gun from her hand.

"We cannot have you carrying a weapon," he told her. Acid nodded and risked a glance at Caesar. He now had both hands raised in surrender, but a quick scan down his back and she was relieved to see his shirt had fallen over the top of his pistol. She released the breath she'd been holding as the guards stepped around the back of them.

"Come with us," the tall guard ordered. "We shall see what the prince wants to do with you. Both of you."

Leading from behind, they herded them through the gates and into the vast courtyard. Acid was glad to see that, except for the four of them, the space was empty. The impressive white building with its domes and turrets looked rather serene in the dusky moonlight. So this was it. They were inside. Except the plan had already gone awry. She was now unarmed and with a sub-machine jabbed between her shoulder blades.

"Hey, careful with that thing," she hissed, snapping her attention over her shoulder.

It only made the guard stab the rifle in harder, but she was able to confirm it was the taller of the two guards. The one that needed taking out first if they were to pull this off.

The tension between her and Caesar was electric as they shuffled their feet, heading for the raised walkway that led to the main entrance of the palace. The plan had been they'd overpower the guards at the gate, but with a rifle pointed at them from the off it hadn't been possible. Now they had a few seconds to do something before more guards appeared. After that it was game over. Acid gnawed on her lip.

Come on, Ceez.

She was ready to act, to strike, but she needed to know he could pull it off too. She jutted her jaw, willing him on. They were now only a few feet from the walkway. A split-second would be all it took. Something. Anything. She slowed her pace but the guard shoved her forward. Then, as they got to the first section of the walkway, Caesar let out a deep, guttural wail and staggered to his knees as if about to faint.

It was all the distraction she needed.

Spinning around she grabbed hold of the agitated guard's rifle, twisting his aim up into the sky whilst simultaneously smashing her boot down against his knee. The impact forced the joint back against itself and the guard screamed out, letting go of the rifle. As he crumpled to the ground, she spun it into her grip and had it pressed against the neck of his open-mouthed colleague before he could act.

"Drop it," she hissed. "The rifle. Drop it. Now."

"I'd do as she says if I was you, lad," Caesar told him, getting to his feet.

Acid regarded him out the corner of one eye. "Was that a play?"

He held up one hand and rotated it from side to side as if to say, *Sort of.* "Let's say it was," he added, before relieving the frightened guard of his weapon and stepping over to the one still whimpering on the floor. "Do put a sock in it, old boy." He leaned over and smashed the rifle butt into the side of his head, knocking him out.

"What about this one?" Acid asked. "He's only a kid."

Caesar dropped the rifle and pulled the TT-33 from his waist-band as he walked over to them. "Kids can be dangerous." He pressed the pistol to the guard's temple. "You were *only a kid* once. Still did a lot of nasty things, if memory serves."

She ignored him, watching as beads of sweat ran down the kid's face. "I sorry, I don't know," he kept saying. "I go home."

"Oh, if t'were so easy." Caesar sighed. "Sorry, my good lad, but we can't have loose ends—"

"Caesar."

He turned to her, his face formed into that expression she always hated, half-way between hammy surprise and intense wickedness, brows arched, lips pursed in a cruel pout. Like a camp demon. Like John Lydon in his prime.

"Fine," he huffed, before flipping the pistol around and smashing the handle across the back of the kid's head. He went down like a handless sock puppet. Caesar shook his head at her. "Happy now?"

She considered the two fallen guards. "Should we tie them up?"

"No. We'll be in and out before they get their acts into gear. Besides, hop-along isn't going to be much of a problem and that little streak of piss will probably run home to be with his goats the second he wakes up."

She knelt down and grabbed up her confiscated pistol, clicking one into the chamber for good measure. "Leave the rifles?"

"I'd say. Too cumbersome. Too noisy." He nudged her playfully. "You know my philosophy, sweetie. A good mission is all about stealth and grace."

"Absolutely. You going to be okay to carry on?"

He pointed his finger in her face, deep lines forming across his brow. "Don't bleeding well start. I'll be fine. You worry about yourself."

"If you're sure."

"I'm sure. But good work there, I've got to say, textbook stuff. I knew you still had it in you." He smiled, a real one. As real as they got with him, at least. "Acid Vanilla gone soft? Not pissing well likely."

Once again her mentor's words lifted her in a way that both surprised and unnerved her. But she wasn't complaining. She glanced over to the stable block. "So we free the ones in the holding cell first and then go for Kendis."

Caesar sighed, but there was a twinkle behind his eyes. He could protest all he liked, but he was enjoying himself. Same as her. "Fine, but once we free them it's down to them what they do next. Agreed? I'm not babysitting a load of old hippies and do-gooders."

"As you wish," she replied, already heading over to the side of the stable block. "Now come on, let's move."

The plan was to approach the entrance from the opposite side, maintaining the element of surprise if there were soldiers on guard. With her back grazing the textured wall of the building, she edged swiftly around the side of the stables, stopping every fifty yards or so to allow Caesar to catch up. It was clear he was struggling, but she was damned if she was going to give him any leeway. Or sympathy.

The bastard.

Brutal annoyance at other people's foibles wasn't an unusual feeling for Acid, but this felt different. Watching Caesar as he hobbled towards her, she realised the overriding emotion driving her wasn't the usual frustration or annoyance, but a deep-rooted resentment. She resented him for getting old, for getting sick – for not being the strong, cocksure man she'd met all those years ago. It was how she'd felt towards her mother too, when the first throes of dementia showed themselves.

How dare these people she cared about be fragile and human! How dare they leave her!

She shook the thought away and raised her gun as they approached the entrance. The play here was to ambush the guards from behind. Pistol into the nape of the neck, relieve them of their guns, bind and gag them, done. But no killing if they could help it, she'd been adamant of that. A quick glance over her shoulder told her Caesar was ready to move. She gave him a nod and slipped around the side of the building, ready to—

"Shit."

She'd been primed for action, playing the scene out in her head the last few minutes. How she'd grab the closest guard, snarling in his ear for him to drop his weapon.

Only there were no guards.

And the doors to the stable block were hanging open.

"Bugger," Caesar whispered over her shoulder. "Doesn't look too good."

She didn't reply as she crept around the side of the doorway. Peering through the gloom she could make out the cot beds, all empty. The table and chairs in the middle of the room, empty too. Down the stone steps to the stable floor, and as her eyes grew accustomed to the darkness she saw two of the chairs had been knocked over. Sign of a struggle perhaps. Also one of the cot beds had been stripped, and walking over to it she could see the thin mattress was stained with blood. It was dry, but a dark crimson colour rather than the rusty brown hue of old blood. Her guess was it was a day old, perhaps less.

"Oh dear."

She flicked her attention back to the doorway to see Caesar

holding something small and shiny up to his face. As she strode over, he held out his hand to show her the spent shell casing, rolling it up and down in his quivering palm.

"Looks like we were too late."

"Do you think he's…"

He shrugged. "Not sure. Like I say, he needs leverage now more than ever. Needs to keep the Americans at arm's length. Threatening to kill hostages is a good way to do that." He nodded over at the blood-stained bed. "I do know he's got himself a studio set up in the palace, for making… home movies, shall we say."

Acid took the shell casing and held it up to the moonlight, looked to be steel, a 7.62 Soviet round. She flung it to the floor before racing up the steps back into the courtyard.

"Oi, where you going?" Caesar called after her.

At the doorway she stopped and glared back at him. "Where do you think? We might be too late to save these guys, but Kendis is still upstairs."

She could hear her old mentor shouting something else but she was already marching across the courtyard. The bats screeched across her consciousness and the pressure in her head was intense. But it was a good feeling. It was what she needed. She felt invincible, ready to burst into flames at any moment.

Soft?

How the hell had she even allowed that thought to enter her head?

She was Acid Vanilla and she always had been. Even back when she was still the young Alice Vandella. Because Acid Vanilla was more than a codename or an alias. She was a state of mind. A way of being. Strong, powerful, uncompromising. She held the gun up beside her face as another surge of manic bat energy fired across her nervous system. The past didn't exist and the future was unwritten. All that mattered was who she was in this moment. Heydari would pay for his actions. And she was the person to make him pay.

CHAPTER 39

Acid was already half-way up the palace walkway when Caesar caught up with her. "Slow down. Jesus," he said. "I thought we were doing this together?"

"We haven't got time to slow down," she said, not turning around.

They marched on in silence with Caesar casting his gaze around the area, searching for threats that might be lurking in the shadows. He didn't spot any, but that in itself wasn't particularly reassuring. Even the main entrance was unguarded. This was far too easy and that worried him. What was the mad prince up to?

Up ahead of him, Acid strode on purposefully towards the palace, back straight, chest out, weapon raised and ready. Seeing her like this, full of spit and vinegar, ready to obliterate anyone who stepped in her path, it made him damn proud. They'd royally fucked each other over and probably deserved the consequences of their actions, yet somehow they'd got over their differences. She'd survived all the punishment he'd sent her way and he was glad of that. But really that was Acid all over. She was a born survivor. Just like him.

Pissing nonce.

He wiped a tear angrily from his face, holding his eyes open in the cool night, trying and failing to stop more from falling.

Not the time, old boy.

Never the bleeding time.

He gritted his teeth as a sudden urge came over him to tell the kid he was proud of her. Not just for what she'd done for him over the years, but for who she'd become without him. He'd denied it for so long – and still would if anyone challenged him on it – but there was a lot of paternal love in his big old belly for Acid Vanilla. She was a part of him. They were a part of each other. Death, murder, betrayal – nothing still could take that away from them.

Screw it.

He was going to tell her.

He opened his mouth, but before he had chance to get the words out she'd spun on her heels and was holding her finger up in the air, eyes wide.

"Listen," she whispered. "Do you hear that?"

He tilted his head to one side as a distinct sound drifted over from the eastern side of the compound. It was a long way off, a few kilometres at least, and distorted somewhat by the breeze, but there was no mistaking the sonic crack of gunshots and the rattle of machine gun fire.

"Do you think that's the Americans?" she asked.

"Possibly. Which means we need to get the girl and get out of here. Pronto."

Acid looked down. "Or we could leave them to save Kendis?"

"I thought we were doing this," he snapped, surprising himself but going with it. "If Heydari is getting antsy she might not survive that long."

"Wow." A thick pout pursed her lips as she looked him up and down. "Did you grow a conscience as well?"

"Not a fucking chance," he told her, raising his gun. "But we're here now, aren't we? I've got the fire in me."

"Okay. So…?"

"So stick to the plan. Let's get inside, see what the hell is going on."

He didn't say anything else, what he'd been planning on saying. The moment had passed and there'd be time later. Once all the fun and games were over.

A few more feet and they reached the top of the walkway, where it opened out onto a wide platform in front of the main entrance. Normally there were at least two armed soldiers standing guard, but they'd already seen from the courtyard that there was no one in sight. Acid got to the doors first and listened at the wood. As he got closer, she shook her head. Nothing. She grabbed the handle and pushed, but the door didn't budge.

"Let me have a go," he told her, shoving her out the way to have a better look. The doors were tall and wide with swirls and scrolls carved around the edges, yet despite their lavish appearance, up close they looked to be made of plywood and the locking mechanism modern. But it made sense – Heydari's world was all about smoke and mirrors. Caesar tried the handle a few times before leaning down to examine it, a typical mortice type. If he'd had his old kit with him he'd have got through it in a second. He listened at the door but couldn't hear anything.

"Right, well, let's go for the old-fashioned method," he told her, putting an arm out to move her away. Taking a step back first, he lunged forward, putting every ounce of his sizeable weight into it as he barged the door. A sharp pain ran down his arm and he felt the lock give way a little but the doors remained shut. He went again, slamming into the point where the two doors met in the hope of splintering the lock from the wood, but they held fast. He was getting angry now. The doors weren't even real wood. Back in his day he'd have been through on the first go.

"Wait," Acid told him, moving in front of the door as he sized up for another go. "I can hear movement on the other side."

Caesar straightened up and listened. No voices could be heard at present, but there was definite movement. It sounded like rubber soles on marble tiles. The scuffle continued for a few seconds then went silent, before they heard a familiar click and the chink of metal.

He and Acid both shot their heads up at the same time to look at each other. The expression on her face was no doubt the same he wore on his. Grim realisation

"Move."

They pushed off against one another, shifting to the opposite sides of the entrance as whoever was inside opened fire and a solid torrent of machine gun rounds blasted through the thin wooden doors like they were made of butter. Caesar pressed his back against the wall as bullets whizzed past him into the night sky and pieces of fibreglass scroll splintered off the framework. His guess was there were at least three shooters inside, possibly more if the seemingly unending burst of hellfire was anything to go by. He caught Acid's eye and held up his pistol. They were sitting ducks out here. He had to do something.

"Wait," she yelled back, as if reading his mind. "They can't go on forever."

But in his head he was already committed, he'd already acted. A second later he noticed the rhythm of the gunfire alter a touch, as if one of the men had stopped momentarily, perhaps to reload. Twisting his torso around, he brought his pistol down in a wide arc and aimed through the now large hole where most of the doors had been. Through the smoke and sawdust he saw three men, all dressed in black army fatigues with black headwear. Two of them were standing upright, their weapons held at waist height, still firing incessantly at the door, while the third, the one nearest to him on this side, was down on one knee shoving a new magazine into his rifle. In one fluid movement, Caesar squeezed the trigger, putting a bullet through the kneeling guard's brain, then moved back around the side of the door and zipped a burst of four rounds across to the other two, catching one of them in the shoulder and sending him jolting backwards but missing the last one entirely.

The whole movement had happened in a split-second and he

was leaning against the cold stone of the palace wall before the soldiers had even seen him. He gasped in a lungful of air as a heavy retaliation of bullets erupted from inside, blasting one of the doors off its hinges and ricocheting off the stonework inches from his cheek.

He raised his head, ready for another attempt, when he heard Acid's voice over the booming rat-a-tat of the assault rifles. Turning, he caught her glare as she snarled at him through gritted teeth. "Mine."

Fine. He held his hand before flattening it and making a fist. It was their in-field communication for when stealth was of the essence. It meant stay low and go on my signal. Acid nodded and slunk to her knees, keeping her back to the wall. From where he was standing, Caesar could see there was a decent-sized hole a few inches from her shoulder. Swallowing hard on a dry throat, he gave her the nod. Then, with a curtain of bullets still whizzing through the doorway at seven hundred meters per second, he shifted his body around and waved an arm across the open doorway.

Everything happened at once.

The first thing he was aware of was a dull thud in his upper shoulder, like someone had hit him with a baseball bat. At the same time, Acid twisted into position, her face distorted in grim determination as she fired through the gap in the door. She yelled out. He did too. Time stopped. The machine gun fire continued. He managed to get himself back behind the cover of the wall as a hail of punishing rounds smashed out the remaining doorframe on his side. But Acid stayed low, still screeching like a banshee and squeezing off round after round towards the soldiers.

Then, as if the tumultuous sea-storm they'd been fighting had suddenly calmed to a still, peaceful ocean, the firing stopped.

As the dust clouds settled, Caesar slumped against the wall and gripped at his shoulder. The dull pain was fast morphing into a sharp burning sensation, but it wasn't as painful as he remembered. He'd been shot only two times before – once in the leg, once in the stomach. Which, considering the life he'd led, wasn't bad going.

"You okay?" Acid asked, moving over to him and breaking his flow of thought. "They get you?"

He lifted his hand from his shoulder. The bullet had gone straight through, ripping his shirt and leaving a furrow of burnt flesh maybe half an inch deep. "Tis but a flesh wound," he told her.

"Well, cheers for the diversion, but I could have handled them."

He hit her with his famous grin, purposefully exposing the gold canines, the way he always did when he wanted to conjure fear in his operatives. "I know," he told her. "But we're a team. You know me, kid. I love teamwork."

She threw up an eyebrow as she stepped past him into the palace. "Well, they've certainly made a mess of Heydari's grand entrance," she muttered. "He won't be happy."

She disappeared into the entrance hall, but Caesar remained outside for a moment, breathing in the cool night air as his heart rate slowed to something more manageable. Over the top of the perimeter wall he could see lights strobing in the distance and played a quick game with himself of gunfire or nightclub. He knew of a decent-sized township in that direction and he might have gone with nightclub but for the distant rumble which followed. He raised his head, nodding solemnly as if somehow this was all fateful.

Pissing hell.

Was this what happened to you when you knew your time was up? You became a simpering, pathetic mess, looking for order and significance where there was none? He sniffed back angrily.

No.

Wasn't happening.

Life was nothing but meaningless chaos, and death was no different. He shoved the pistol into his waistband and slipped inside the palace after Acid.

CHAPTER 40

cid didn't look up as she sensed Caesar standing over her. She'd chucked her spent pistol away and was inspecting the dead guards for any weapons they might utilize. Not the AK-47s, they were too cumbersome, but she'd found a tasty-looking stiletto blade. She held it over her shoulder, releasing her grip on it as Caesar took the handle.

"Lovely stuff," he purred. "My blade of choice."

"I always preferred something meatier," she responded, unclipping the guard's gun holster and releasing a fully loaded TT-33 from its clutches.

"Yes, I heard that rumour."

She gave him the mother of all eyes-rolls, knowing that even with her back to him he'd pick up on it. She shoved the gun in her jeans and threw her gaze down the empty entrance hall. "Surely someone would have heard that."

"Just what I was thinking. I don't think we should stay still if we can help it."

"Not a problem."

She moved over to another of the guards and relieved him of his pistol, keeping this one in her hand. As she joined Caesar, she found him surveying the room's length with narrow eyes. The double doors at the far end led to the room with the marble columns and modern art displays, but there were also doors standing at intervals along the left-hand wall. Some of them were hanging open, others locked.

"Heydari's suite," Caesar muttered, speaking as if to himself.

"You think that's there where they are? Where Kendis is?"

He rocked his head from side to side. "I reckon. He'll be holed up in his little cave like a timid animal. The pathetic lump of arse cancer. Come on."

They moved across the room, sticking close to the left-hand wall and approaching each of the open doorways with caution. Caesar was first to reach the fourth set and, after peering around the side, held his hand up.

"What is it?" she whispered.

He shifted places with her so she could look, and with her breath frozen in her throat she leaned around the doorframe. The room beyond was vast and the ceiling at least three storeys high, ending in the huge qubba dome which, along with the minaret tower on the opposite wing, could be seen from miles around. But that wasn't what drew Acid's attention or made her suck back a sharp breath. Filling the space were lines of young soldiers standing in formation with rifles held at chest height. In front of the throng, five men were addressing them in loud voices, sharp angry eyes the only features visible beneath their black face coverings, worn to match the black army fatigues. To complete the look, each of the men was wearing a harness with destructive weaponry attached – grenades, pipe bombs – as well as bandoliers slung around their waists.

Like with most things in the civilian world – celebrity culture, Netflix, modern music – Acid didn't keep abreast of the news, but even she knew an ISIS fighter when she saw one. The sight of them standing there with their hands on their hips, addressing the hordes of timid but eager youths, sent a chill running down her back.

She glanced over her shoulder at Caesar, but he knew what

she was thinking and shook his head. Not worth it. He jutted his chin over to the doors on the far side of the room and traced an arc in the air with two fingers. *Move out.*

The soldiers were standing side-on to them, so fully engaged with their new commanders' rhetoric that no one saw as Acid and Caesar slipped away. Still, the pair gave the doorway a wide berth, shifting over to the wall on the opposite side and not stopping until they'd reached the back of the room.

"Did you know about this?" Acid whispered.

"I knew Heydari was in communication with the ISIS lot – been a middle-man for them in some arms deal – but that was it, as far as I could tell. He talks a lot of shit about uniting the region, but he's just a chancer. Wants power and infamy at any cost."

"Sounds familiar." She put one ear to the door, trying to ignore Caesar's spluttering protests.

"Are you comparing me to me to that mad fucker?"

She considered him, the deep lines in his brow, the sweat pouring down his face, the trembling hands. "I think perhaps you lost sense of what was important."

"I see." He cricked his neck to one side. The way he always did when he was pissed off but didn't have a comeback.

"We can talk about it later," she told him, leaning against the door and discovering it was open. "I can't hear any movement, but keep your aim up regardless."

"Yes, thank you, I am aware." He scowled at her, and it wasn't for effect. "I might have been blowing smoke up your perky little arse for the last few hours but I taught you everything you know. Don't you forget that."

"Perky little arse? Jesus, it *has* been a while." She grabbed the second pistol from out of her jeans, holding one in each hand. "More like big fat arse these days."

"Oh come on, you were never one to fish for compliments."

"I'm not doing," she rasped, turning back to the door and preparing to push on through.

"Well you're still doing something right," he whispered over her shoulder. "Heydari clearly thought you were worth letting his guard down for. Stupid fucker."

A smile teased at the corner of her mouth, but she caught it and shook it away. "Come on, you silvery-tongued dickhead," she said. "Let's do this."

Raising both guns up to her face, she put her shoulder to the door and leaned against it. Making no sound, the door swung open to reveal the next room, the ornate tiled floor, the rows of white marble columns. But as Acid's focus shot across the room, she saw two guards at the far end bustling to move their rifles into shooting position.

She ran for the cover of the first column with Caesar close behind, reaching it as the first wave of bullets thudded into the hard marble on the other side.

"Bollocks."

Dropping to her knee she threw an arm around the column and returned fire. But her aim was off and the guards parted, taking cover behind each of the two columns at the far end of the room.

Well, shit.

There goes the element of surprise.

As the sound of machine gun fire echoed through the room, she stayed low, throwing her attention over to the far wall and wondering if the nearest marble plinth – this one displaying an embossed metal shield – would provide suitable cover.

"Well, sweetie, only one way to find out."

She glanced up at Caesar, but he wasn't looking at her and hadn't spoken. It was just his voice in her head. What that meant she wasn't sure, but right now she didn't have time to worry about insurmountable questions. She waited until the soldiers had spluttered out another burst of rounds before pushing off from the column and running as fast as her fatigued muscles allowed. A trail of bullets followed her path, bouncing off the highly polished tiles and sending dust and marble particles up into the air. She reached the plinth and leaned against the side of it. With the bats screaming for blood, she cast her aim around the side and took out the nearest guard. One in the neck, two in the head. As his body slumped to the floor, she pressed herself against the plinth while the second guard emptied his magazine in her direction. The bullets pounded the marble and thudded like a stud gun into the metal plate, which fell to the floor and rolled around on its circumference before coming to a stop a few metres from her right foot.

The moment she heard the bullets stop and the impotent click-clack of an unresponsive trigger, she leapt to her feet and ran towards him. He already had a new magazine in his grip, desperately trying to release the spent one. As she raised both pistols towards him she noticed how young he was, and the look of sheer terror in his eyes. For a split-second she hesitated, but the bats were in control and she was in kill mode. No mercy. No prisoners. No respite. The soldier locked eyes with her and she fired. Two rounds out of each pistol. Four chest shots. The impact knocked the rifle from his hands and all the life out of his body. As he stumbled back his eyes fell on hers once more. Then all the light went out of them, and he dropped to the ground.

"Wonderful shooting, my dear." Caesar appeared alongside her, wheezing conspicuously, both hands shaking like he was on the wrong side of an alcohol binge. "But let's not sit around basking in our glory. We need to get out of here."

She gulped back a deep breath as the frantic bat energy subsided enough that she could think. "Shit. The ISIS troops."

"Exactly. Come on."

He grabbed hold of her shoulder as she set off, her pulling him along until he matched her pace.

They got to the doors at the far end just as a deep voice roared: "Stop!"

Without turning around Acid yanked open the doors. Behind her she heard more voices and the sound of jackboots, followed by the clank-clink of rifles being armed.

"In here, quick," she yelled, shoving Caesar's immense bulk into the empty bathing suite.

Once inside, they moved to opposite sides of the doorframe and each got behind one of the heavy mahogany doors. With a surge of energy that belied their weariness, they slammed them shut as a hail of bullets slammed into the thick wood on the other side.

"Help me with this," Acid called out, grappling with the timber joist propped up against the wall.

Caesar came to her aide and together they manoeuvred the wooden slide bolt into position across both doors.

"Should hold them for a while," he growled. "But that's our only exit."

"We'll worry about that later." She looked over to the door to Heydari's suite. "Why is no one coming out? You don't think he's...?"

"What? Escaped?"

"Maybe. I was thinking suicide pact."

"Not a chance. He loves himself too much." Caesar released the magazine from his pistol and examined it before shoving it back with the heel of his palm. "I suppose there's only one way to find out."

Cautiously they stepped over to the door and got into position either side of it. As before, Acid could hear little sound coming from inside, but that meant nothing. Gripping both pistols like they were extensions of her, she moved in front of the door. There was no way of knowing what was waiting on the other side: twenty guards, armed and ready to fill her with holes; the lone Heydari, cowering behind his pillow; a pile of dead bodies. But whatever it was, she was ready for it.

"You can do it, kiddo," Caesar told her. "I believe in you."

With a grunt she brought her leg up and kicked down on the lock, dropping into shooting position as the door swung open to reveal a room full of people.

"Hey, hey, hey..."

Everyone shouted at once, yelling over each other as chaos descended on the scene.

"What is this…?"

Swiping her heightened awareness around the room and keeping her aim high, Acid saw Heydari over to her left. He was standing against the wall flanked by Kendis on one side and his sisters on the other.

"Go away… leave me…"

"It's over, Cyrus."

Lars and the rest of the prisoners were huddled together against the adjacent wall. Heydari had them bound and gagged and each one of them looked broken and terrified, but at least they still had their heads.

Acid shot her attention back to Heydari.

"I'll kill them," he said. He was holding a small pistol and swaying it erratically around the room.

"Stop. It's over."

"You stop it."

The bats chewed on her nervous system.

"Don't be stupid."

Her fingers tightened on the triggers.

"Drop it."

"You drop it." Saliva sprayed from his mouth as he yelled, a repellent mix of fear and madness in his frozen face.

"Acid," Kendis whimpered. "He's gone crazy. Please. Help—"

She shut up when Heydari shoved the gun at her. "I'll kill her."

"No."

Acid aimed one of the 33s between his eyes, her finger tensing on the trigger as he snapped his pistol towards her.

"What are you waiting for?" he cried. "Shoot her, you fool."

What?

Snapping her attention across the room, she now saw the young guard hidden in the corner. He was holding an AK-47 to his chest like it was a security blanket, like his life depended on it, yet he was also doing a brilliant impression of someone who really didn't want to be there – or even know what he was supposed to be doing. Good. She could work with that.

"Drop your weapon," she said, pointing the second gun at him.

His eyes darted from her back to Heydari. She could see his fingers were loose on the trigger and the bats screamed for her to take the shot. He'd never see it coming. She sucked back a deep breath. Remained still.

"Let them go," she hissed, relaxing into the moment and shifting her focus back to Heydari. "Give us the prisoners, we won't hurt you."

"It's too late," he barked back. "The Americans are outside. They are here for me."

As the bat chatter filled her psyche, Acid held her ground, guns raised but with limbs fluid, ready to act if and when required. Looking straight forward she had both men in her peripheral vision and could drop either of them at the merest suggestion they might shoot. Standing this way it also had the added advantage of making her look batshit crazy – not looking at either man, just staring out the window in front of her with the 33s aimed in opposite directions.

"Drop your weapons," she tried again. "No one else has to get hurt. We might all get out of this in one piece. Before the Americans arrive."

"Liar. The minute we lower our guns you will kill me."

"I told you before," she sneered towards the window. "I don't even have an opinion on what you're trying to do here. I just want to go home. That's all anyone in this room wants."

"Please," Kendis pleaded. "We won't tell anyone what we've seen or what you've done, we just—"

"Oh for bleeding hell's sake, what the fuck are you all jabbering about?"

The room erupted in pandemonium as she sensed the substantial presence of her old boss entering the room. Before anyone could speak, a sonic crack blew all the sound out of her hearing and the young guard's head exploded in a cloud of red mist.

Shit.

No.

Heydari was already firing while Acid dived for cover behind the end of the bed. Bullets whizzed overhead as the mad bastard waved the pistol around, shooting indiscriminately and taking out one of his long-suffering sisters with the bullets he sprayed around the room. Acid returned fire but the angle was off and she sent the shots high. Beneath the ringing in her ears, she could hear muted screams, Caesar roaring in anger (and… pain?). The wet splatter of blood hit her in the face and she looked up to see Kendis had taken a bullet in the upper chest. The young American fell face down onto the bed. Then Acid lost all sense of who she was.

The bats screamed.

She screamed louder.

In full-on kill mode – no thoughts, no feelings, driven by instinct and rage– she leapt to her feet and aiming both guns at the mad prince fired a zipper line up his torso, emptying one of the magazines into his chest. He staggered back and raised his own gun, but only managed to get it to navel-height before she took aim and blew out the back of his head with an expertly placed shot between the eyes.

"Stupid bastard," she said, as she watched his body slump to the floor.

"Acid…"

Shit.

Caesar.

As her sentient bearing fought to control her relentless blood-lust, she turned to take in the room. She saw Lars and the others, cowering in terror, fine blood spatter covering their faces and clothes. Saw the young guard in the corner, his body twisted awkwardly where he fell. And she saw her old boss, lying on the ground clutching at his leg, thick blood bubbling from a wound in his upper thigh. He looked up at her and his face was white. The parts of it not covered in blood, at least. Because it was everywhere. Up the walls. Across the floor. Over the bed…

No.

The recall slapped her across the face.

"Kendis."

She scrambled over to the grand double-king-size and grabbed the young American by the shoulders, shifting her over onto her back.

"Ah, Kendis, no…"

She was dead. Heydari had shot her twice – once through the neck, once through the heart. She'd have bled out in seconds. No one survived those kinds of injuries.

"You rotten bastard." She raised the gun at the prince's prone form, ready to fire off a few more rounds into his ridiculous face.

"Hey," Caesar called over. "Don't waste your ammo on that prick."

She looked across at him, not even bothering that there were tears rolling down her cheeks. She was about to respond (something nasty and pithy, something juvenile and mean) when he shook his head.

"Listen," he said, pausing from tying a piece of ripped shirt around the top of his leg.

"What?"

What could he possibly want to inform her of in this moment? Kendis was dead. Another innocent. Someone else who'd been dragged into Acid's orbit and had suffered the worst fate because of it. She wanted to scream, to put a bullet in Caesar's head and then her own.

Still gripping the pistols tight, she wiped the heel of her thumb across her cheeks.

What a waste.

What a damn waste.

She turned back to Heydari, fighting the urge to kick the crap out of his mangled, bullet-ridden corpse. It would make her feel better, at least.

"Acid, calm down. This isn't helping."

"Go to hell."

"Listen," he told her, more forceful now. "Listen to what's going on."

The intensity in his eyes shook her out of herself, and as the mayhem in her head diminished, her awareness spread out from the mad swirling energy in the room. She could hear gunfire – lots of it – as well as the distinct rumble of explosives being denotated. Then, through the window she heard voices. It was hard to pick out what they were saying but she could tell they were males, speaking English.

She could tell they were American.

"Shitting hell," she said, going to him. "They're here."

"Yes they bloody well are," he said, speaking through gritted teeth as he got himself upright. "Which means if we don't want to spend the rest of our lives in a windowless cell, we have to get of here. And fast."

CHAPTER 41

As Caesar finished off his makeshift tourniquet, Acid ran over to untie the other prisoners, starting with Lars who helped her free the rest.

"We have to get out of here," she told him. "The Americans are here." She focused on untying a middle-aged German woman whose name she didn't know. But she'd done that on purpose, kept the other prisoners at arm's length. It was easier that way. She glanced up to see Lars considering her with kind, watery eyes.

"But this is a good thing," he said. "The Americans are here to save us."

She finished off the knot and pulled the rope free from the woman who thanked her with a series of meek nods.

"Oh. Yes. Of course."

The way Lars was looking at her – eyes darting from her to Caesar and back again – it made her feel smaller than she'd ever felt. Her first impulse was to punch the gentle doctor in the face. Her second impulse was to fight that first impulse with everything she had.

"Heydari has a lot of men out there," she told him. "And ISIS soldiers leading them. I think you should come with—"

"Leave them if they want to stay," Caesar's voice boomed over her shoulder. "Like the man says, this is a good thing for them."

Acid stepped out the way as Caesar limped over and held out a quivering and bloody hand towards Lars. "Cheers, doc. Lars. I appreciate what you did for me."

"You will be okay?" he asked, taking his hand. "I can have a look at your leg. Maybe stitch it up for you?"

"No time, doc. But it's fine, the bullet went right through, missed the main artery. I'll live. Well... you know..."

"If you stay I can ask the Americans to get more of the drugs," Lars told him. "It will make life bearable again."

"Until when?"

Lars' mouth twitched but he held his ground. "There is no reason why—"

"Leave it, doc. We both know it's a losing battle." He glanced at Acid as an explosion rocked the foundations of the palace. "And we really can't stay."

Acid, who had been watching the exchange with a storm of chaotic thoughts swirling around her head, stepped forward. "Are you sure you won't come?" she asked Lars. "It's about to get messy here. Not to mention, if the Americans lose this battle, the ISIS soldiers will take you. That doesn't bear—"

She could hear herself babbling, so was glad when Lars held up his hand and gave her one of those beatific smiles of his. "Thank you, Acid. But we'll take our chances." He looked around at the other prisoners, at Kendis' lifeless body. "The American soldiers are resilient and so are we. We will be safe inside this chamber until we are rescued."

"Have it your way." She moved to the door, examining the ornate ivory handle. "Lock yourselves in once we leave, and... shit... why is there no bloody lock?"

Lars shrugged. "Cyrus Heydari was a strange man. Who knows what his reasoning was. But you have freed the world from him and I thank you." He smiled again, except this time she noticed a glimmer of something else in the lines around his eyes. It looked a lot like relief but also vindication.

Revenge. It could eat away at the best of us.

"Push the bed against the door," she told him. "That should hold them enough, and grab the guard's rifle if you need it."

"Thank you," Lars said. "Now go. Both of you. I understand."

Acid hurried over and prised Heydari's pistol from the dead man's clutches. Stuffing it down the back of her jeans, she turned back to Caesar. His leg had stopped bleeding, but the way he gnashed his teeth as he hobbled towards the door, the way his whole body was shaking, it didn't fill her with confidence.

She joined him at the door and shoved her head under his armpit, wrapping his big arm around her shoulders. "Ready, you old fucker?"

He looked down at her and raised his pistol to his chest. "Come on, Sundance," he said. "Let's do this."

They left Heydari's room through the white-tiled bathing suite, finding a way of walking together that worked, despite looking as if they were taking part in some macabre three-legged race. As they got to the door Acid left Caesar's side and, putting all her weight under it, lifted the timber slide bolt off its hinges. The sound of gunfire was much louder now, as if the fighting had already spread to the next room, and as she opened the door a rush of air brought with it the crash and crack of assault rifles and handguns being discharged at a rapid rate. Now, in such close proximity to the fray, the voices were clearer and more distinct. She could hear men barking orders at each other, telling each other to back off, to drop their weapons, to surrender – usual stuff for these sorts of situations, and like always neither side were taking any heed of the other.

"Are you good to move?" she asked, gripping Caesar around the waist.

"Stick to the walls," he told her. "The pillars will provide cover."

"Got you."

With a whirlwind of manic *fuck-the-world* energy filling her soul, she dragged Caesar into the smoke and dust-filled room. The air was so thick with the vapours of war she could hardly see where she was heading, but with Caesar leaning on her, and her leaning against the wall, they were able to move steadily along the nearside wall.

She could now make out vague figures at the far end of the long room, about twenty of them, all Heydari's soldiers. They were standing or lying beside the wide pillars or knelt behind the huge marble plinths on which Heydari displayed his art and antiquities – most of which were now riddled with bullet holes or blown into tiny pieces. Narrowing her eyes through the gloom she counted around twenty more soldiers – US troops this time – in the room beyond. Each was dressed in full battle gear, almost like robots these days, with their heat-vision helmets and high-tech body armour. They made Heydari's men look like a bunch of ill-equipped goat farmers – which, it had to be said, they probably were once. Poor bastards.

"Come on," Acid said, quickening her pace and gripping onto Caesar as they took the corner and headed down the side of the room, away from the action. An immense pressure pounded in her chest as they got to the first pillar and rested up.

"If we can get to the next pillar, we can slip through there," she said, pointing to an open door twenty feet away. "It leads to the bottom of the tower where we saw the troops assembling."

"I see it," Caesar growled.

"How's the leg?"

He sniffed and then grimaced, as if even this was painful. "It's not too bad. Don't worry about me."

"You've left it a bit late to tell me that, haven't you?" She followed the statement with a grin but it elicited nothing in return. Tightening her resolve, she asked, "We ready?"

"Ready as ever, my dear. Slow and steady."

Together they shuffled around the side of the pillar and headed for the door. But they'd only taken a few steps when a dark figure stepped out of the smoke in front of them. He was short and skinny in stature, but the way he looked at them, with such vile contempt and hatred in his eyes, it made her blood run cold. That and the assault rifle he was carrying. He lifted it to his shoulder but Acid already had her pistol drawn and, pushing Caesar towards the open door, shot the man three times in the chest. Three bullets. Each one finding its target. Except the bastard was wearing a vest, and from this distance they didn't even knock him off his feet. Thankfully, however, the impact did knock off his aim, meaning a wave of Kalashnikov bullets meant for Acid whizzed overhead. As the soldier steadied himself, she dropped to the floor, took aim and shot him through the head. But not before he'd fired another wave of shots that wiped across the doorway, the one Caesar had stumbled through seconds earlier. As the man's body fell to the ground, Acid scrambled to her feet and leapt for cover.

"Got the bastard," she said, skidding into a turn and getting behind the heavy door. "Help me close— Shit."

Caesar was down on one knee, holding his chest. At first she thought he was having a heart attack, but then she saw the blood gushing out over his hand.

"Fuck, wait there." Gritting her teeth she pushed the door closed and bolted the metal rivet-lock through the clasp. She was over to hm in two strides. "Let me see."

He lifted his shaking hand away to show her. The bullet had gone straight through between his top two ribs. Too high for his heart but it could have grazed the top of his lung. Perhaps he saw what she was thinking because he shook his head. "I don't think it hit anything important."

With the bats still spurring her on, and the veins in her neck and legs pulsing ferociously, she looked around, searching for another exit, stairs to another level, anything. At one end of the room was a row of windows that looked down onto the court-yard. Leaving Caesar for a moment, she ran over to inspect the drop.

"Fucking shitting bastard."

This part of the room jutted out over the main courtyard and she guessed the drop to be around ten foot. A fair height, but survivable. Except they had a bigger issue to deal with, in the shape of the ten or more US Special Forces soldiers standing below the window and more coming in through a large hole that had been blown in the palace wall.

"Shitting bastard fuck."

"Not very ladylike," Caesar called over. "What filthy bastard taught you to swear like that?"

She spun around to see he'd dragged himself over to the side of the room, leaving a trail of blood in his wake. He was sitting against the wall with his head back, staring at the ceiling.

"What the hell are you doing?" she asked, walking back over. "Get up. We need to get out of here."

He let out a deep sigh but didn't look at her. "It's over, kid."

She scowled, willing him to look at her so he could see the determination in her face. Because this was far from over. One final push and they'd be out of here. They'd be free. They'd be…

"Look at me, Acid," he sneered. "I'm fucked. I can hardly feel my legs."

"No. We can do this. We can—"

"No, Acid. *We* can't. But you can." He looked up at her and smiled, and just then she wanted to punch him he looked so pathetic.

"I'm not going to leave you here. Not now." She knelt beside him. "Not after everything."

He tilted his head back to take her in. "I'll only slow you down. Get us both killed. No, sweetie. Your only chance of getting out of here is to leave me. You can do it. You've done it before."

"I'll bloody well drag you out of here if I have to." Next door a huge explosion went off, rattling the walls. She didn't take her eyes off him. "Get the fuck up off the floor."

"I can't walk. I can't do anything. Look at the bleeding state of me."

Another explosion rocked the room. Acid got to her feet as dust and plaster residue drifted down from the domed ceiling. "Okay, but you'll be fine. The American troops are taking control, but you'll be able to negotiate some sort of…"

She trailed off as she saw the look in his eyes. Her stomach turned upside down.

"Oh no."

"Yes, Acid."

"No. No, I can't."

"Of course you bleeding well can. It's all you've thought about for the last two years."

"Yes, but things have changed. You know they have. I was hurt, angry… confused. I still am, but I… I…" She swiped her hand angrily across her eyes. "You'll be able to sort something out, make a deal."

"Not likely, kiddo." He held up his quivering hand. "Look at that. I'm not putting it on. I've got – what – five years left if I'm lucky? Five years being a pathetic, shivering mess, in and out of detention centres and courtrooms. Not a fucking chance." He held her gaze, his eyes steely and determined. "Do this for me, Acid. If it has to happen, I'm glad it's you."

She sniffed back a whole lifetime of emotion. "I don't know if I can."

"I killed your mum. I deserve it."

"But I need you."

"No. She was such an angry little thing, Alice Vandella. All that fire and fury and nowhere to put it. But look at you now, all grown up. You don't need me. You don't need anyone."

"Ceez, this isn't how it should go." The hoarseness of her throat made the words sound little more than a gasp.

"It's the only way, kid. It's not so bad, I promise."

"You promise?"

His mouth twisted into a crooked grin. "Here, let me give you this." With a quivering hand, he reached into his trouser pocket and pulled out a scrap of paper. "The contact details of the guy who can get you out of the country. Tell him what happened. Tell him I sent you. You'll be fine."

In the next room the fighting had died down, or moved further into the palace perhaps. She could still hear the faint sound of gunshots, but calmer voices too, coming through from the next room.

"Caesar… please."

"We've been through this," he snapped. "I don't want to die in custody. Or as some CIA asset."

She looked down at him without blinking, perhaps trying to snapshot the moment. Nothing felt real to her. She tightened her grip on the handle of her gun.

"Right between the eyes," he said, with a smile. "I'll never feel a thing."

Stepping back, she raised the pistol at his head. Her fingers trembled on the grip. A tear rolled down her cheek. "I'll miss you," she whispered.

"Nah," Caesar replied. "You won't. Because I am you. You're me."

She sniffed. "I know."

"We had a good run, kid. It's been a blast. Just promise me one thing."

"What's that?" she asked, lowering her aim.

"You won't become too much of a bleeding do-gooder."

She smiled through the pain. Even managed a brief wink. "Not a bloody chance."

"That's my girl."

He relaxed his body against the wall and gave her a nod as she stiffened her aim. Over the top of the gun their eyes met, and for a brief moment she was transported back to a different place and a different time. Back to when all was possible and life was nothing but a wild thrill ride. When she still believed Beowulf Caesar to be the most amazing and mysterious man she'd ever met.

But that was normal, right?

What young girl didn't believe her father was king of the world?

"Now, Acid. Do it."

She closed her eyes, sensing the bond they'd shared circling back through time and meeting itself at this exact point.

It was time, the bats said.

Do it.

She opened her eyes, and pulled the trigger before she had chance to talk herself out of it. One bullet. Straight between the eyes. He never felt a thing.

And just like that, Beowulf Caesar was dead.

Closure.

CHAPTER 42

The pain of what she'd done reverberated through Acid's entire being. But there was no time to try and make sense of the ocean of emotions bubbling up inside of her. As she was laying Caesar's body down, another explosion ripped through the palace, causing huge cracks to splinter up the walls like bolts of lightning. Above her the domed roof shook as more plaster and rubble fell into the room. It was time for her to get out of here.

She chucked away her spent pistol and pulled the almost fully loaded one from out of Caesar's waistband. Gripping it in her right hand, she held her left up to his still warm cheek.

"Goodbye, Ceez," she whispered. "You were right, it has been a blast."

As if to slam an ironic exclamation mark on the end of her words, another explosion rocked the room. Getting to her feet, she hurried over to the door and yanked the metal rivet from out of the clasp. Without looking back, and with the 33 leading the way, she eased open the door and peered around the side of the frame. The room beyond was still foggy with smoke, but as she moved through the doorway towards the nearest pillar she could make sense of the situation. The walls were crumbling with the scars of a hundred bullet holes and the floor littered with the broken and bloody bodies of fallen soldiers. Most of them were Heydari's men, young wide-eyed kids from the local towns. All dead. Pawns in the futile but never-ending game of egos and world-politics. On the far side of the room she saw a group of US troops standing in front of the doors that led to Heydari's suite. Lars would be safe, and the others, but with the palace and the court-yard outside swarming with more American soldiers, it didn't help her own situation.

Sticking close to the pillars and staying out of sight as much as possible, she wove between the dead until she got to the next room. Once there, she slid behind a large marble plinth as two US soldiers ran out from a side door a few feet in front of her. A second later the place erupted in gunfire as three ISIS fighters burst into the room with machine guns blazing. Shifting along on her backside, she got to the wall and pressed her back against it as a veil of bullets thudded into the marble on the opposite side of the plinth. A primal scream of pain seized her attention and she looked up to see an American soldier staggering backwards, clutching his throat under his visor. As she watched on, another trail of bullets ripped across his thighs and torso and he dropped to the floor in front of her. Bad news for him, but the opening she'd been hoping for.

Staying out of sight behind the plinth, she stretched out with her foot so that she could kick the soldier's limp arm close enough to reach. Grabbing hold of it, she dragged him towards her as more bullets whizzed overhead. As his comrade kept the ISIS fighters at bay, she removed the fallen soldier's helmet and put it on. It felt loose but wasn't ridiculously big for her, and now she had a plan. Removing the man's body armour and combat fatigues, she lay down flat and wriggled his trousers on over her jeans. It was awkward as hell putting on the heavy combat gear without revealing her position, but after a few attempts and fighting through a stiff cramp in her shoulder she managed to get the jacket on, followed by the body armour. Every item was too big for her, but it was the intense heat inside the helmet and the weight of all the equipment which gave her pause, wondering how the hell soldiers operated effectively under such conditions. But maybe that was the point. Not everyone could do it. It took resolve and patience. Only certain people were cut out for army life. People like Kendis' brother.

Ah, shit... Kendis.

She pushed the thought away. There was a whole host of confusing, shitty emotions for her to deal with when she got home. But first she had to get home. And she wasn't out of danger yet.

The soldier had dropped his rifle, an M16, but it was a good metre or so from where she was, and to reach it she'd have to expose herself. Lying flat on the ground behind the plinth, she reached her foot out but only managed to spin it away from her.

Shit.

She scuttled back against the wall as more shots pounded against the marble plinth. As she did, she saw the remaining American soldier throw his arms up in the air and his head lurch back violently. He was dead before he hit the ground. Three bullets, straight through the visor of his helmet. His head lolled to one side, and through the cracked screen she saw his eyes were open, looking straight at her. It should have been unsettling, but the sight only made the bats shriek louder in her head.

Get out.

Get out now.

Kill... Kill... Kill...

The ISIS goons had stopped firing and she could hear them advancing steadily across the room. A second went by. And another. Her skin burned and her nerve endings fizzed with electric energy. In her head she heard Caesar's voice, the words echoing through the chattering chaos. One of the last things he'd said to her.

You're Acid bleeding Vanilla... The toughest person I've ever met... You can do anything...

He was right.

She could.

Every cell in her body burned with fiery intensity as she rolled over and grabbed up the M16. In front of her the ISIS fighters (two of them now, the American must have taken one out) were moving swiftly through the space, sweeping the area with their rifles drawn at waist height. They saw Acid and snapped their rifles towards her, but by then it was already too late. Letting out a visceral scream that emanated from somewhere deep inside of her, she stepped into a wide-legged stance and squeezed the trigger. As the M16 burst into life she moved her aim around in a circular motion, taking them both out in less than one second. While their bullet-ravaged bodies dropped to the floor, she was already running towards them, squeezing off another deluge of bullets to finish the job. It wasn't needed. But now she was having fun. Because she could. And because these bastards deserved it.

Once satisfied they were both dead, she glanced back over her shoulder to make sure no one else was coming, then ran over to the main entrance. With the doors gone, she could already see down to the courtyard where the last of Heydari's men were lined up on their knees with their hands on their heads, watched over by armed US soldiers. The battle was over. The Americans had won.

Stepping through the open doorway, she blinked into the sun, bright even behind the dark visor. She paused, attempting to centre herself and get her head around the situation. Down in front of her she counted five US soldiers positioned at intervals along the walkway. At the bottom, three more men were standing around peering at a tablet as one of them swiped at the screen. With the M16 held tight to her chest and her head held high, she set off past the sentries, nodding curtly to each one as she passed by and not daring to breathe until she reached ground level.

"How we doing in there?" The man holding the tablet looked her up and down as she got closer. He looked to be in his mid-fifties and was dressed in the same desert camo fatigues as her, but wore no helmet or body armour. Possibly he was one of the commanding officers. His bright blue eyes narrowed as he noticed the state of her uniform. "You injured, soldier?"

"Not my blood, sir," she said, lowering her tone and putting on a mid-American accent. "We're all good. No more threats."

Under the circumstances, it wasn't her best accent-work, but she hoped the muffled nature of the helmet would go some way to masking any tells. She remained still as the officer considered her. Over his shoulder she could see the hole in the wall where the soldiers had breached the compound. She guessed it to be around a hundred metres away, give or take. A thirty-second walk to freedom.

"How many of them are left?" he asked.

"That's it, sir. We're done. We won."

He frowned and her heart froze in her chest. *We won?* Did US soldiers say stuff like that?

Shit. Shit. Shit.

The officer looked her up and down again, but then a smile curled the corner of his mouth. "Go report in with your commanding officer and get debriefed, soldier. You did well today."

"Thank you, sir."

With her finger still rigid on the rifle trigger, she stepped away and began the short walk over to the hole in the wall. She walked steadily at first, trying to remain calm and soldier-like, but as she got closer she couldn't help but quicken her pace. Ten feet from the wall she turned around, walking backwards to take in the scene – the expansive courtyard, Heydari's foot soldiers being herded into the back of US trucks, and then up to Heydari's palace where she could see Lars and the rest of the prisoners being escorted out of the main entrance.

It wasn't the ending she'd hoped for, but it was an ending. An exit of sorts too. Caesar was dead and a part of her had died with him. But maybe that wasn't a bad thing. Maybe some parts needed to die.

A large plume of black smoke rose ominously from the top of the domed tower, drifting up into the unbroken blue of the Iranian sky. She watched it for a moment before shooting a cautionary glance at the officers standing at the foot of the walkway, but none of them were looking her way. Turning around, she stepped over a pile of rubble and in one, two steps, was over the other side of the compound. Freedom. In front of her a wide, dusty road stretched out towards the horizon with just the occasional tree or mound of rocks for scenery. If she narrowed her eyes, she could make out what looked like a shanty town over to the west. Somewhere she could stop and get directions, hopefully trade the M16 for some supplies. It was going to be a long trek home, but she'd already made peace with that, and she could do it. Of course she could.

She was *Acid bleeding Vanilla.*

She could do anything.

CHAPTER 43

The sun was setting over the horizon, casting long shadows across the desert and highlighting the mounds and hollows in the sand as far as the eye could see, as Acid got comfortable on the soft dunes. It was a warm night and she lay back in the sand, resting up on one elbow to gulp back a long drink of water from the canteen she'd procured two days earlier. In the valley below, she could make out the white buildings of Kukh, a small village of less than four hundred inhabitants, all of them Kurds. Being the northernmost town in the country and standing as it was on the Iranian-Turkish border, it was the perfect place for their rendezvous.

It had taken Acid six days to get here and most of the travelling had been done by car, hitching rides with locals in return for some of the money she'd made from the sale of the M16 rifle and the US Special Forces uniform. Despite the horrors that many Iranians had endured over the last thirty-some years, they all still went crazy for war memorabilia. Especially, it seemed, American war memorabilia. Even more so if the clothes were covered in real blood and had real bullet holes in them. You didn't get more authentic than that.

After some bartering, she'd raised enough money to buy supplies and get herself here. Now she had to wait until the cover of nightfall to meet Caesar's contact. The arrangement was he'd take her through the mountains, across the eastern side of Turkey, and over the Aras river into Armenia. From there she could get a train over to Georgia, and then onto Eastern Europe where she'd arranged to meet her old pal Sonny who was loaning her enough cash for a plane ticket home, along with a new alias and passport. She'd pay him back, of course, she'd have to. In her world, friendships only lasted for as long as you both played nice. The first hint of double-cross and a comrade quickly became an adversary, became a threat.

She closed her eyes, enjoying the last rays of the warm sun on her face before it disappeared over the edge of the Earth. It would take her another week at least until she was back home in London. Back with Spook. But that was okay. Despite planning for a one-way trip, she was indeed going home and the ensuing break would do her good. Give her the opportunity to consider what she might do next. Because now more than ever she understood where Caesar was coming from. She wasn't soft. She never had been. But she was also stupid to think she could ever fit into civilian life. And why should she? For the first time in a long time she liked who she was and who she'd become. She was sharp, tough as hell, and still had an incredibly short temper (as one local farmer had learnt to his cost when haggling over some flatbread a day earlier). But she was also looking to the future for the first time in her life. She could only do that by leaving the past behind.

So it hadn't happened the way she'd wanted it – it certainly hadn't happened the way she'd planned it – but she'd gotten closure. Caesar was dead and that part of her life was over. What happened next, she wasn't sure. But she was done beating herself up about who she was and what she'd done.

Because she didn't have to change.

Hell, she couldn't even if she wanted to.

She gazed out over the expansive terrain, letting her soul absorb all the silence and stillness of the harsh but stunning vista. It felt like the first time in many years she could truly relax, and for a glorious moment she felt free of everything, unencumbered not only from the pain of her past but from the stresses and strains of modern life. She felt amazing, strong in both body and mind, and it was a hell of a long time since she'd been able to say that.

The story she'd told herself these last few years was that she was a bad person and people had got hurt because of her. But that wasn't true. She wasn't the problem. As she'd stared down at Kendis' lifeless body, the realisation had hit her like a claw hammer to the guts. The poor girl wasn't dead because of her. She was dead because of that evil piece of shit, Cyrus Heydari. And as long as there were creeps like him in the world, her mission wasn't over. Her life still had purpose.

She was Acid Vanilla.

And she was ready for whatever came next.

The end

But Acid Vanilla will return in

Never Say Die.

Order your copy now click here

————

GET YOUR FREE BOOK

Discover how Acid Vanilla transformed from a typical London teenager into the world's deadliest female assassin.

Get the Acid Vanilla Prequel Novel:
Making a Killer available FREE at:

www.matthewhattersley.com/mak

CAN YOU HELP?

Enjoyed this book? You can make a big difference

Honest reviews of my books help bring them to the attention of other readers. If you've enjoyed this book I would be very grateful if you could spend just five minutes leaving a review (it can be as short as you like) on the book's Amazon page.

ALSO BY MATTHEW HATTERSLEY

Have you read them all?

————

The Acid Vanilla series

Acid Vanilla

Acid Vanilla is an elite assassin, struggling with her mental health. Spook Horowitz is a mild-mannered hacker who saw something she shouldn't. Acid needs a holiday. Spook needs Acid Vanilla to NOT be coming to kill her. But life rarely works out the way we want it to.

BUY IT HERE

Seven Bullets

Acid Vanilla was the deadliest assassin at Annihilation Pest Control. That was until she was tragically betrayed by her former colleagues. Now, fuelled by an insatiable desire for vengeance, Acid travels the globe to carry out her bloody retribution. After all, a girl needs a hobby...

BUY IT HERE

Making a Killer

How it all began. Discover Acid Vanilla's past, her meeting with Caesar and how she became the deadliest female assassin in the world.

FREE TO DOWNLOAD HERE

————

Stand-alone novels

Double Bad Things

All undertaker Mikey wants is a quiet life and to write his comics. But then he's conned into hiding murders in closed-casket burials by a gang who are also trafficking young girls. Can a gentle giant whose only friends are a cosplay-obsessed teen and an imaginary alien really take down the gang and avoid arrest himself?

Double Bad Things is a dark and quirky crime thriller - for fans of Dexter and Six Feet Under.

BUY IT HERE

Cookies

Will Miles find love again after the worst six months of his life? The fortune cookies say yes. But they also say commit arson and murder, so maybe it's time to stop believing in them? If only he could...

"If you life Fight Club, you'll love Cookies." - TL Dyer, Author

BUY IT HERE

For Suzanne and Alba

ABOUT THE AUTHOR

Over the last twenty years Matthew Hattersley has toured Europe in rock n roll bands, trained as a professional actor and founded a theatre and media company. He's also had a lot of dead end jobs…

Now he writes high-octane pulp action thrillers and crime fiction.

He lives with his wife and daughter in Derbyshire, UK and doesn't feel that comfortable writing about himself in the third person.

COPYRIGHT

Printed in Great Britain
by Amazon

19012929R00174